P9-DCR-815

PEANUTS CLASSICS

Dr. Beagle and Mr. Hyde
Fly, You Stupid Kite, Fly!
How Long, Great Pumpkin, How Long?
It's Great to Be a Superstar
Kiss Her, You Blockhead!
My Anxieties Have Anxieties
Speak Softly, and Carry a Beagle
There Goes the Shutout
Summers Fly, Winters Walk
Thank Goodness for People
The Beagle Has Landed
What Makes You Think You're Happy?
And a Woodstock in a Birch Tree
A Smile Makes a Lousy Umbrella
The Mad Punter Strikes Again
There's a Vulture Outside
Here Comes the April Fool!
What Makes Musicians So Sarcastic?
A Kiss on the Nose Turns Anger Aside
It's Hard Work Being Bitter
I'm Not Your Sweet Babboo!
Stop Snowing on My Secretary
Always Stick Up for the Underbird
What's Wrong with Being Crabby?
Don't Hassle Me with Your Sighs, Chuck
The Way of the Fussbudget Is Not Easy
You're Weird, Sir!
It's a Long Way to Tipperary
Who's the Funny-Looking Kid with the Big Nose?
Sunday's Fun Day, Charlie Brown
You're Out of Your Mind, Charlie Brown!
You're the Guest of Honor, Charlie Brown
You Can't Win, Charlie Brown
Peanuts Every Sunday
The Unsinkable Charlie Brown
Good Grief, More Peanuts
You've Come a Long Way, Charlie Brown
The Cheshire Beagle
Duck, Here Comes Another Day!
Sarcasm Does Not Become You, Ma'am
Nothing Echoes Like an Empty Mailbox
I Heard A D Minus Call Me

MY ANXIETIES HAVE ANXIETIES

Copr. © 1950, 1958 United Feature Syndicate, Inc.

Cartoons from *You've Had It, Charlie Brown*

by Charles M. Schulz

An Owl Book
Henry Holt and Company / New York

Henry Holt and Company, Inc.
Publishers since 1866
115 West 18th Street
New York, New York 10011

Henry Holt ® is a registered
trademark of Henry Holt and Company, Inc.

Copyright © 1968, 1969 by
United Feature Syndicate, Inc.
All rights reserved.
Published in Canada by Fitzhenry & Whiteside Ltd.,
195 Allstate Parkway, Markham, Ontario L3R 4T8.

Library of Congress Catalog Card Number: 77-71353

ISBN 0-8050-1691-0 (An Owl Book: pbk.)

Henry Holt books are available for special promotions
and premiums. For details contact: Director, Special Markets.

Originally published as *You've Had It, Charlie Brown*
in 1969 by Holt, Rinehart and Winston. Published in an expanded
edition under the title *My Anxieties Have Anxieties* in 1977, and
included strips from *You're You, Charlie Brown*, published in 1968
by Holt, Rinehart and Winston.

New Owl Book Edition—1991

Printed in the United States of America
All first editions are printed on acid-free paper.∞

3   5   7   9   10   8   6   4

Copr. © 1958 United Feature Syndicate, Inc.

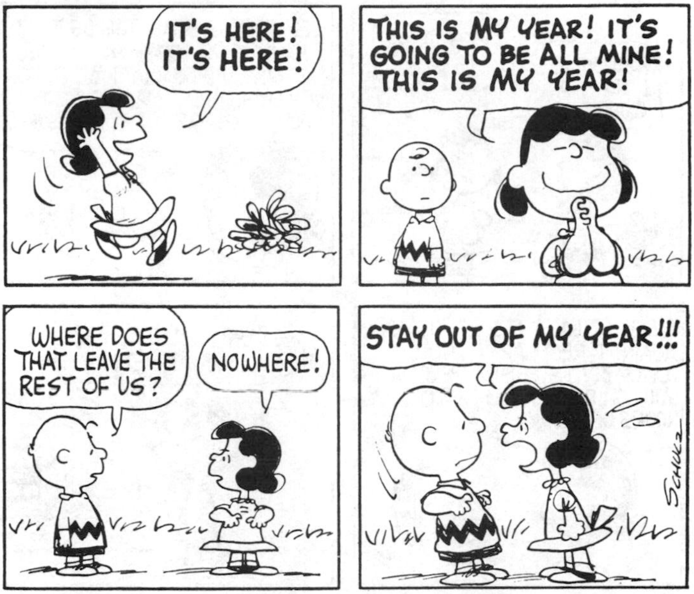
IT'S HERE! IT'S HERE!
THIS IS MY YEAR! IT'S GOING TO BE ALL MINE! THIS IS MY YEAR!
WHERE DOES THAT LEAVE THE REST OF US?
NOWHERE!
STAY OUT OF MY YEAR!!!
SCHULZ

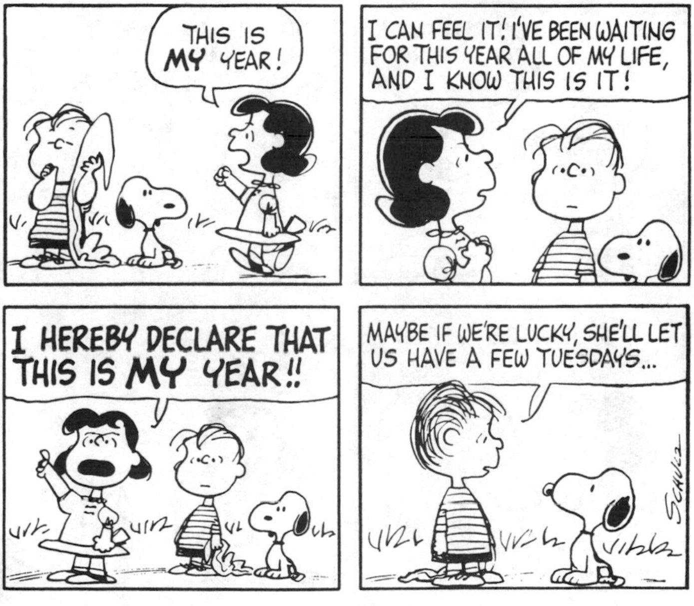
THIS IS MY YEAR!
I CAN FEEL IT! I'VE BEEN WAITING FOR THIS YEAR ALL OF MY LIFE, AND I KNOW THIS IS IT!
I HEREBY DECLARE THAT THIS IS MY YEAR!!
MAYBE IF WE'RE LUCKY, SHE'LL LET US HAVE A FEW TUESDAYS...
SCHULZ

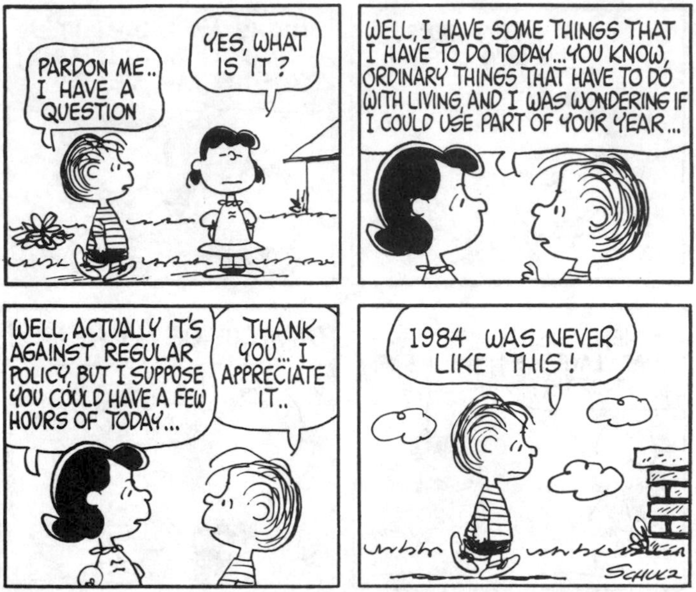
PARDON ME.. I HAVE A QUESTION
YES, WHAT IS IT ?
WELL, I HAVE SOME THINGS THAT I HAVE TO DO TODAY...YOU KNOW, ORDINARY THINGS THAT HAVE TO DO WITH LIVING, AND I WAS WONDERING IF I COULD USE PART OF YOUR YEAR...
WELL, ACTUALLY IT'S AGAINST REGULAR POLICY, BUT I SUPPOSE YOU COULD HAVE A FEW HOURS OF TODAY...
THANK YOU... I APPRECIATE IT..
1984 WAS NEVER LIKE THIS !
SCHULZ

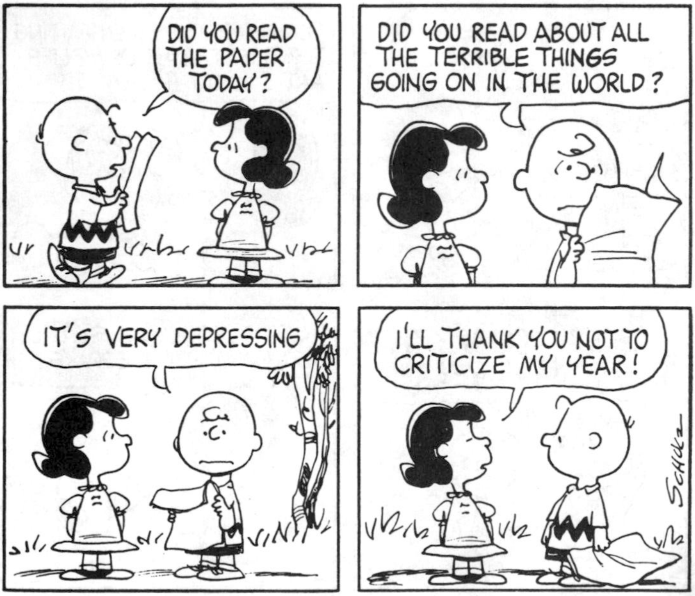
DID YOU READ THE PAPER TODAY ?
DID YOU READ ABOUT ALL THE TERRIBLE THINGS GOING ON IN THE WORLD ?
IT'S VERY DEPRESSING
I'LL THANK YOU NOT TO CRITICIZE MY YEAR !
SCHULZ

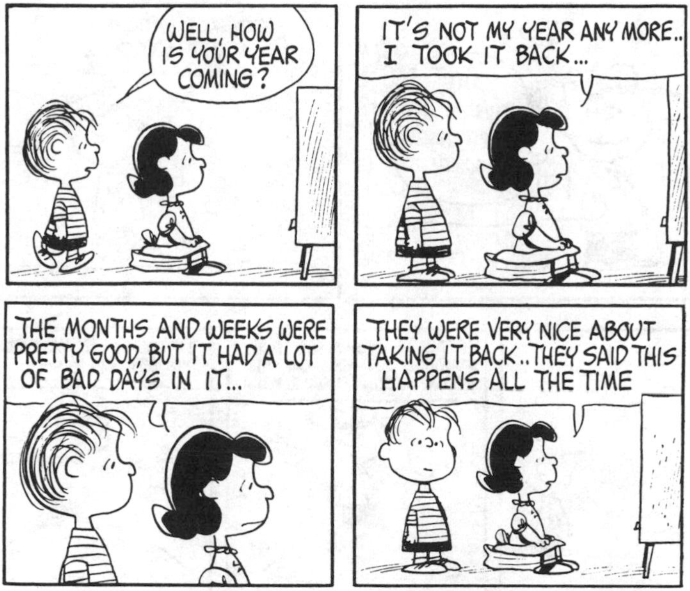
WELL, HOW IS YOUR YEAR COMING?
IT'S NOT MY YEAR ANY MORE.. I TOOK IT BACK...
THE MONTHS AND WEEKS WERE PRETTY GOOD, BUT IT HAD A LOT OF BAD DAYS IN IT...
THEY WERE VERY NICE ABOUT TAKING IT BACK..THEY SAID THIS HAPPENS ALL THE TIME

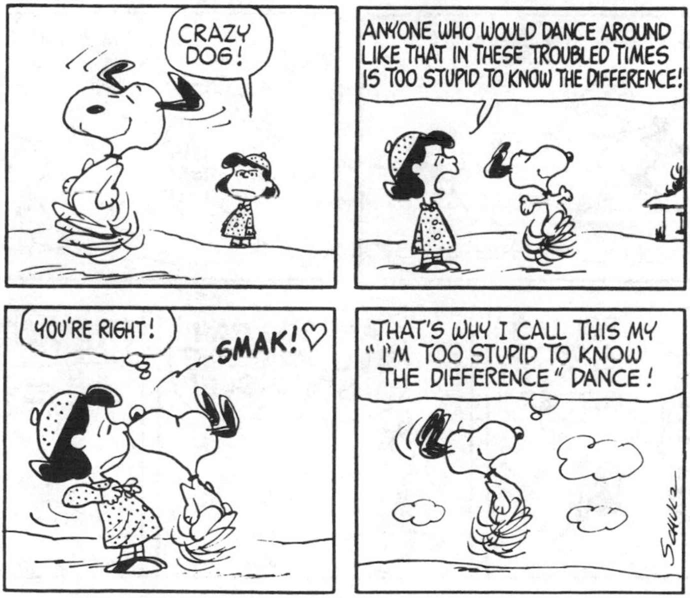
CRAZY DOG!
ANYONE WHO WOULD DANCE AROUND LIKE THAT IN THESE TROUBLED TIMES IS TOO STUPID TO KNOW THE DIFFERENCE!
YOU'RE RIGHT!
SMAK! ♡
THAT'S WHY I CALL THIS MY "I'M TOO STUPID TO KNOW THE DIFFERENCE" DANCE!

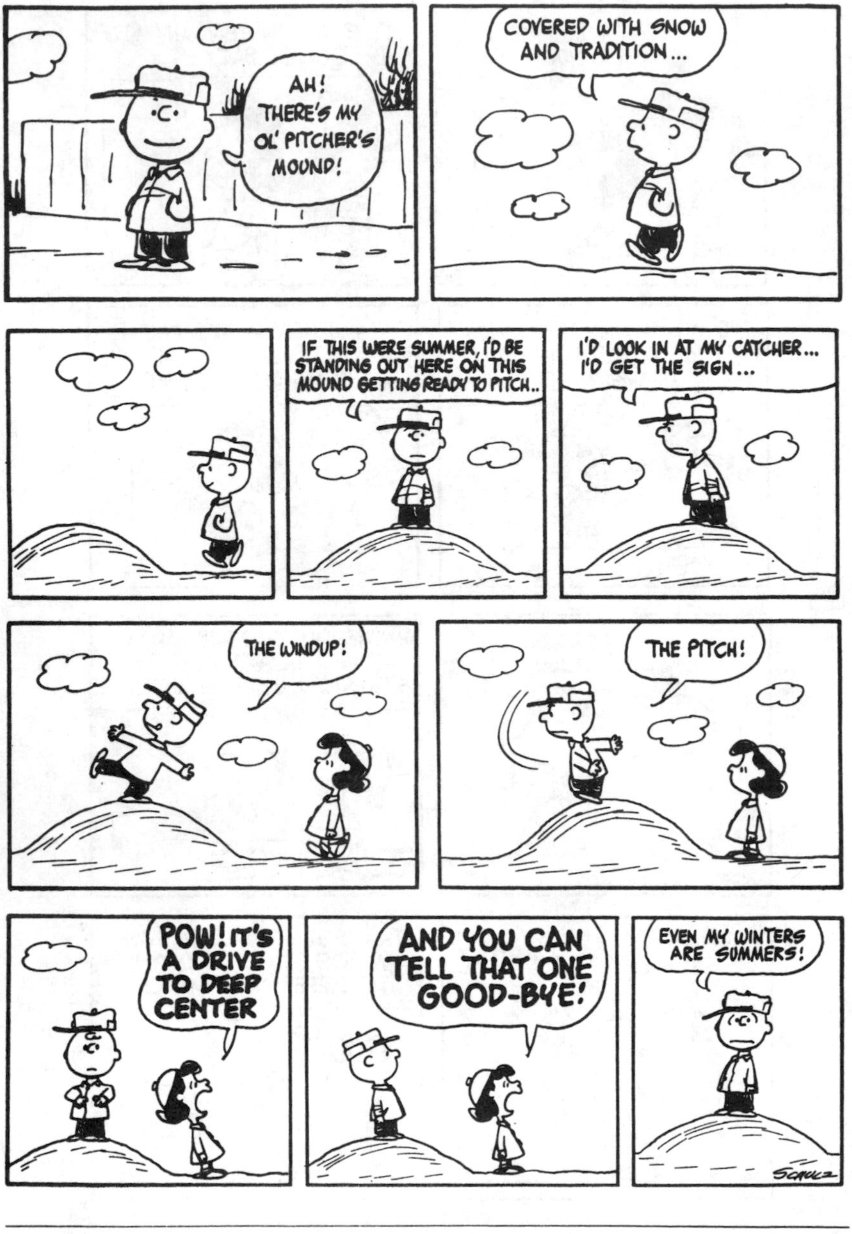
AH! THERE'S MY OL' PITCHER'S MOUND!
COVERED WITH SNOW AND TRADITION...
IF THIS WERE SUMMER, I'D BE STANDING OUT HERE ON THIS MOUND GETTING READY TO PITCH..
I'D LOOK IN AT MY CATCHER... I'D GET THE SIGN...
THE WINDUP!
THE PITCH!
POW! IT'S A DRIVE TO DEEP CENTER
AND YOU CAN TELL THAT ONE GOOD-BYE!
EVEN MY WINTERS ARE SUMMERS!
SCHULZ

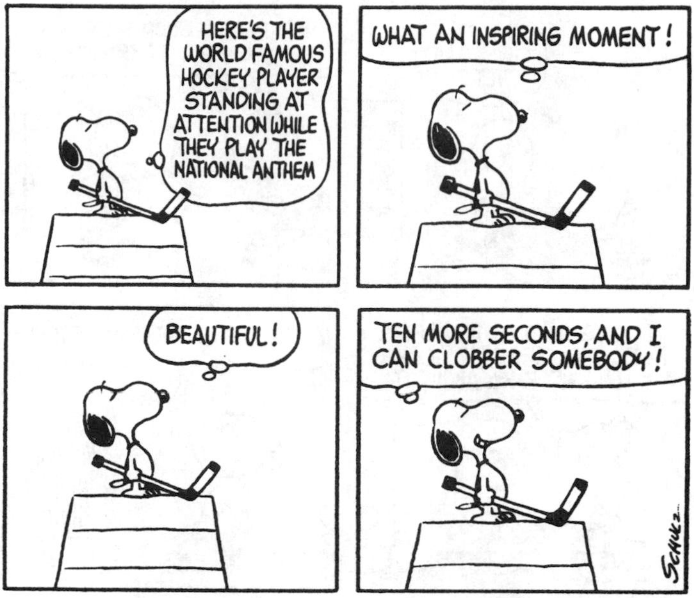
HERE'S THE WORLD FAMOUS HOCKEY PLAYER STANDING AT ATTENTION WHILE THEY PLAY THE NATIONAL ANTHEM
WHAT AN INSPIRING MOMENT!
BEAUTIFUL!
TEN MORE SECONDS, AND I CAN CLOBBER SOMEBODY!
SCHULZ

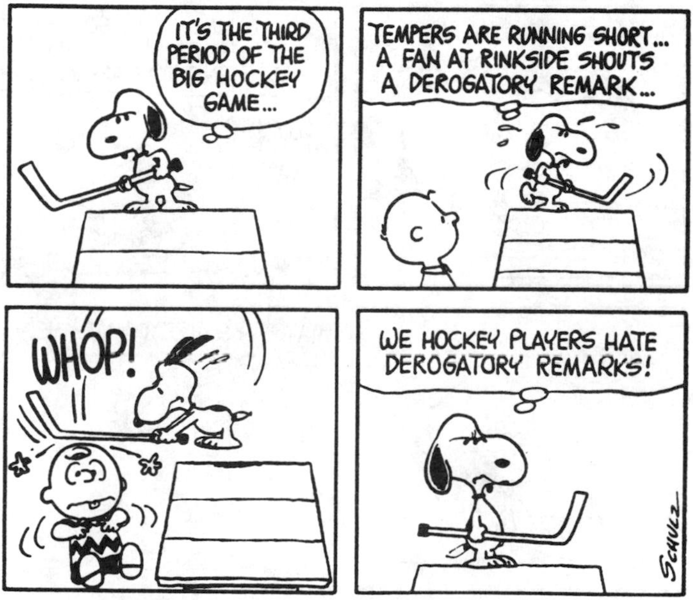
IT'S THE THIRD PERIOD OF THE BIG HOCKEY GAME...
TEMPERS ARE RUNNING SHORT... A FAN AT RINKSIDE SHOUTS A DEROGATORY REMARK...
WHOP!
WE HOCKEY PLAYERS HATE DEROGATORY REMARKS!
SCHULZ

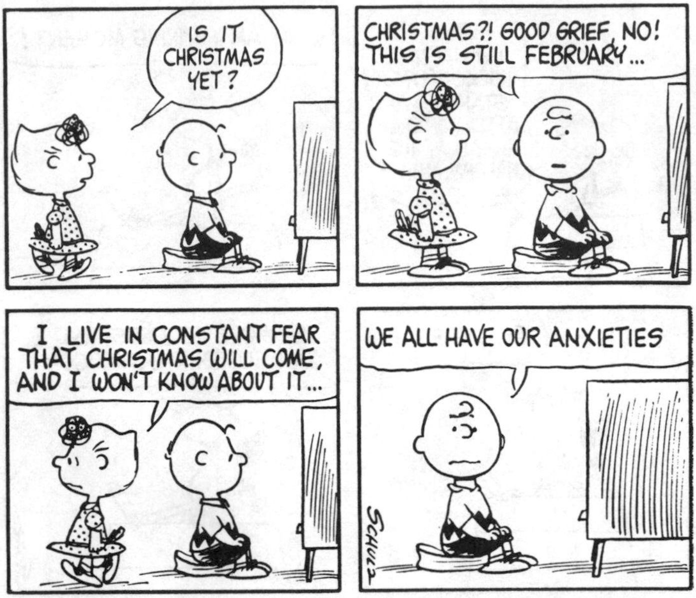
IS IT CHRISTMAS YET?
CHRISTMAS?! GOOD GRIEF, NO! THIS IS STILL FEBRUARY...
I LIVE IN CONSTANT FEAR THAT CHRISTMAS WILL COME, AND I WON'T KNOW ABOUT IT...
WE ALL HAVE OUR ANXIETIES
SCHULZ

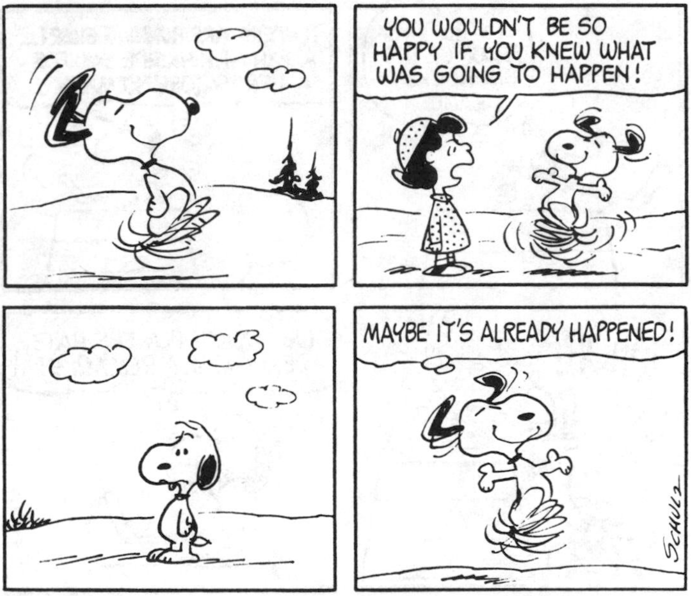
YOU WOULDN'T BE SO HAPPY IF YOU KNEW WHAT WAS GOING TO HAPPEN!
MAYBE IT'S ALREADY HAPPENED!
SCHULZ

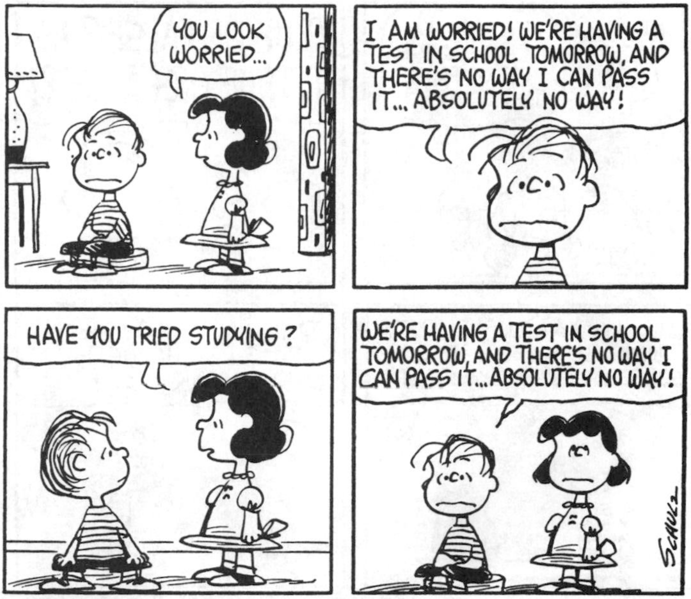
YOU LOOK WORRIED...
I AM WORRIED! WE'RE HAVING A TEST IN SCHOOL TOMORROW, AND THERE'S NO WAY I CAN PASS IT... ABSOLUTELY NO WAY!
HAVE YOU TRIED STUDYING?
WE'RE HAVING A TEST IN SCHOOL TOMORROW, AND THERE'S NO WAY I CAN PASS IT... ABSOLUTELY NO WAY!
SCHULZ

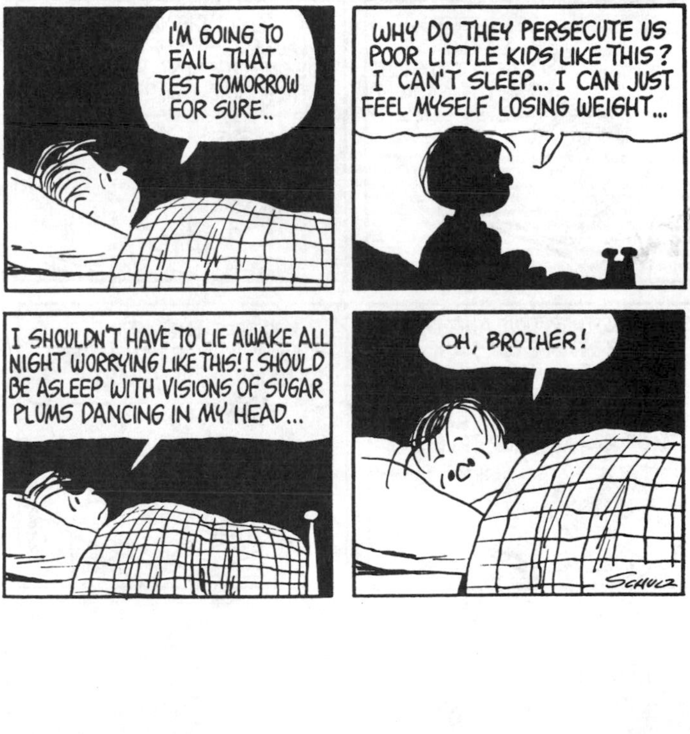
I'M GOING TO FAIL THAT TEST TOMORROW FOR SURE..
WHY DO THEY PERSECUTE US POOR LITTLE KIDS LIKE THIS? I CAN'T SLEEP... I CAN JUST FEEL MYSELF LOSING WEIGHT...
I SHOULDN'T HAVE TO LIE AWAKE ALL NIGHT WORRYING LIKE THIS! I SHOULD BE ASLEEP WITH VISIONS OF SUGAR PLUMS DANCING IN MY HEAD...
OH, BROTHER!
SCHULZ

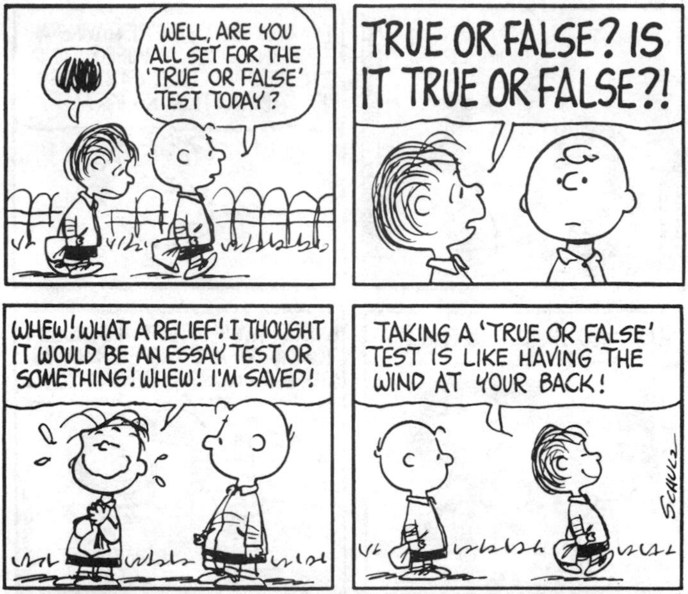
WELL, ARE YOU ALL SET FOR THE 'TRUE OR FALSE' TEST TODAY?
TRUE OR FALSE? IS IT TRUE OR FALSE?!
WHEW! WHAT A RELIEF! I THOUGHT IT WOULD BE AN ESSAY TEST OR SOMETHING! WHEW! I'M SAVED!
TAKING A 'TRUE OR FALSE' TEST IS LIKE HAVING THE WIND AT YOUR BACK!
SCHULZ

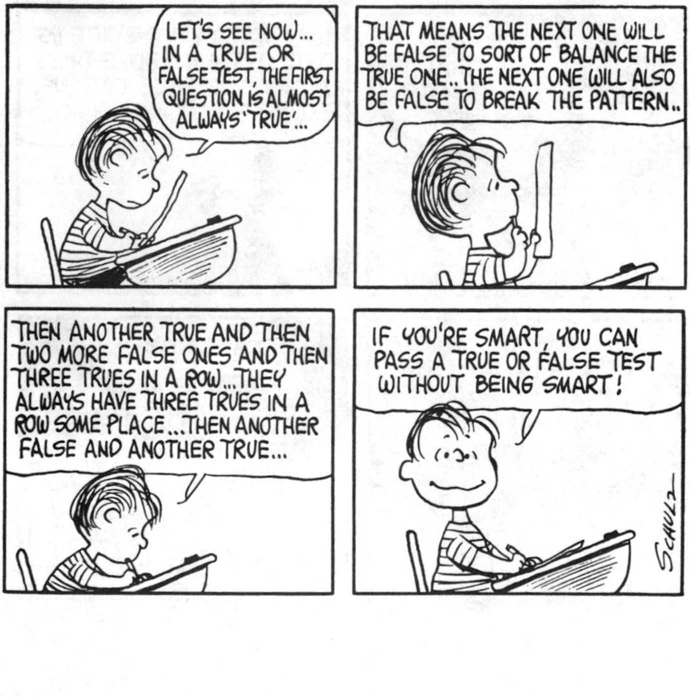
LET'S SEE NOW... IN A TRUE OR FALSE TEST, THE FIRST QUESTION IS ALMOST ALWAYS 'TRUE'...
THAT MEANS THE NEXT ONE WILL BE FALSE TO SORT OF BALANCE THE TRUE ONE.. THE NEXT ONE WILL ALSO BE FALSE TO BREAK THE PATTERN..
THEN ANOTHER TRUE AND THEN TWO MORE FALSE ONES AND THEN THREE TRUES IN A ROW... THEY ALWAYS HAVE THREE TRUES IN A ROW SOME PLACE... THEN ANOTHER FALSE AND ANOTHER TRUE...
IF YOU'RE SMART, YOU CAN PASS A TRUE OR FALSE TEST WITHOUT BEING SMART!
SCHULZ

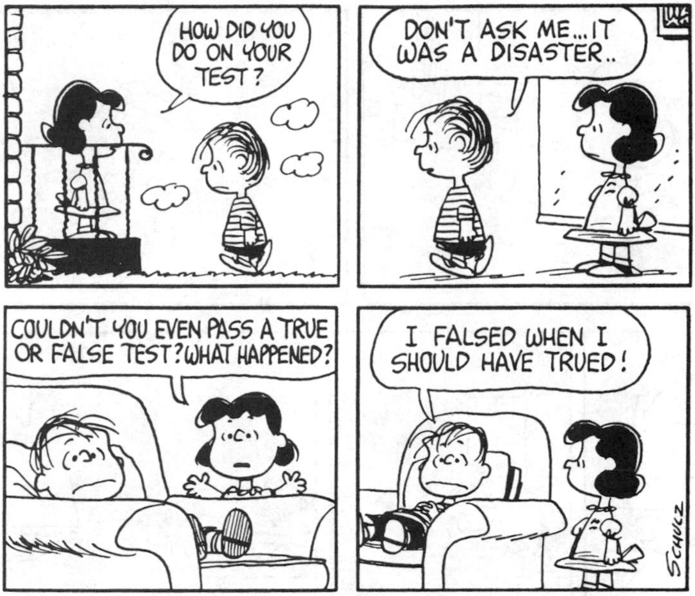
HOW DID YOU DO ON YOUR TEST?
DON'T ASK ME... IT WAS A DISASTER..
COULDN'T YOU EVEN PASS A TRUE OR FALSE TEST? WHAT HAPPENED?
I FALSED WHEN I SHOULD HAVE TRUED!
SCHULZ

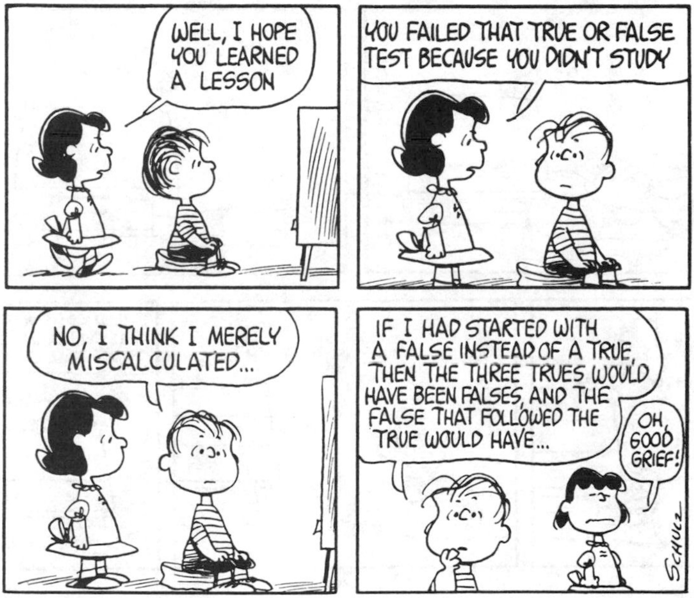
WELL, I HOPE YOU LEARNED A LESSON
YOU FAILED THAT TRUE OR FALSE TEST BECAUSE YOU DIDN'T STUDY
NO, I THINK I MERELY MISCALCULATED...
IF I HAD STARTED WITH A FALSE INSTEAD OF A TRUE, THEN THE THREE TRUES WOULD HAVE BEEN FALSES, AND THE FALSE THAT FOLLOWED THE TRUE WOULD HAVE...
OH, GOOD GRIEF!
SCHULZ

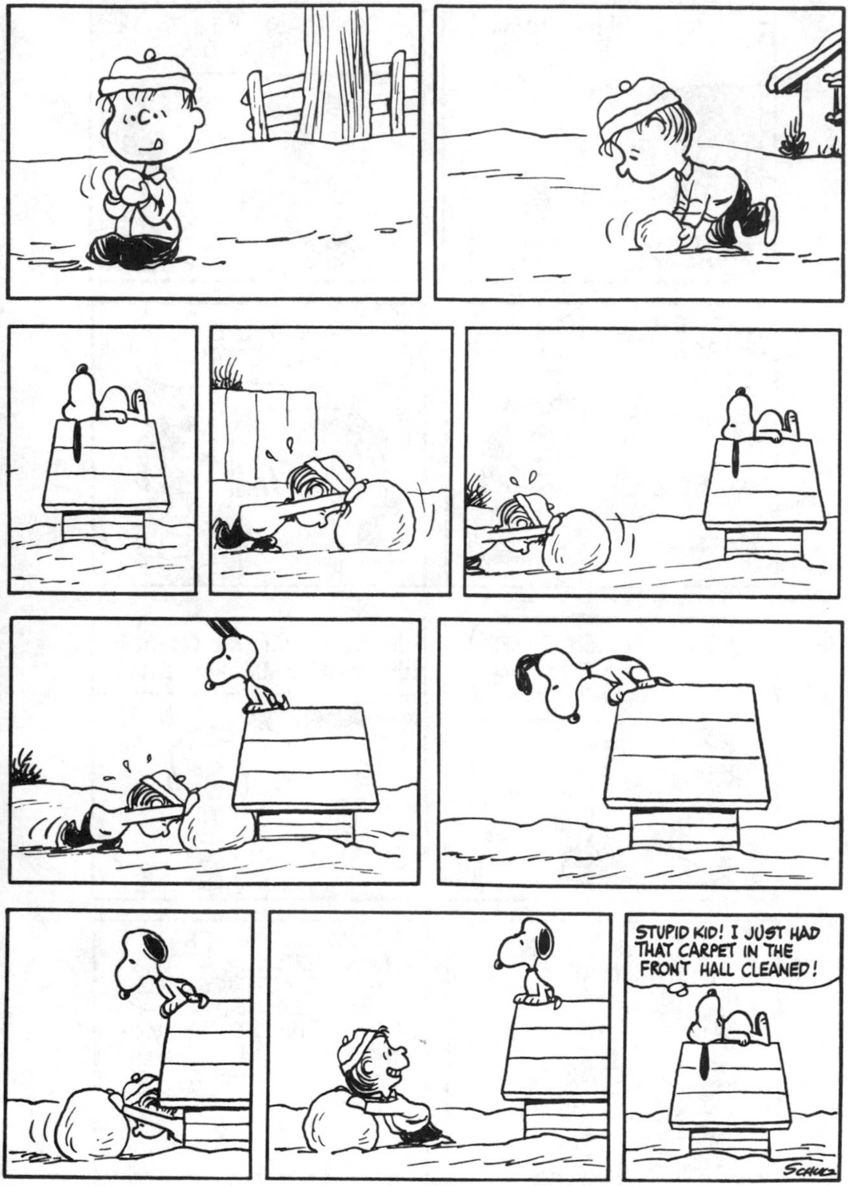
STUPID KID! I JUST HAD THAT CARPET IN THE FRONT HALL CLEANED!
SCHULZ

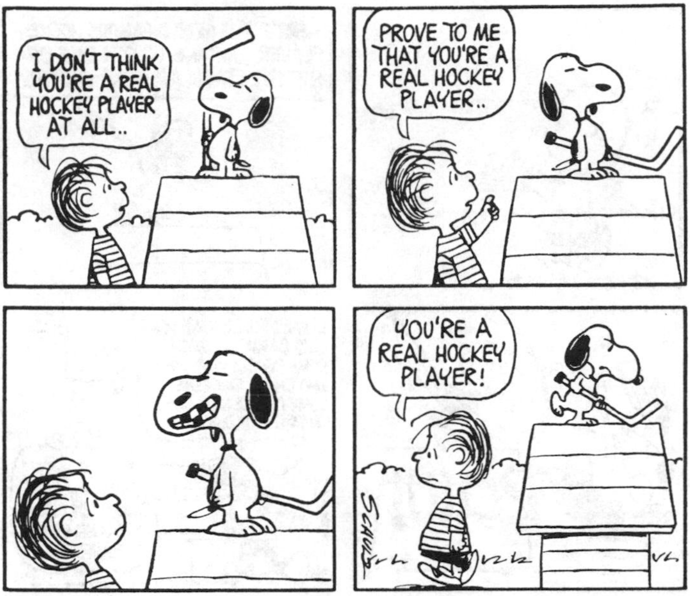
I DON'T THINK YOU'RE A REAL HOCKEY PLAYER AT ALL..
PROVE TO ME THAT YOU'RE A REAL HOCKEY PLAYER..
YOU'RE A REAL HOCKEY PLAYER!

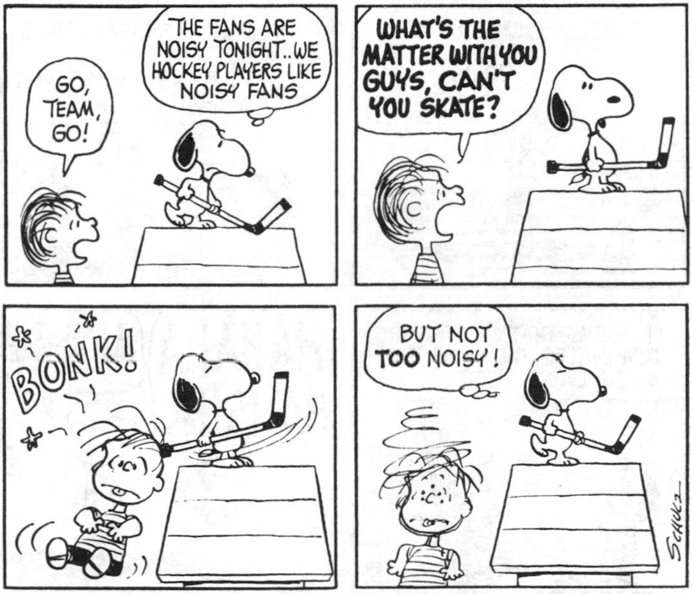
GO, TEAM, GO!
THE FANS ARE NOISY TONIGHT..WE HOCKEY PLAYERS LIKE NOISY FANS
WHAT'S THE MATTER WITH YOU GUYS, CAN'T YOU SKATE?
BONK!
BUT NOT TOO NOISY!

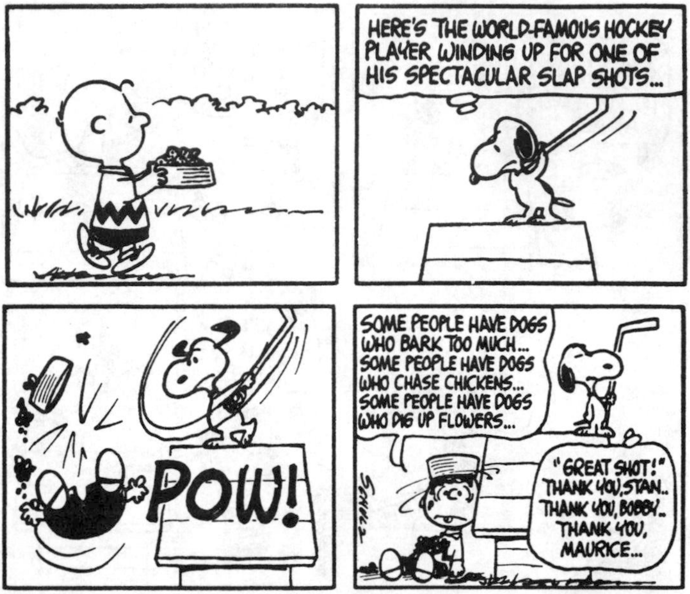
HERE'S THE WORLD-FAMOUS HOCKEY PLAYER WINDING UP FOR ONE OF HIS SPECTACULAR SLAP SHOTS...
POW!
SOME PEOPLE HAVE DOGS WHO BARK TOO MUCH... SOME PEOPLE HAVE DOGS WHO CHASE CHICKENS... SOME PEOPLE HAVE DOGS WHO DIG UP FLOWERS...
"GREAT SHOT!" THANK YOU, STAN.. THANK YOU, BOBBY.. THANK YOU, MAURICE...
SCHULZ

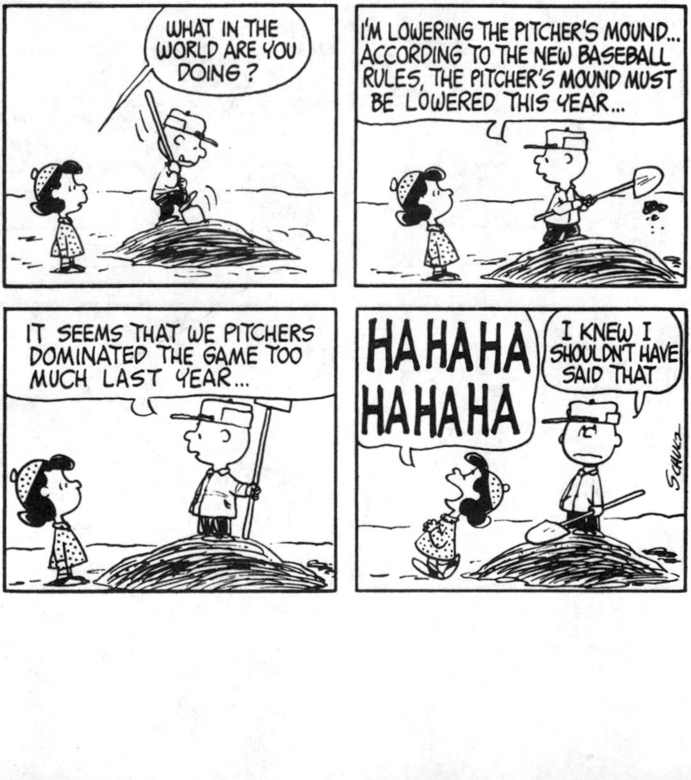
WHAT IN THE WORLD ARE YOU DOING?
I'M LOWERING THE PITCHER'S MOUND... ACCORDING TO THE NEW BASEBALL RULES, THE PITCHER'S MOUND MUST BE LOWERED THIS YEAR...
IT SEEMS THAT WE PITCHERS DOMINATED THE GAME TOO MUCH LAST YEAR...
HAHAHA HAHAHA
I KNEW I SHOULDN'T HAVE SAID THAT
SCHULZ

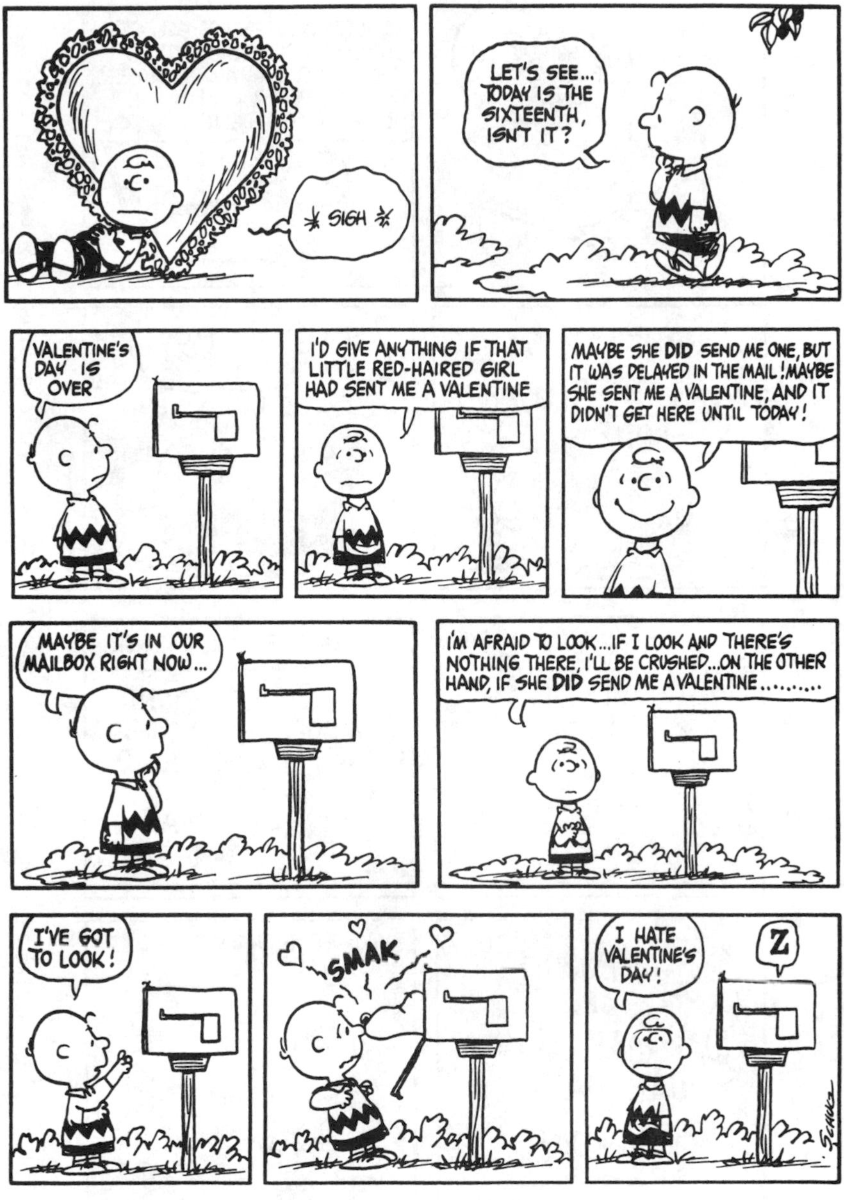

* SIGH *
LET'S SEE... TODAY IS THE SIXTEENTH, ISN'T IT?
VALENTINE'S DAY IS OVER
I'D GIVE ANYTHING IF THAT LITTLE RED-HAIRED GIRL HAD SENT ME A VALENTINE
MAYBE SHE DID SEND ME ONE, BUT IT WAS DELAYED IN THE MAIL! MAYBE SHE SENT ME A VALENTINE, AND IT DIDN'T GET HERE UNTIL TODAY!
MAYBE IT'S IN OUR MAILBOX RIGHT NOW...
I'M AFRAID TO LOOK...IF I LOOK AND THERE'S NOTHING THERE, I'LL BE CRUSHED...ON THE OTHER HAND, IF SHE DID SEND ME A VALENTINE.........
I'VE GOT TO LOOK!
SMAK
I HATE VALENTINE'S DAY!
Z
SCHULZ

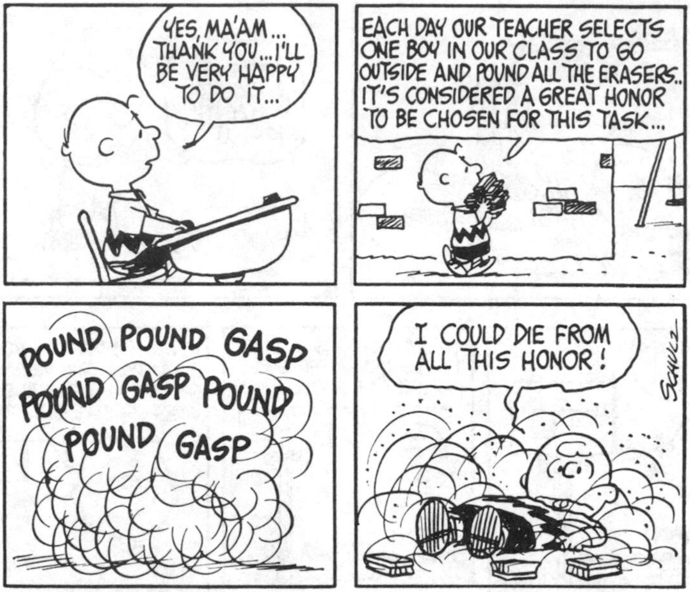
YES, MA'AM... THANK YOU...I'LL BE VERY HAPPY TO DO IT...
EACH DAY OUR TEACHER SELECTS ONE BOY IN OUR CLASS TO GO OUTSIDE AND POUND ALL THE ERASERS.. IT'S CONSIDERED A GREAT HONOR TO BE CHOSEN FOR THIS TASK...
POUND POUND GASP
POUND GASP POUND
POUND GASP
I COULD DIE FROM ALL THIS HONOR!
SCHULZ
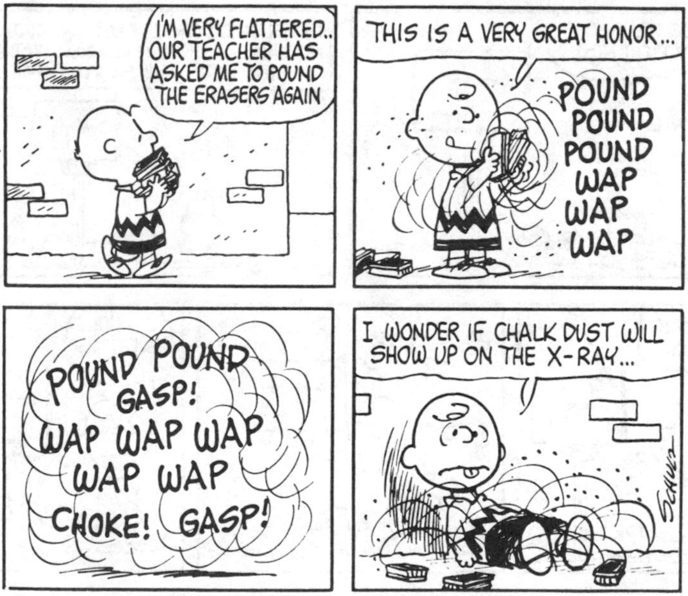
I'M VERY FLATTERED.. OUR TEACHER HAS ASKED ME TO POUND THE ERASERS AGAIN
THIS IS A VERY GREAT HONOR...
POUND POUND POUND WAP WAP WAP
POUND POUND
GASP!
WAP WAP WAP
WAP WAP
CHOKE! GASP!
I WONDER IF CHALK DUST WILL SHOW UP ON THE X-RAY...
SCHULZ

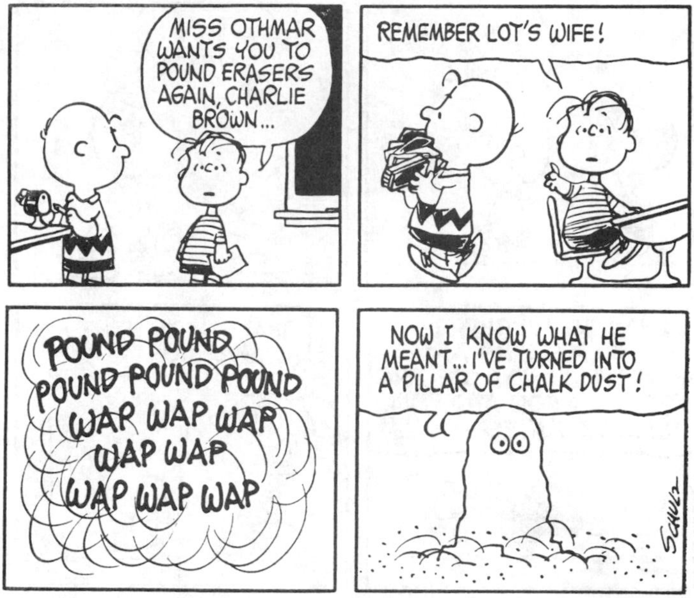
MISS OTHMAR WANTS YOU TO POUND ERASERS AGAIN, CHARLIE BROWN...
REMEMBER LOT'S WIFE!
POUND POUND POUND POUND POUND WAP WAP WAP WAP WAP WAP WAP WAP
NOW I KNOW WHAT HE MEANT... I'VE TURNED INTO A PILLAR OF CHALK DUST!
SCHULZ

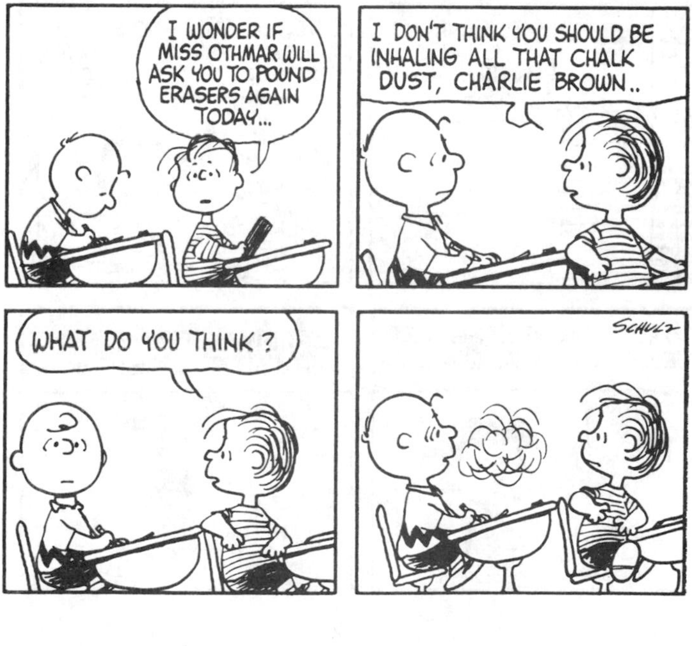
I WONDER IF MISS OTHMAR WILL ASK YOU TO POUND ERASERS AGAIN TODAY...
I DON'T THINK YOU SHOULD BE INHALING ALL THAT CHALK DUST, CHARLIE BROWN..
WHAT DO YOU THINK?
SCHULZ

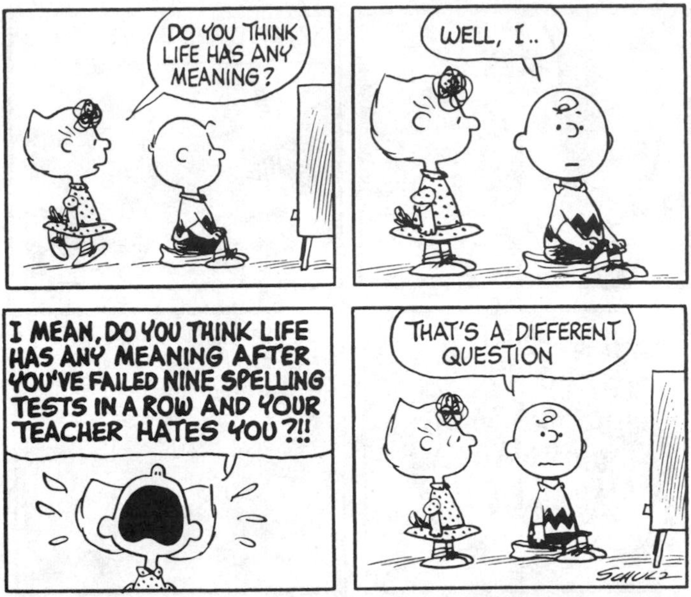
DO YOU THINK LIFE HAS ANY MEANING?
WELL, I..
I MEAN, DO YOU THINK LIFE HAS ANY MEANING AFTER YOU'VE FAILED NINE SPELLING TESTS IN A ROW AND YOUR TEACHER HATES YOU?!!
THAT'S A DIFFERENT QUESTION
SCHULZ

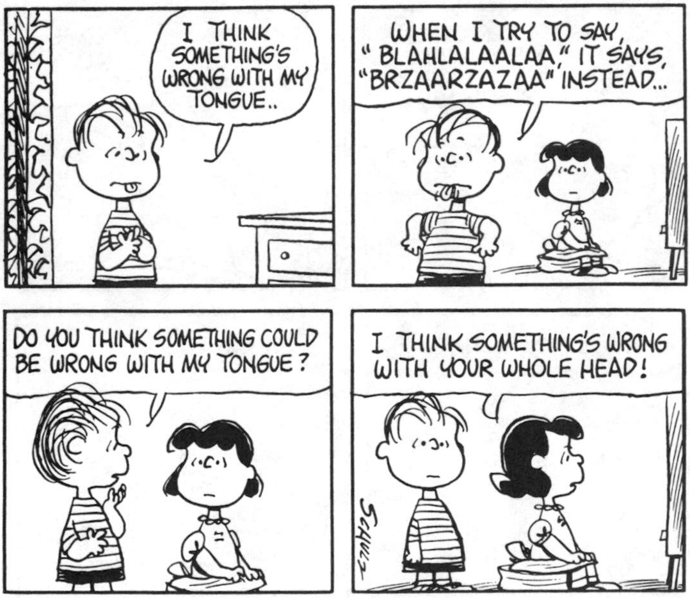
I THINK SOMETHING'S WRONG WITH MY TONGUE..
WHEN I TRY TO SAY, "BLAHLALAALAA," IT SAYS, "BRZAARZAZAA" INSTEAD...
DO YOU THINK SOMETHING COULD BE WRONG WITH MY TONGUE?
I THINK SOMETHING'S WRONG WITH YOUR WHOLE HEAD!
SCHULZ

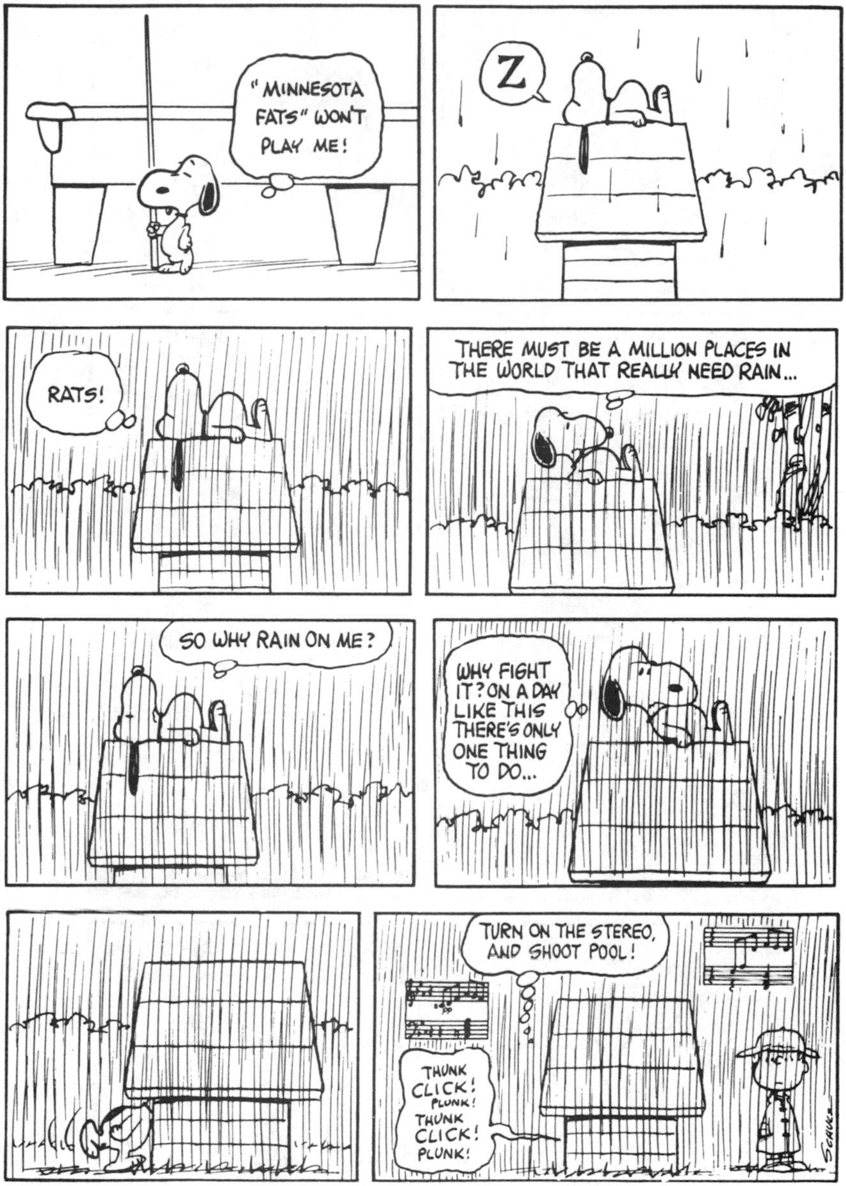
"MINNESOTA FATS" WON'T PLAY ME!
Z
RATS!
THERE MUST BE A MILLION PLACES IN THE WORLD THAT REALLY NEED RAIN...
SO WHY RAIN ON ME?
WHY FIGHT IT? ON A DAY LIKE THIS THERE'S ONLY ONE THING TO DO...
TURN ON THE STEREO, AND SHOOT POOL!
THUNK CLICK! PLUNK! THUNK CLICK! PLUNK!
SCHULZ

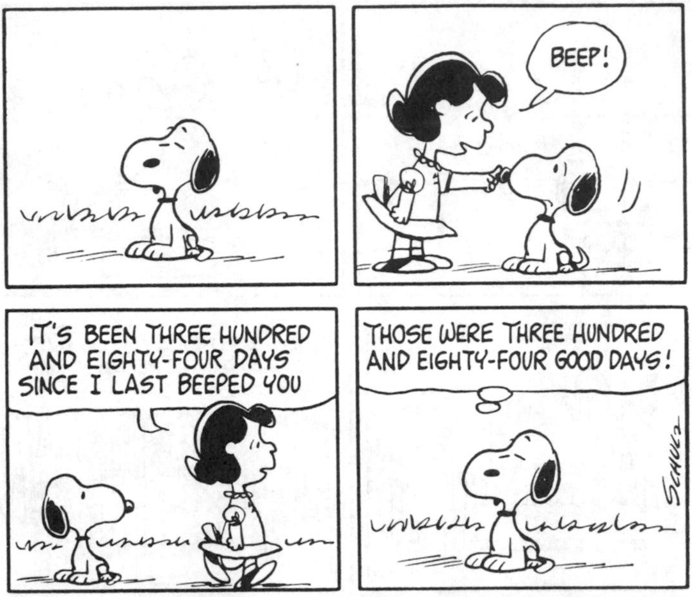
BEEP!
IT'S BEEN THREE HUNDRED AND EIGHTY-FOUR DAYS SINCE I LAST BEEPED YOU
THOSE WERE THREE HUNDRED AND EIGHTY-FOUR GOOD DAYS!
SCHULZ

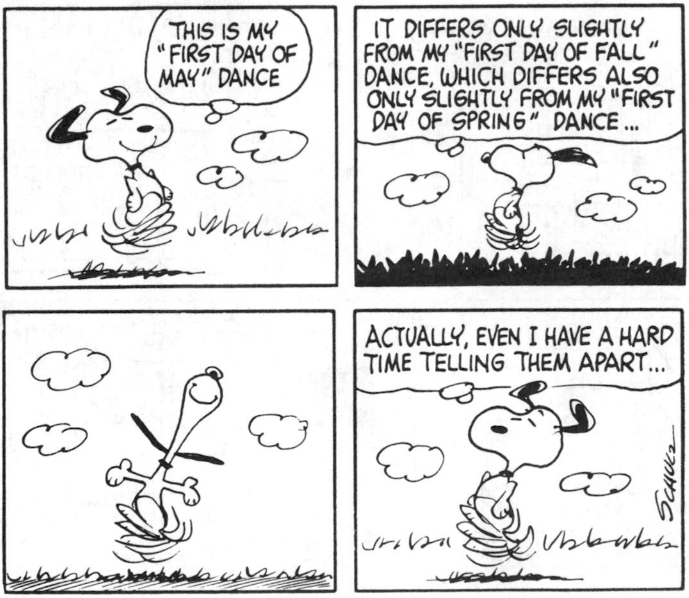
THIS IS MY "FIRST DAY OF MAY" DANCE
IT DIFFERS ONLY SLIGHTLY FROM MY "FIRST DAY OF FALL" DANCE, WHICH DIFFERS ALSO ONLY SLIGHTLY FROM MY "FIRST DAY OF SPRING" DANCE...
ACTUALLY, EVEN I HAVE A HARD TIME TELLING THEM APART...
SCHULZ

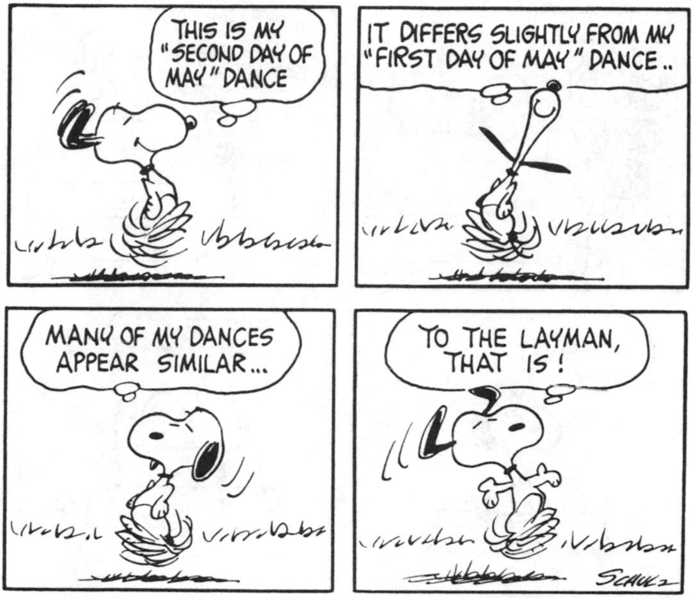

THIS IS MY "SECOND DAY OF MAY" DANCE
IT DIFFERS SLIGHTLY FROM MY "FIRST DAY OF MAY" DANCE..
MANY OF MY DANCES APPEAR SIMILAR...
TO THE LAYMAN, THAT IS!
SCHULZ

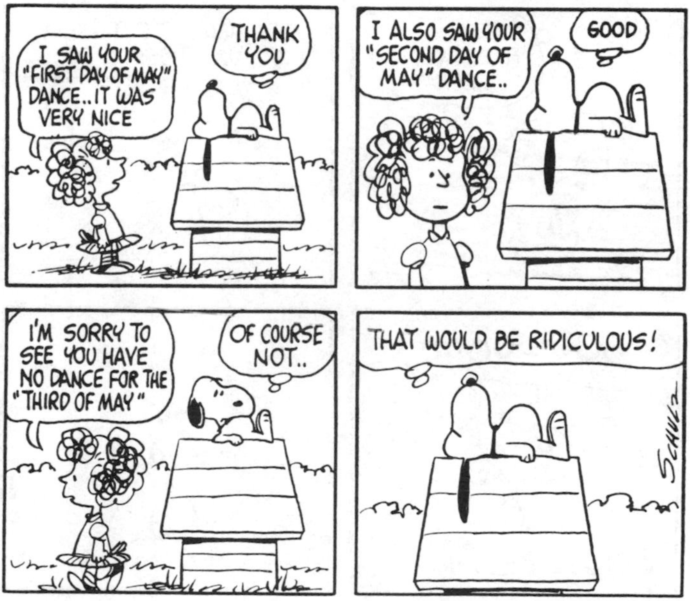

I SAW YOUR "FIRST DAY OF MAY" DANCE..IT WAS VERY NICE
THANK YOU
I ALSO SAW YOUR "SECOND DAY OF MAY" DANCE..
GOOD
I'M SORRY TO SEE YOU HAVE NO DANCE FOR THE "THIRD OF MAY"
OF COURSE NOT..
THAT WOULD BE RIDICULOUS!
SCHULZ

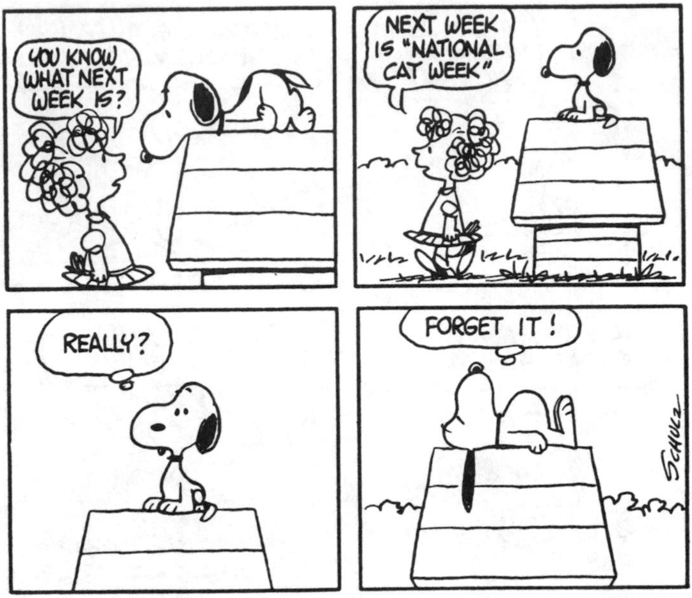
YOU KNOW WHAT NEXT WEEK IS?
NEXT WEEK IS "NATIONAL CAT WEEK"
REALLY?
FORGET IT!
SCHULZ

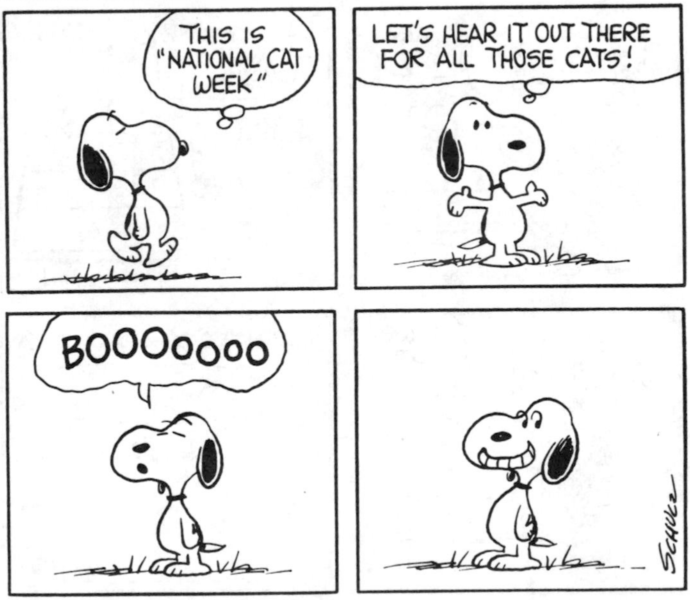
THIS IS "NATIONAL CAT WEEK"
LET'S HEAR IT OUT THERE FOR ALL THOSE CATS!
BOOOoooo
SCHULZ

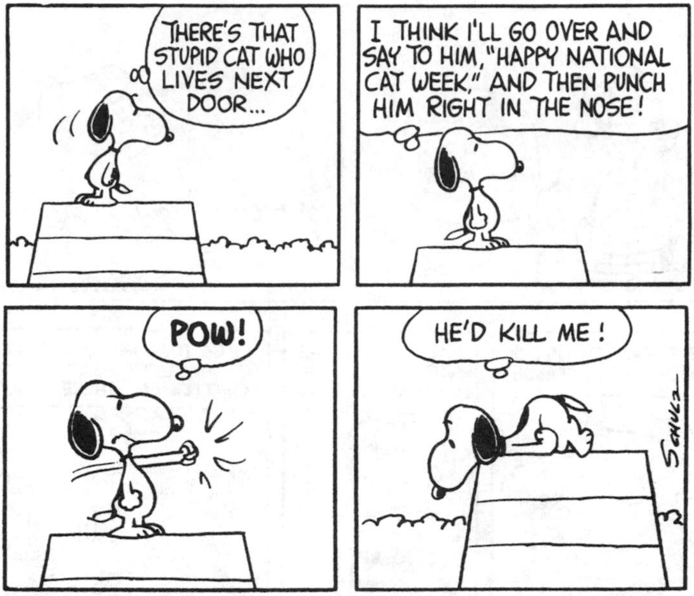
THERE'S THAT STUPID CAT WHO LIVES NEXT DOOR...
I THINK I'LL GO OVER AND SAY TO HIM, "HAPPY NATIONAL CAT WEEK," AND THEN PUNCH HIM RIGHT IN THE NOSE!
POW!
HE'D KILL ME!
SCHULZ

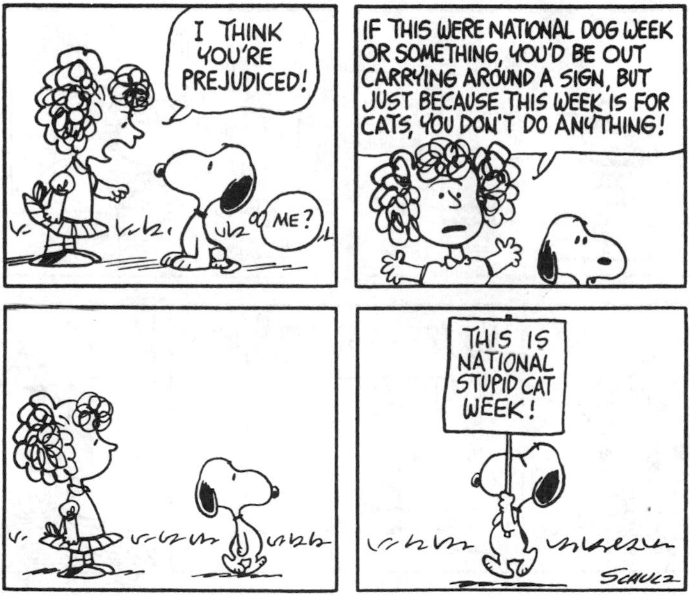
I THINK YOU'RE PREJUDICED!
ME?
IF THIS WERE NATIONAL DOG WEEK OR SOMETHING, YOU'D BE OUT CARRYING AROUND A SIGN, BUT JUST BECAUSE THIS WEEK IS FOR CATS, YOU DON'T DO ANYTHING!
THIS IS NATIONAL STUPID CAT WEEK!
SCHULZ

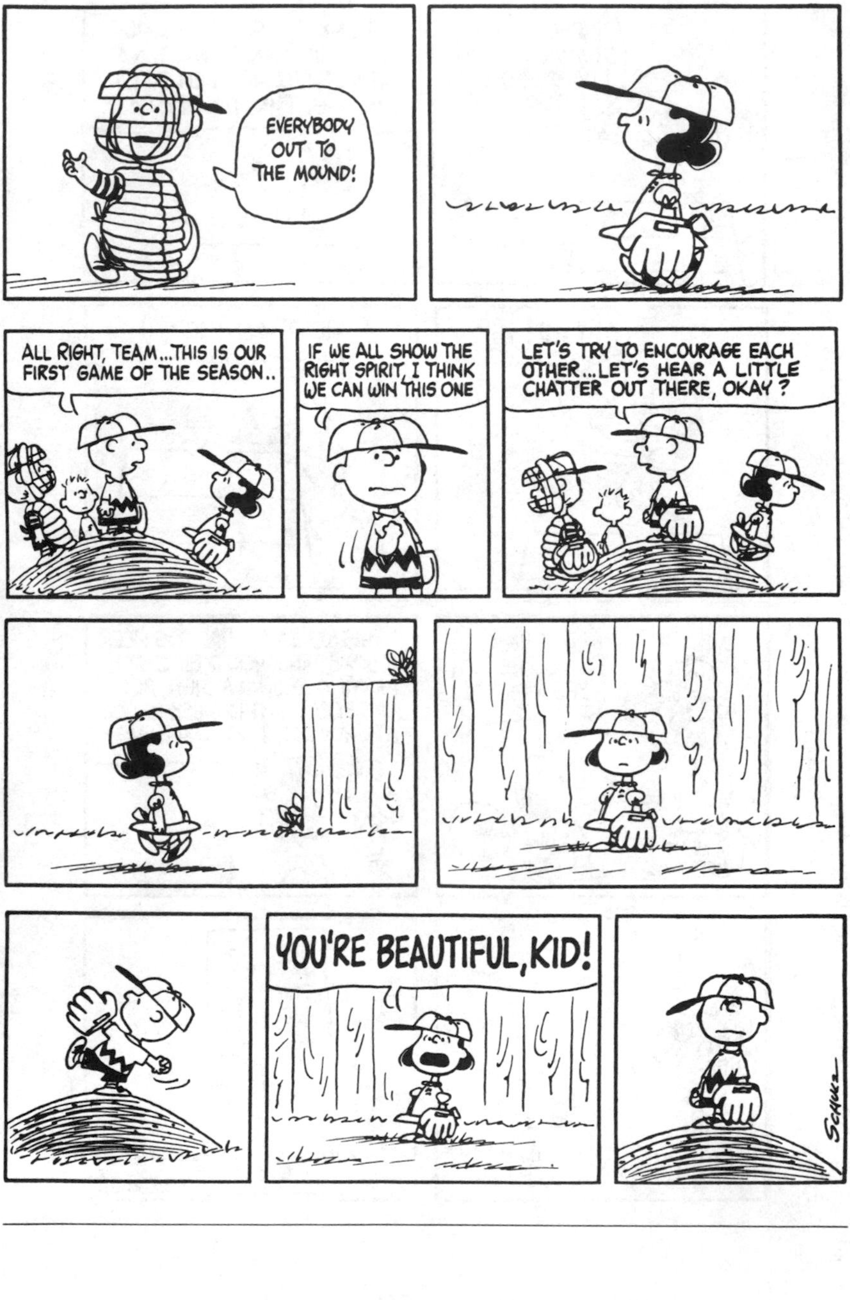
EVERYBODY OUT TO THE MOUND!
ALL RIGHT, TEAM...THIS IS OUR FIRST GAME OF THE SEASON..
IF WE ALL SHOW THE RIGHT SPIRIT, I THINK WE CAN WIN THIS ONE
LET'S TRY TO ENCOURAGE EACH OTHER...LET'S HEAR A LITTLE CHATTER OUT THERE, OKAY?
YOU'RE BEAUTIFUL, KID!
SCHULZ

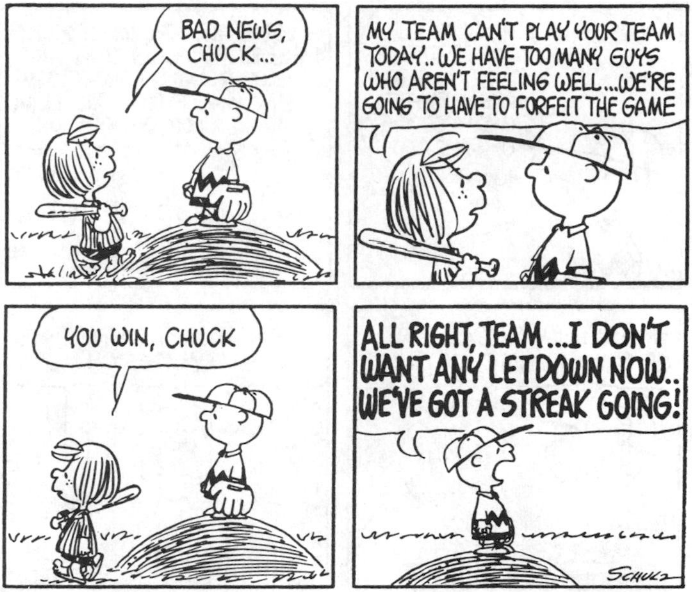
BAD NEWS, CHUCK...
MY TEAM CAN'T PLAY YOUR TEAM TODAY.. WE HAVE TOO MANY GUYS WHO AREN'T FEELING WELL...WE'RE GOING TO HAVE TO FORFEIT THE GAME
YOU WIN, CHUCK
ALL RIGHT, TEAM...I DON'T WANT ANY LETDOWN NOW.. WE'VE GOT A STREAK GOING!

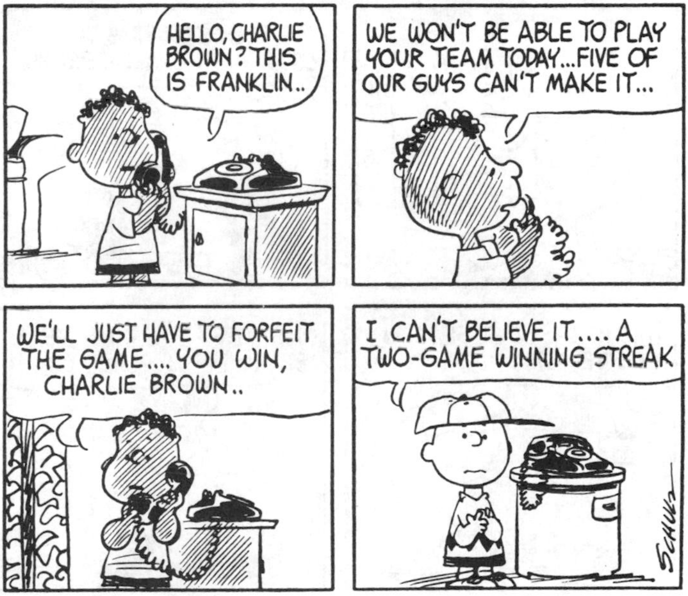
HELLO, CHARLIE BROWN? THIS IS FRANKLIN..
WE WON'T BE ABLE TO PLAY YOUR TEAM TODAY...FIVE OF OUR GUYS CAN'T MAKE IT...
WE'LL JUST HAVE TO FORFEIT THE GAME.... YOU WIN, CHARLIE BROWN..
I CAN'T BELIEVE IT.... A TWO-GAME WINNING STREAK

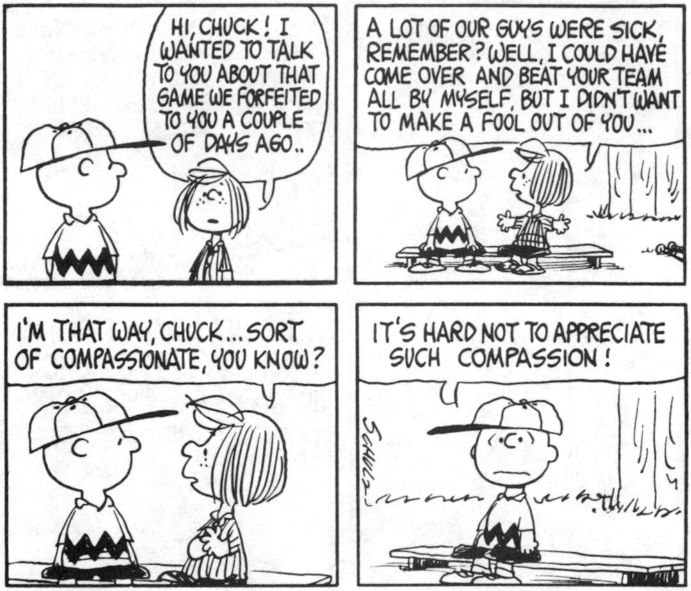
HI, CHUCK! I WANTED TO TALK TO YOU ABOUT THAT GAME WE FORFEITED TO YOU A COUPLE OF DAYS AGO..
A LOT OF OUR GUYS WERE SICK, REMEMBER? WELL, I COULD HAVE COME OVER AND BEAT YOUR TEAM ALL BY MYSELF, BUT I DIDN'T WANT TO MAKE A FOOL OUT OF YOU...
I'M THAT WAY, CHUCK... SORT OF COMPASSIONATE, YOU KNOW?
IT'S HARD NOT TO APPRECIATE SUCH COMPASSION!
SCHULZ

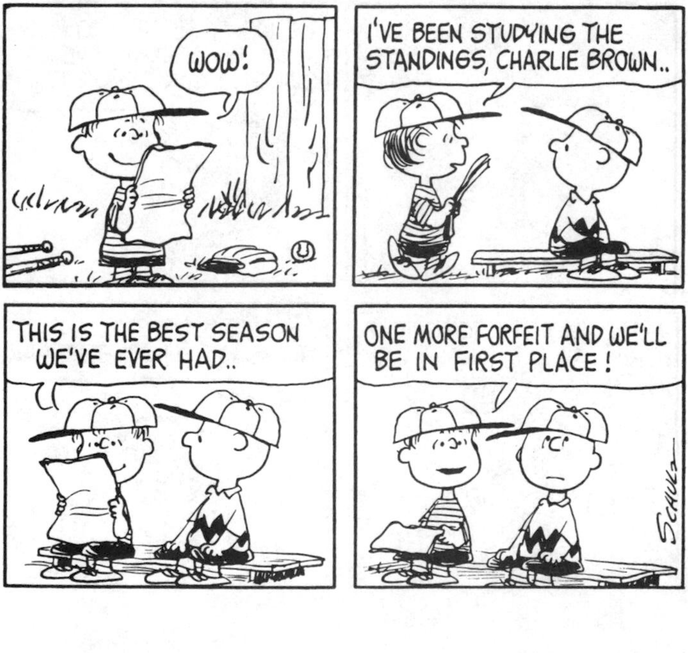
WOW!
I'VE BEEN STUDYING THE STANDINGS, CHARLIE BROWN..
THIS IS THE BEST SEASON WE'VE EVER HAD..
ONE MORE FORFEIT AND WE'LL BE IN FIRST PLACE!
SCHULZ

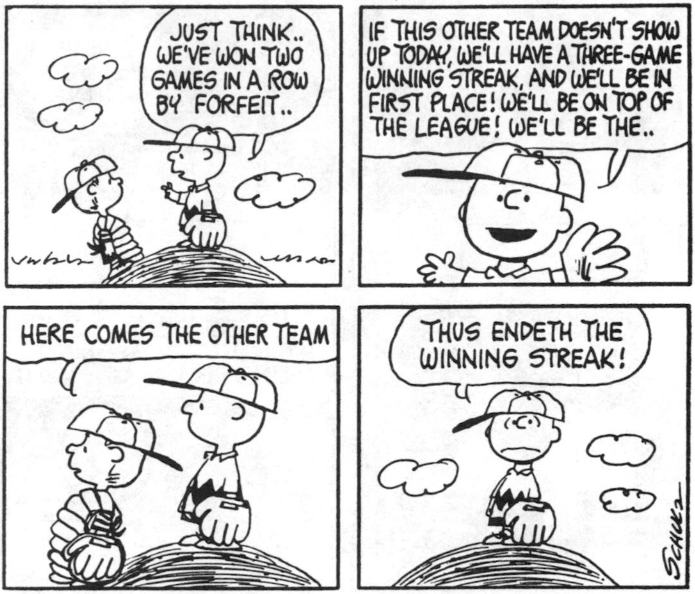
JUST THINK.. WE'VE WON TWO GAMES IN A ROW BY FORFEIT..
IF THIS OTHER TEAM DOESN'T SHOW UP TODAY, WE'LL HAVE A THREE-GAME WINNING STREAK, AND WE'LL BE IN FIRST PLACE! WE'LL BE ON TOP OF THE LEAGUE! WE'LL BE THE..
HERE COMES THE OTHER TEAM
THUS ENDETH THE WINNING STREAK!

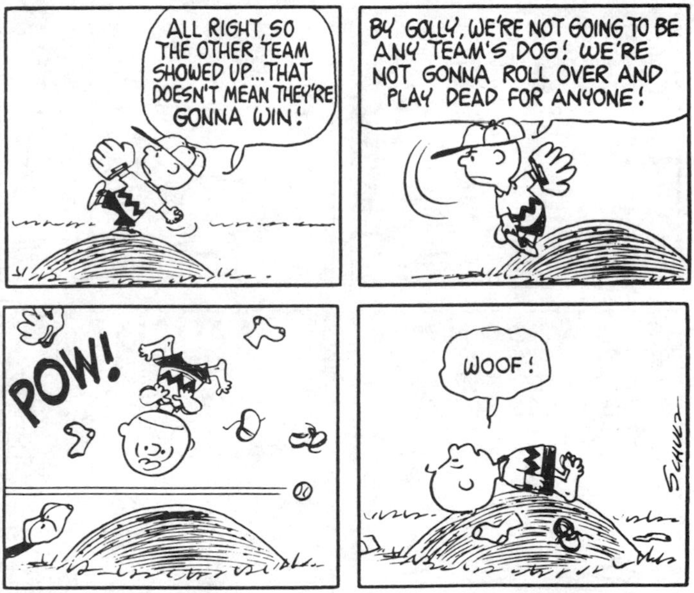
ALL RIGHT, SO THE OTHER TEAM SHOWED UP... THAT DOESN'T MEAN THEY'RE GONNA WIN!
BY GOLLY, WE'RE NOT GOING TO BE ANY TEAM'S DOG! WE'RE NOT GONNA ROLL OVER AND PLAY DEAD FOR ANYONE!
POW!
WOOF!

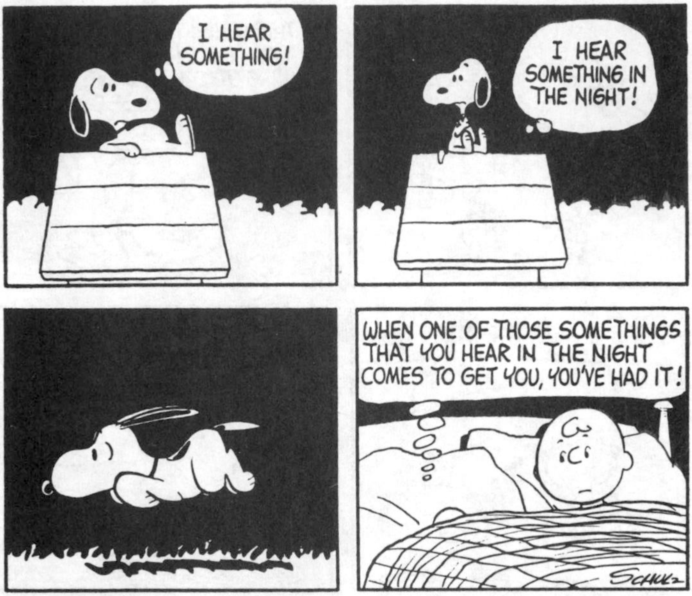
I HEAR SOMETHING!
I HEAR SOMETHING IN THE NIGHT!
WHEN ONE OF THOSE SOMETHINGS THAT YOU HEAR IN THE NIGHT COMES TO GET YOU, YOU'VE HAD IT!
SCHULZ

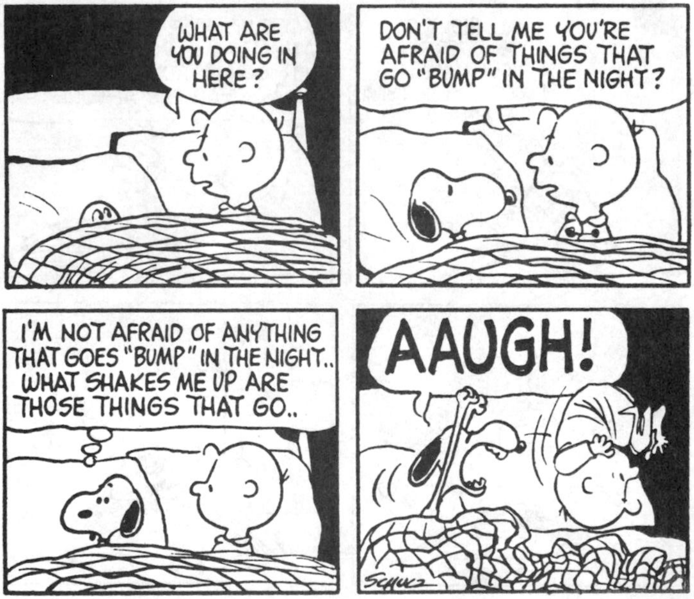
WHAT ARE YOU DOING IN HERE?
DON'T TELL ME YOU'RE AFRAID OF THINGS THAT GO "BUMP" IN THE NIGHT?
I'M NOT AFRAID OF ANYTHING THAT GOES "BUMP" IN THE NIGHT.. WHAT SHAKES ME UP ARE THOSE THINGS THAT GO..
AAUGH!
SCHULZ

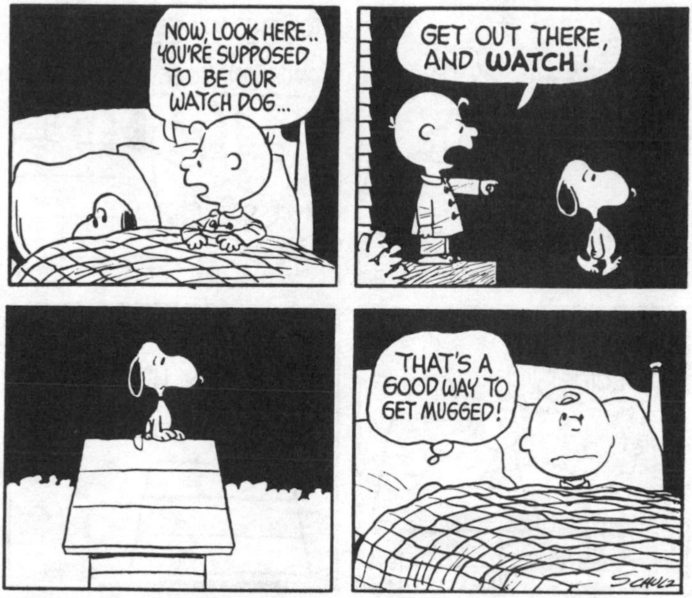
NOW, LOOK HERE.. YOU'RE SUPPOSED TO BE OUR WATCH DOG...
GET OUT THERE, AND WATCH!
THAT'S A GOOD WAY TO GET MUGGED!
SCHULZ

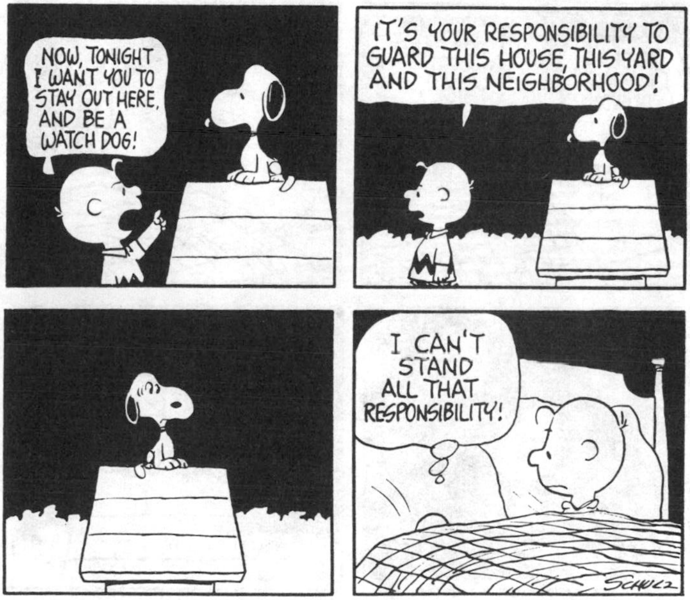
NOW, TONIGHT I WANT YOU TO STAY OUT HERE, AND BE A WATCH DOG!
IT'S YOUR RESPONSIBILITY TO GUARD THIS HOUSE, THIS YARD AND THIS NEIGHBORHOOD!
I CAN'T STAND ALL THAT RESPONSIBILITY!
SCHULZ

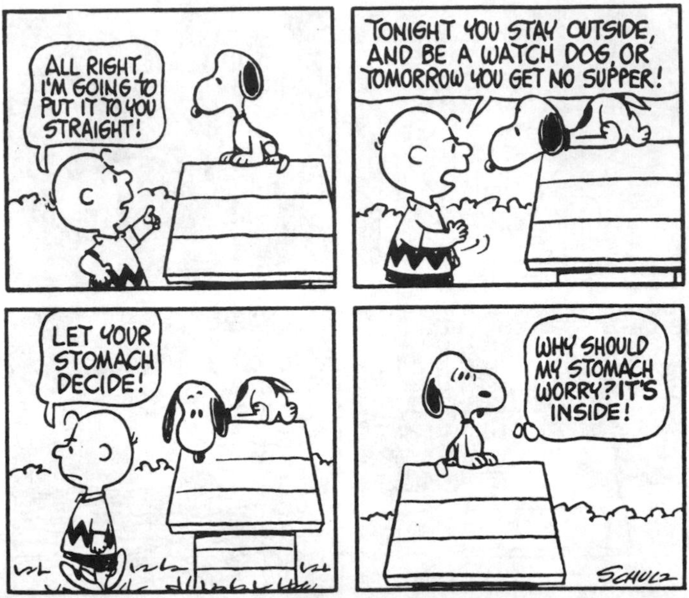
ALL RIGHT, I'M GOING TO PUT IT TO YOU STRAIGHT!
TONIGHT YOU STAY OUTSIDE, AND BE A WATCH DOG, OR TOMORROW YOU GET NO SUPPER!
LET YOUR STOMACH DECIDE!
WHY SHOULD MY STOMACH WORRY? IT'S INSIDE!
SCHULZ

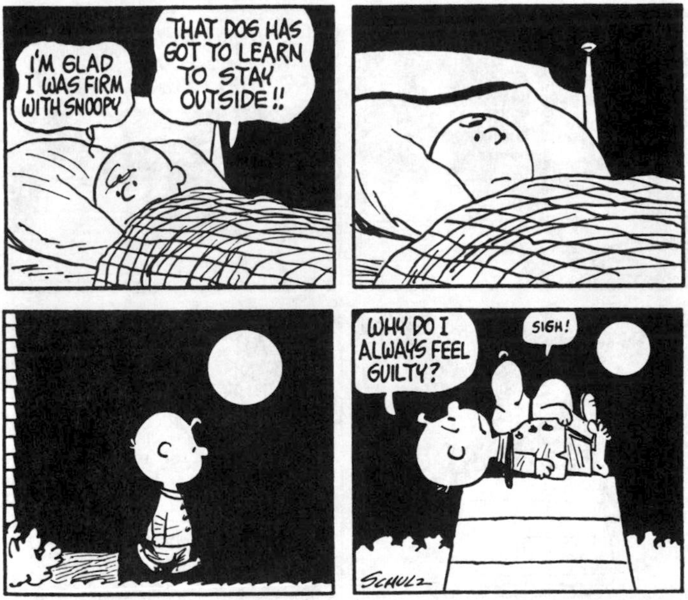
I'M GLAD I WAS FIRM WITH SNOOPY
THAT DOG HAS GOT TO LEARN TO STAY OUTSIDE!!
WHY DO I ALWAYS FEEL GUILTY?
SIGH!
SCHULZ

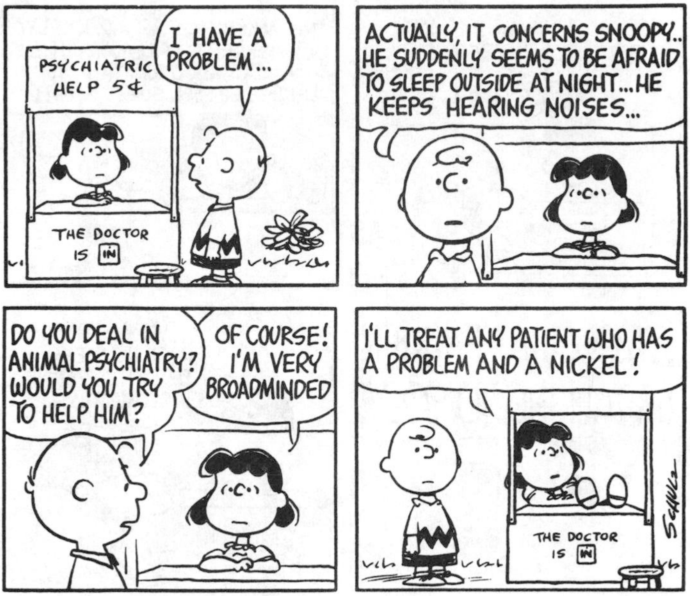
I HAVE A PROBLEM...
PSYCHIATRIC HELP 5¢
THE DOCTOR IS IN
ACTUALLY, IT CONCERNS SNOOPY.. HE SUDDENLY SEEMS TO BE AFRAID TO SLEEP OUTSIDE AT NIGHT... HE KEEPS HEARING NOISES...
DO YOU DEAL IN ANIMAL PSYCHIATRY? WOULD YOU TRY TO HELP HIM?
OF COURSE! I'M VERY BROADMINDED
I'LL TREAT ANY PATIENT WHO HAS A PROBLEM AND A NICKEL!
THE DOCTOR IS IN
SCHULZ

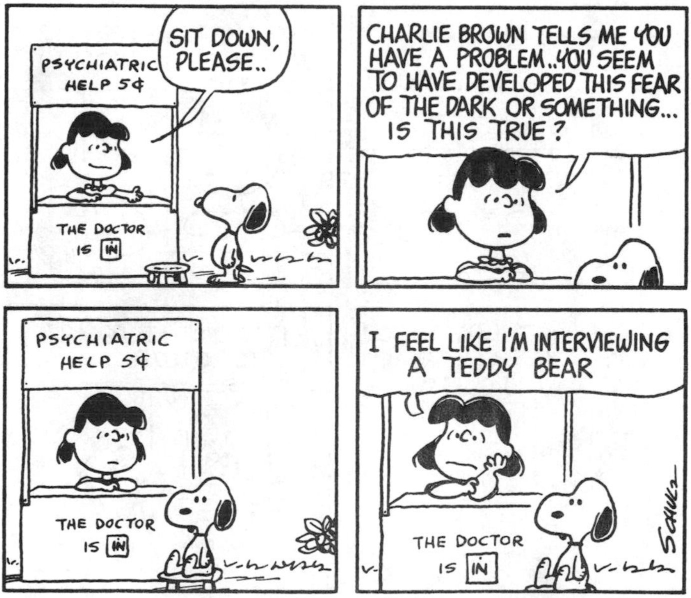
PSYCHIATRIC HELP 5¢
SIT DOWN, PLEASE..
THE DOCTOR IS IN
CHARLIE BROWN TELLS ME YOU HAVE A PROBLEM..YOU SEEM TO HAVE DEVELOPED THIS FEAR OF THE DARK OR SOMETHING... IS THIS TRUE?
PSYCHIATRIC HELP 5¢
THE DOCTOR IS IN
I FEEL LIKE I'M INTERVIEWING A TEDDY BEAR
THE DOCTOR IS IN
SCHULZ

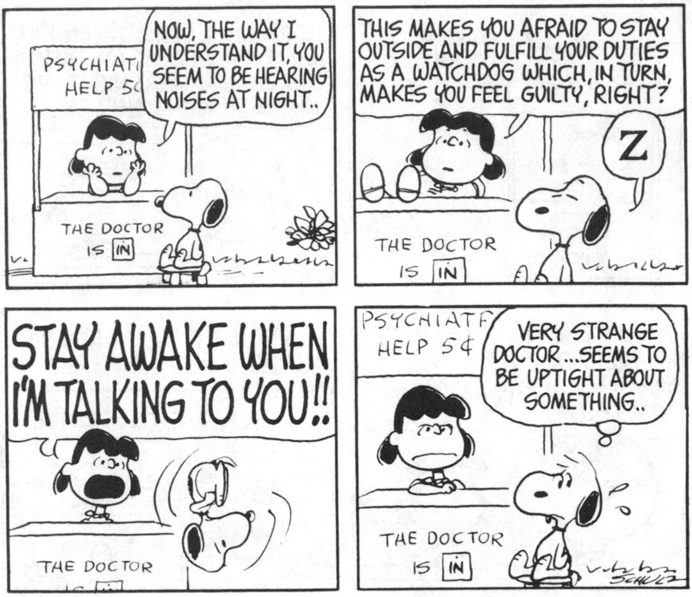
NOW, THE WAY I UNDERSTAND IT, YOU SEEM TO BE HEARING NOISES AT NIGHT..
THIS MAKES YOU AFRAID TO STAY OUTSIDE AND FULFILL YOUR DUTIES AS A WATCHDOG WHICH, IN TURN, MAKES YOU FEEL GUILTY, RIGHT?
Z
STAY AWAKE WHEN I'M TALKING TO YOU!!
VERY STRANGE DOCTOR...SEEMS TO BE UPTIGHT ABOUT SOMETHING..

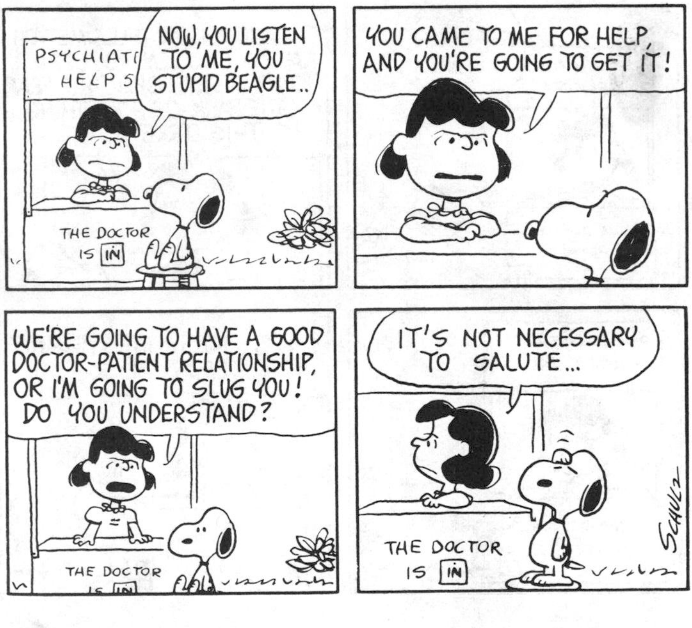
NOW, YOU LISTEN TO ME, YOU STUPID BEAGLE..
YOU CAME TO ME FOR HELP, AND YOU'RE GOING TO GET IT!
WE'RE GOING TO HAVE A GOOD DOCTOR-PATIENT RELATIONSHIP, OR I'M GOING TO SLUG YOU! DO YOU UNDERSTAND?
IT'S NOT NECESSARY TO SALUTE...

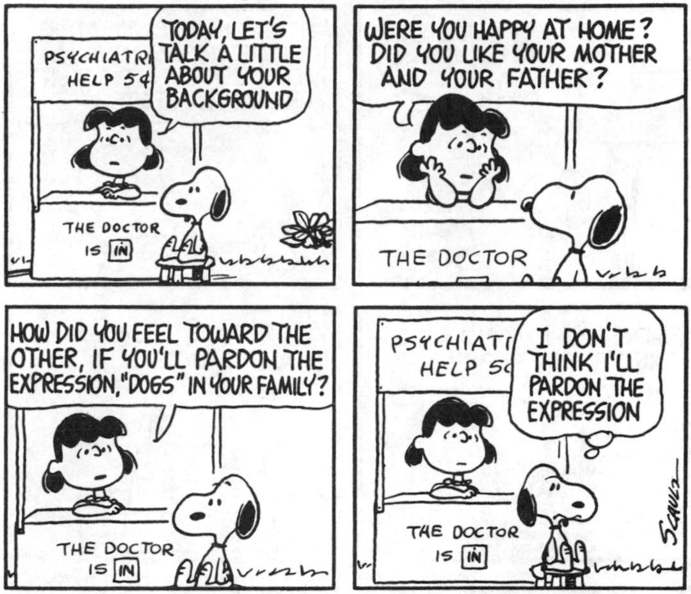
PSYCHIATR
HELP 5¢
TODAY, LET'S TALK A LITTLE ABOUT YOUR BACKGROUND
THE DOCTOR IS IN
WERE YOU HAPPY AT HOME? DID YOU LIKE YOUR MOTHER AND YOUR FATHER?
THE DOCTOR
HOW DID YOU FEEL TOWARD THE OTHER, IF YOU'LL PARDON THE EXPRESSION, "DOGS" IN YOUR FAMILY?
THE DOCTOR IS IN
PSYCHIATI
HELP 5¢
I DON'T THINK I'LL PARDON THE EXPRESSION
THE DOCTOR IS IN
SCHULZ

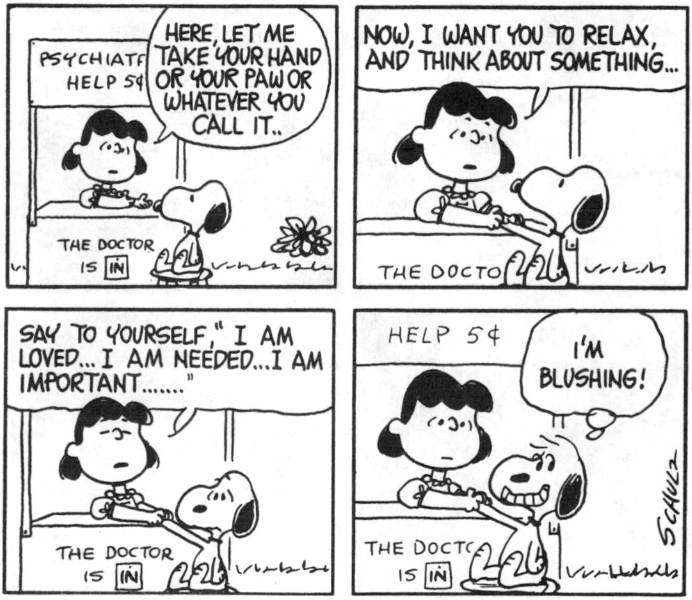
PSYCHIATR
HELP 5¢
HERE, LET ME TAKE YOUR HAND OR YOUR PAW OR WHATEVER YOU CALL IT..
THE DOCTOR IS IN
NOW, I WANT YOU TO RELAX, AND THINK ABOUT SOMETHING...
THE DOCTO
SAY TO YOURSELF, "I AM LOVED... I AM NEEDED...I AM IMPORTANT......."
THE DOCTOR IS IN
HELP 5¢
I'M BLUSHING!
THE DOCTC IS IN
SCHULZ

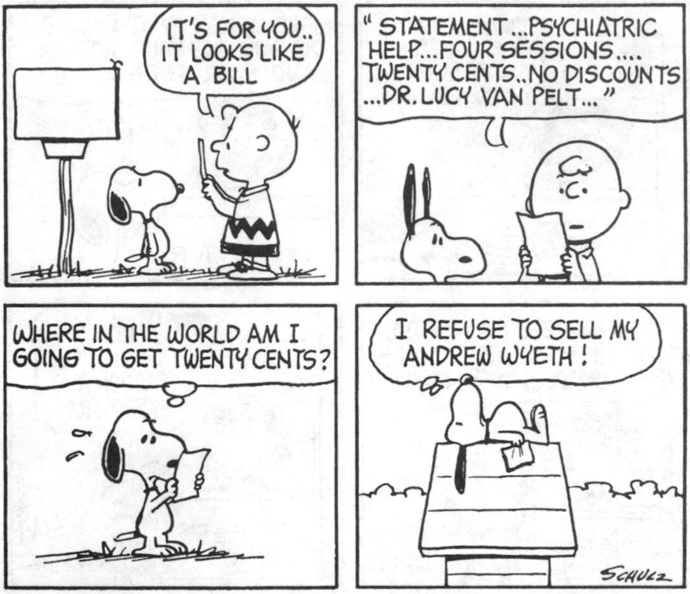
IT'S FOR YOU..
IT LOOKS LIKE
A BILL
" STATEMENT...PSYCHIATRIC HELP...FOUR SESSIONS.... TWENTY CENTS..NO DISCOUNTS ...DR. LUCY VAN PELT..."
WHERE IN THE WORLD AM I GOING TO GET TWENTY CENTS?
I REFUSE TO SELL MY ANDREW WYETH!
SCHULZ

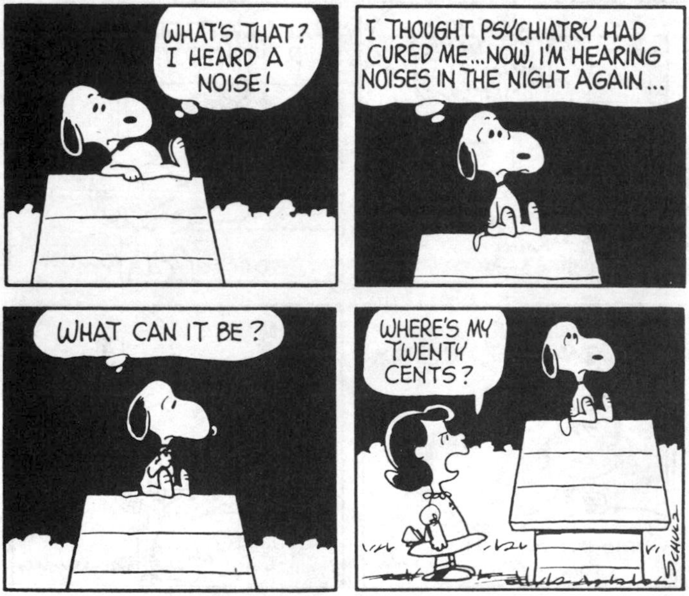
WHAT'S THAT? I HEARD A NOISE!
I THOUGHT PSYCHIATRY HAD CURED ME...NOW, I'M HEARING NOISES IN THE NIGHT AGAIN...
WHAT CAN IT BE?
WHERE'S MY TWENTY CENTS?
SCHULZ

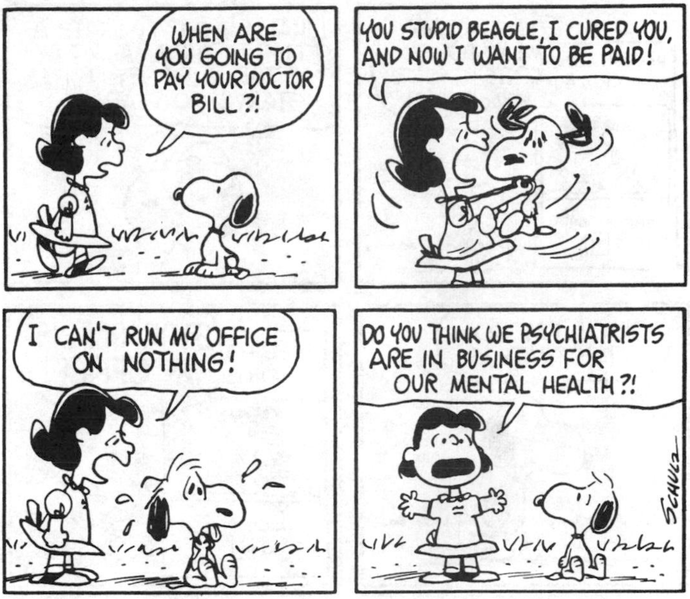
WHEN ARE YOU GOING TO PAY YOUR DOCTOR BILL ?!
YOU STUPID BEAGLE, I CURED YOU, AND NOW I WANT TO BE PAID!
I CAN'T RUN MY OFFICE ON NOTHING!
DO YOU THINK WE PSYCHIATRISTS ARE IN BUSINESS FOR OUR MENTAL HEALTH ?!
SCHULZ

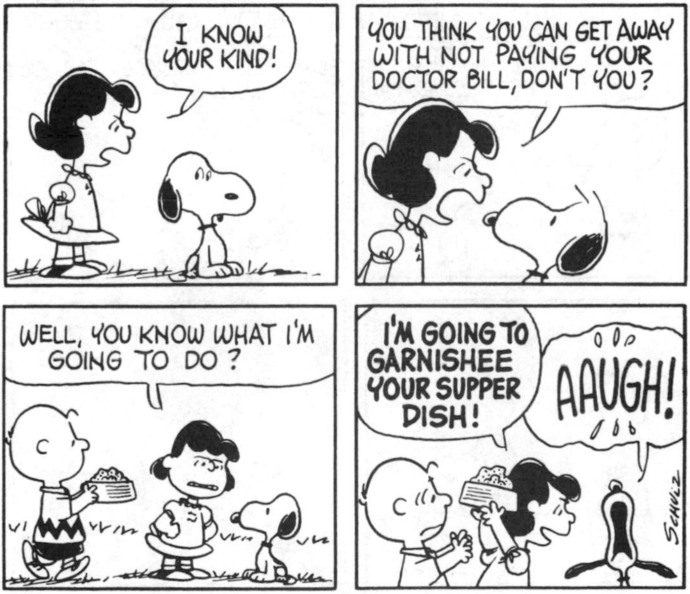
I KNOW YOUR KIND!
YOU THINK YOU CAN GET AWAY WITH NOT PAYING YOUR DOCTOR BILL, DON'T YOU?
WELL, YOU KNOW WHAT I'M GOING TO DO?
I'M GOING TO GARNISHEE YOUR SUPPER DISH!
AAUGH!
SCHULZ

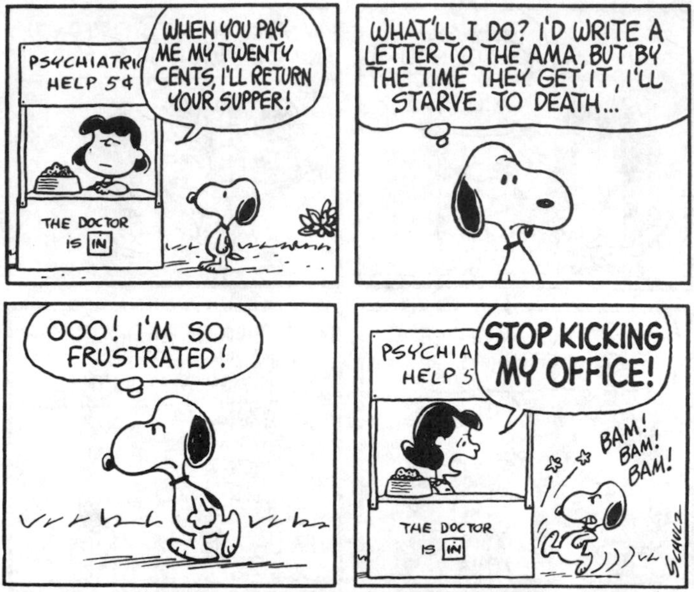
PSYCHIATRI
HELP 5¢
WHEN YOU PAY ME MY TWENTY CENTS, I'LL RETURN YOUR SUPPER!
THE DOCTOR IS IN
WHAT'LL I DO? I'D WRITE A LETTER TO THE AMA, BUT BY THE TIME THEY GET IT, I'LL STARVE TO DEATH...
OOO! I'M SO FRUSTRATED!
PSYCHIA
HELP 5
STOP KICKING MY OFFICE!
THE DOCTOR IS IN
BAM! BAM! BAM!
SCHULZ

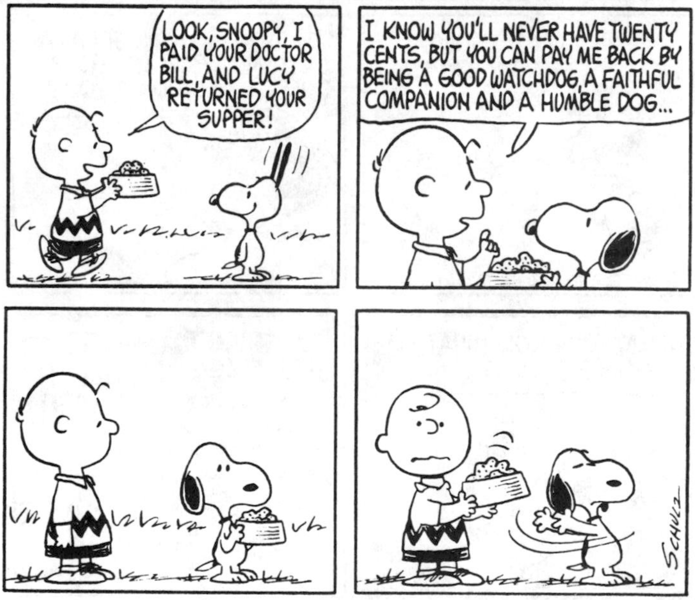
LOOK, SNOOPY, I PAID YOUR DOCTOR BILL, AND LUCY RETURNED YOUR SUPPER!
I KNOW YOU'LL NEVER HAVE TWENTY CENTS, BUT YOU CAN PAY ME BACK BY BEING A GOOD WATCHDOG, A FAITHFUL COMPANION AND A HUMBLE DOG...
SCHULZ

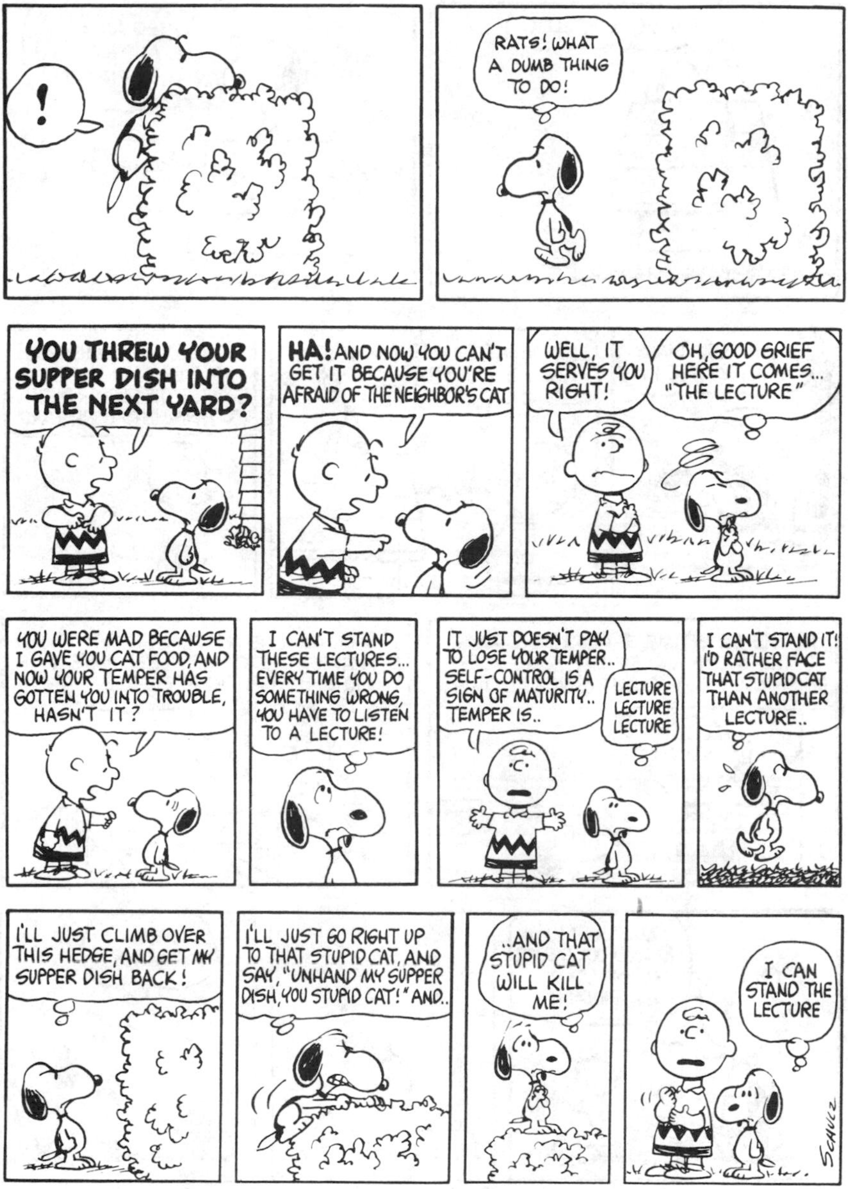
!
RATS! WHAT A DUMB THING TO DO!
YOU THREW YOUR SUPPER DISH INTO THE NEXT YARD?
HA! AND NOW YOU CAN'T GET IT BECAUSE YOU'RE AFRAID OF THE NEIGHBOR'S CAT
WELL, IT SERVES YOU RIGHT!
OH, GOOD GRIEF HERE IT COMES... "THE LECTURE"
YOU WERE MAD BECAUSE I GAVE YOU CAT FOOD, AND NOW YOUR TEMPER HAS GOTTEN YOU INTO TROUBLE, HASN'T IT?
I CAN'T STAND THESE LECTURES... EVERY TIME YOU DO SOMETHING WRONG, YOU HAVE TO LISTEN TO A LECTURE!
IT JUST DOESN'T PAY TO LOSE YOUR TEMPER.. SELF-CONTROL IS A SIGN OF MATURITY.. TEMPER IS..
LECTURE LECTURE LECTURE
I CAN'T STAND IT! I'D RATHER FACE THAT STUPID CAT THAN ANOTHER LECTURE..
I'LL JUST CLIMB OVER THIS HEDGE, AND GET MY SUPPER DISH BACK!
I'LL JUST GO RIGHT UP TO THAT STUPID CAT, AND SAY, "UNHAND MY SUPPER DISH, YOU STUPID CAT!" AND..
..AND THAT STUPID CAT WILL KILL ME!
I CAN STAND THE LECTURE
SCHULZ

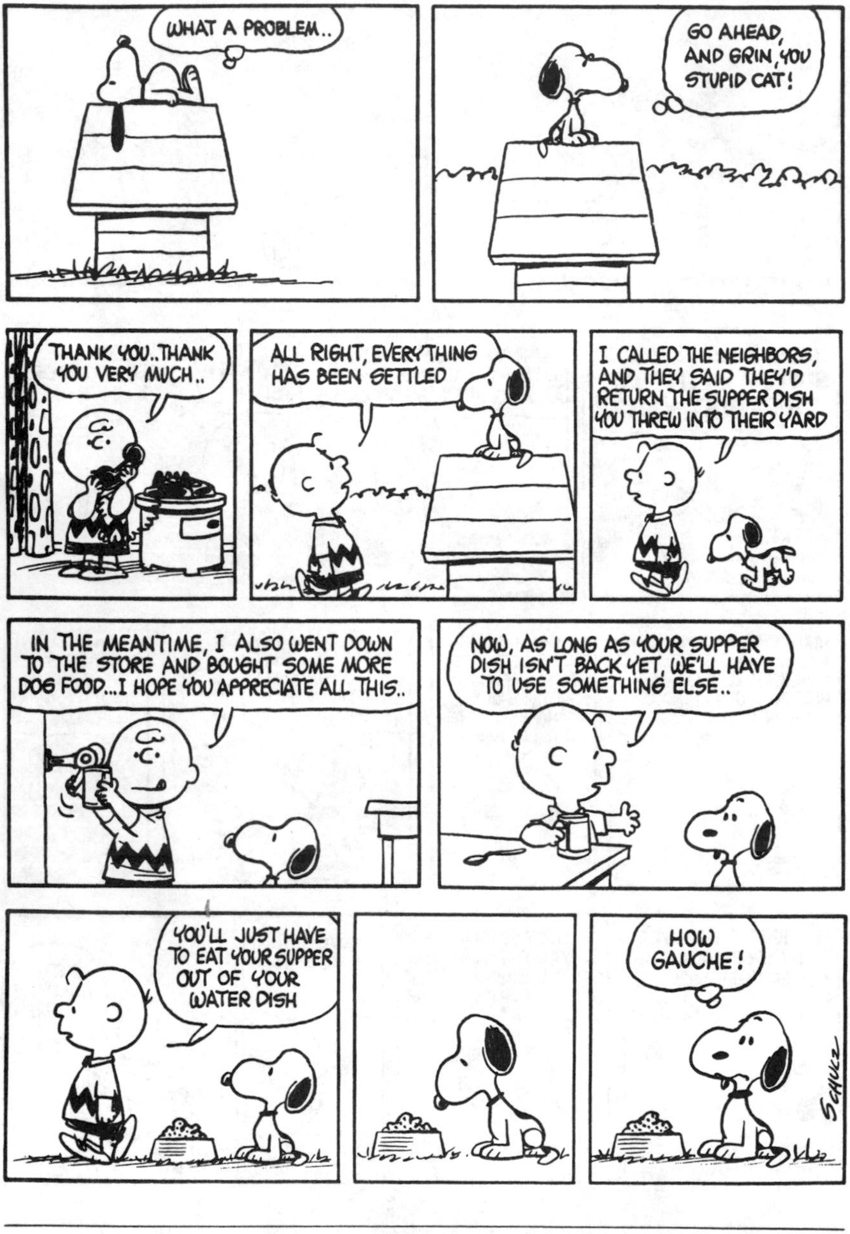
WHAT A PROBLEM..
GO AHEAD, AND GRIN, YOU STUPID CAT!
THANK YOU..THANK YOU VERY MUCH..
ALL RIGHT, EVERYTHING HAS BEEN SETTLED
I CALLED THE NEIGHBORS, AND THEY SAID THEY'D RETURN THE SUPPER DISH YOU THREW INTO THEIR YARD
IN THE MEANTIME, I ALSO WENT DOWN TO THE STORE AND BOUGHT SOME MORE DOG FOOD...I HOPE YOU APPRECIATE ALL THIS..
NOW, AS LONG AS YOUR SUPPER DISH ISN'T BACK YET, WE'LL HAVE TO USE SOMETHING ELSE..
YOU'LL JUST HAVE TO EAT YOUR SUPPER OUT OF YOUR WATER DISH
HOW GAUCHE!
SCHULZ

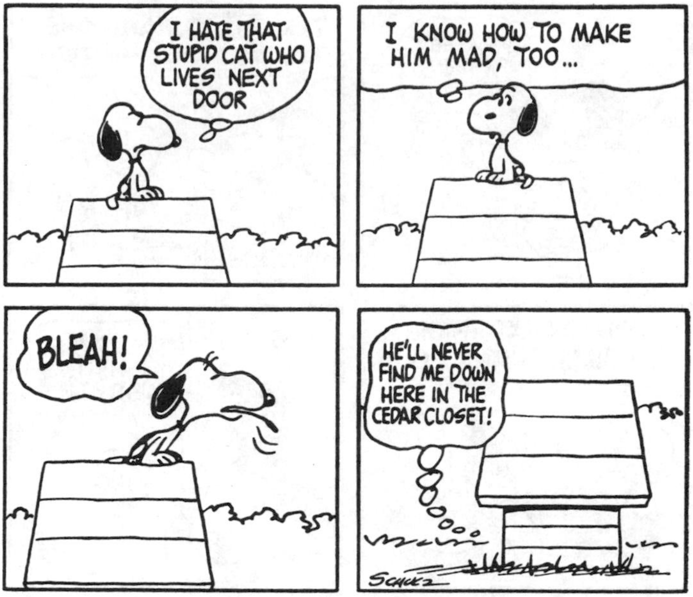
I HATE THAT STUPID CAT WHO LIVES NEXT DOOR
I KNOW HOW TO MAKE HIM MAD, TOO...
BLEAH!
HE'LL NEVER FIND ME DOWN HERE IN THE CEDAR CLOSET!
SCHULZ

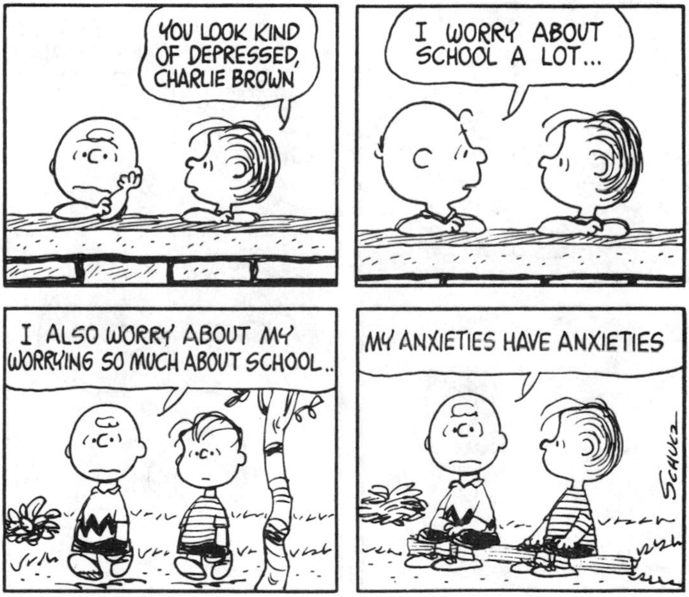
YOU LOOK KIND OF DEPRESSED, CHARLIE BROWN
I WORRY ABOUT SCHOOL A LOT...
I ALSO WORRY ABOUT MY WORRYING SO MUCH ABOUT SCHOOL...
MY ANXIETIES HAVE ANXIETIES
SCHULZ

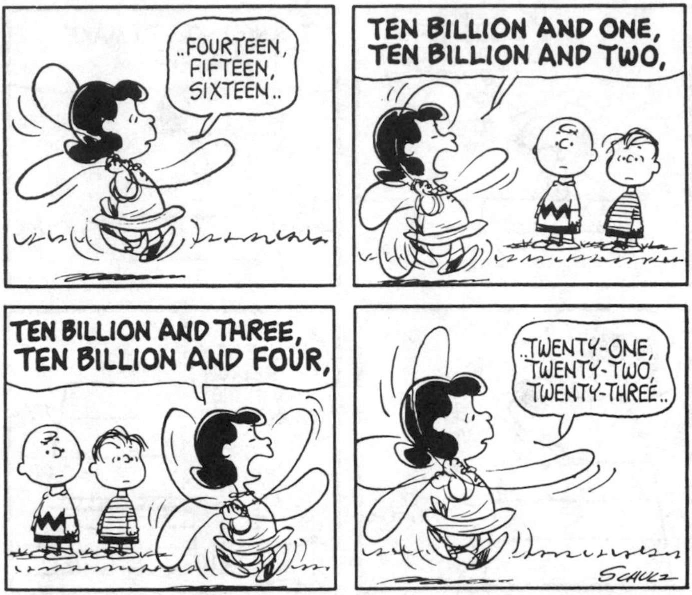
..FOURTEEN, FIFTEEN, SIXTEEN..
TEN BILLION AND ONE, TEN BILLION AND TWO,
TEN BILLION AND THREE, TEN BILLION AND FOUR,
..TWENTY-ONE, TWENTY-TWO, TWENTY-THREE..
SCHULZ

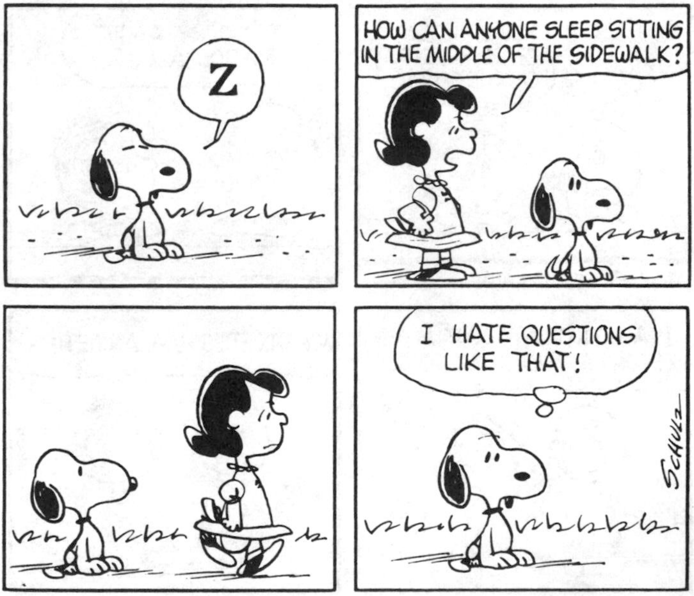
Z
HOW CAN ANYONE SLEEP SITTING IN THE MIDDLE OF THE SIDEWALK?
I HATE QUESTIONS LIKE THAT!
SCHULZ

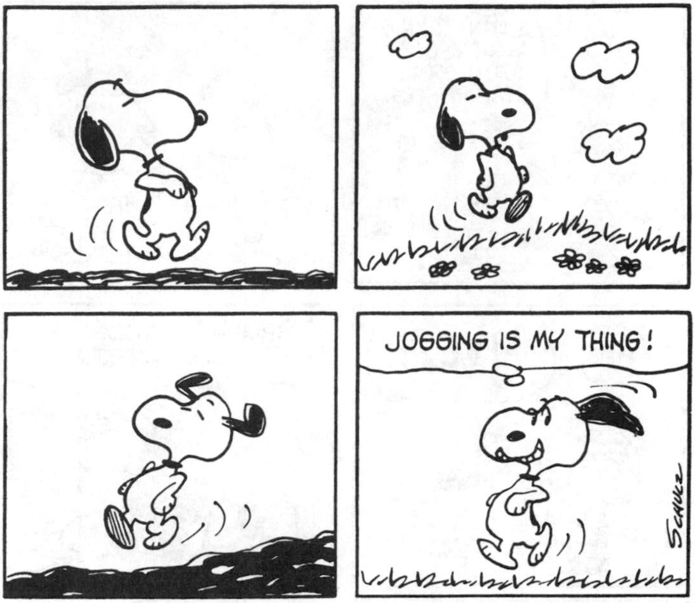
JOGGING IS MY THING!

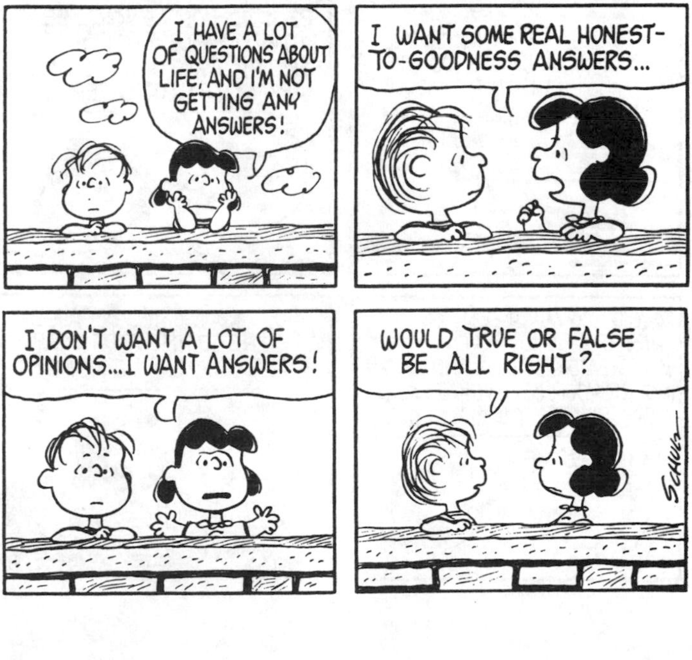
I HAVE A LOT OF QUESTIONS ABOUT LIFE, AND I'M NOT GETTING ANY ANSWERS!
I WANT SOME REAL HONEST-TO-GOODNESS ANSWERS...
I DON'T WANT A LOT OF OPINIONS...I WANT ANSWERS!
WOULD TRUE OR FALSE BE ALL RIGHT?

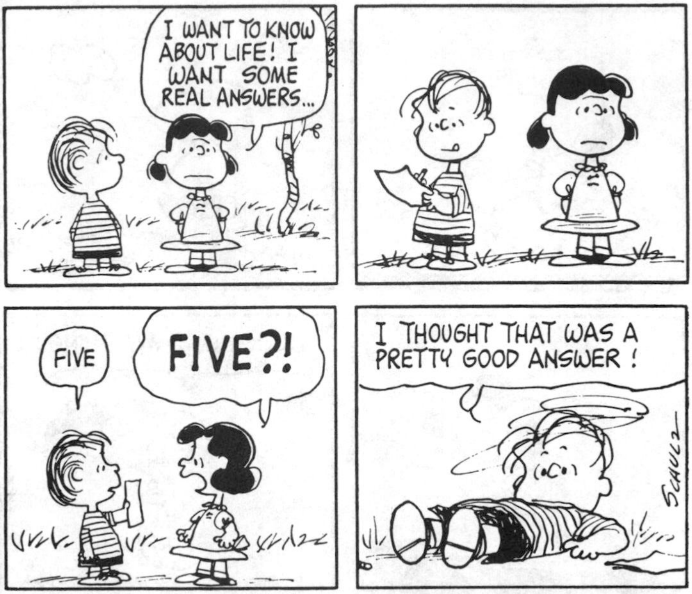
I WANT TO KNOW ABOUT LIFE! I WANT SOME REAL ANSWERS...
FIVE
FIVE?!
I THOUGHT THAT WAS A PRETTY GOOD ANSWER!
SCHULZ

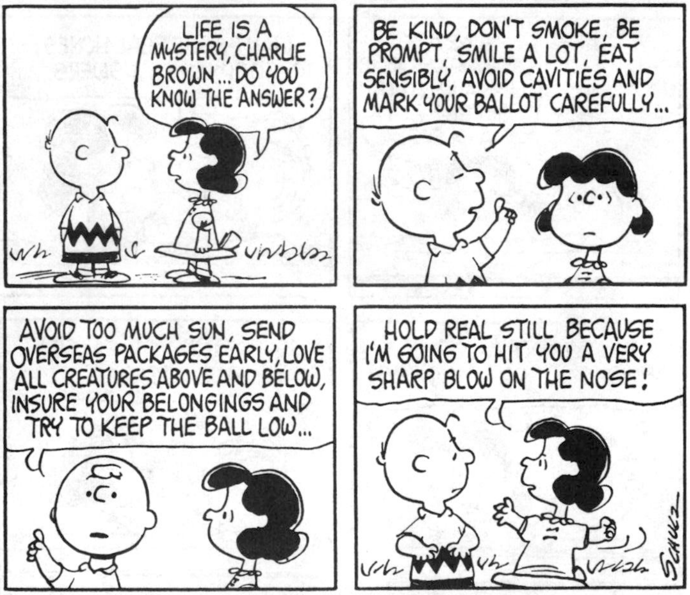
LIFE IS A MYSTERY, CHARLIE BROWN... DO YOU KNOW THE ANSWER?
BE KIND, DON'T SMOKE, BE PROMPT, SMILE A LOT, EAT SENSIBLY, AVOID CAVITIES AND MARK YOUR BALLOT CAREFULLY...
AVOID TOO MUCH SUN, SEND OVERSEAS PACKAGES EARLY, LOVE ALL CREATURES ABOVE AND BELOW, INSURE YOUR BELONGINGS AND TRY TO KEEP THE BALL LOW...
HOLD REAL STILL BECAUSE I'M GOING TO HIT YOU A VERY SHARP BLOW ON THE NOSE!
SCHULZ

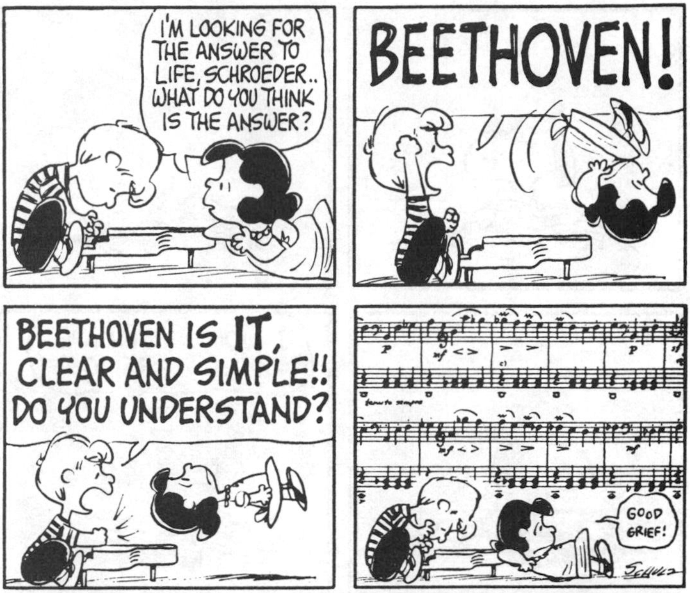
I'M LOOKING FOR THE ANSWER TO LIFE, SCHROEDER.. WHAT DO YOU THINK IS THE ANSWER?
BEETHOVEN!
BEETHOVEN IS IT, CLEAR AND SIMPLE!! DO YOU UNDERSTAND?
GOOD GRIEF!
SCHULZ

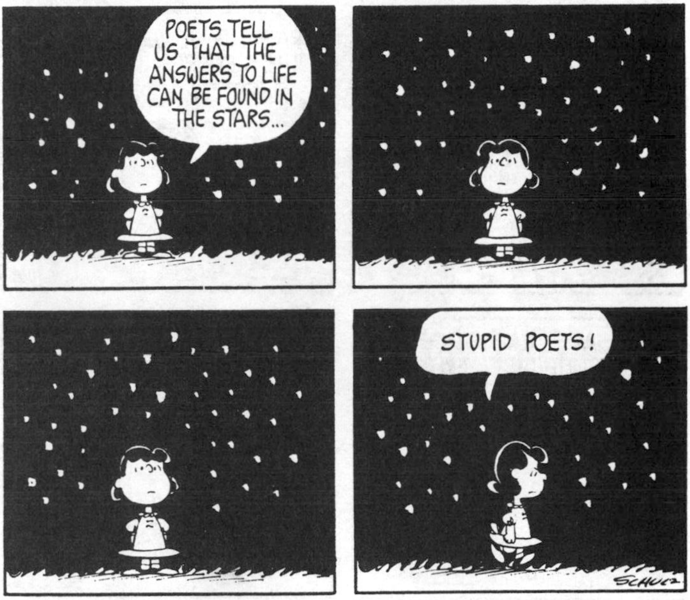
POETS TELL US THAT THE ANSWERS TO LIFE CAN BE FOUND IN THE STARS...
STUPID POETS!
SCHULZ

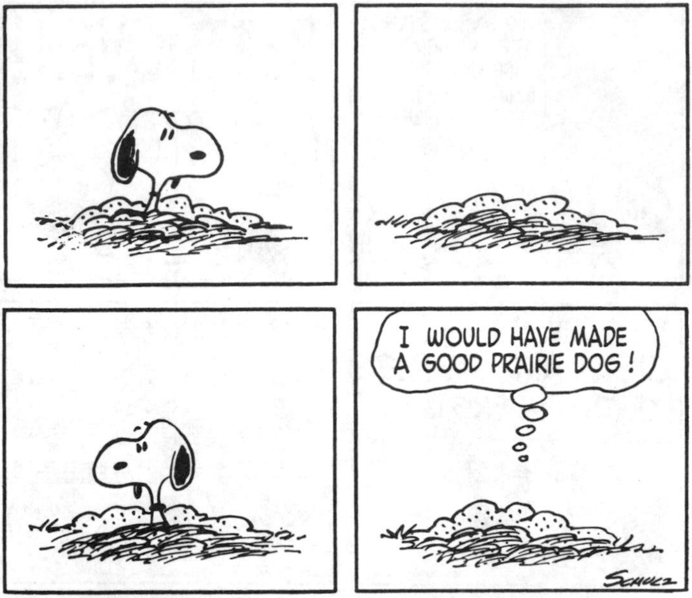
I WOULD HAVE MADE A GOOD PRAIRIE DOG!
SCHULZ

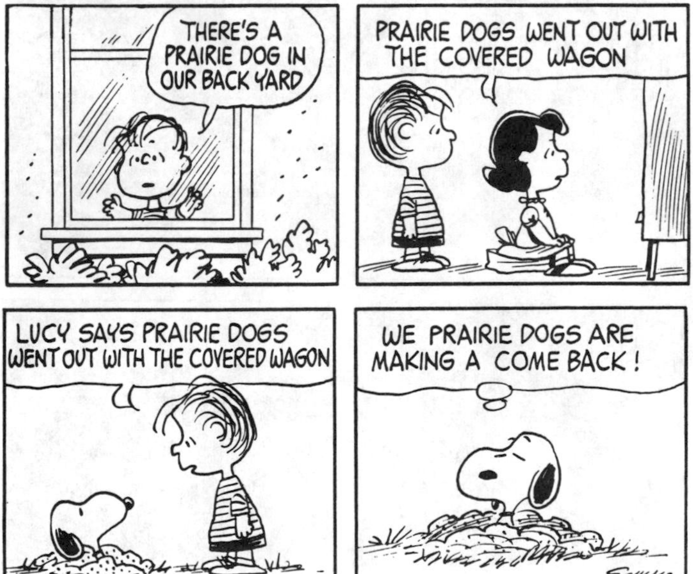
THERE'S A PRAIRIE DOG IN OUR BACK YARD
PRAIRIE DOGS WENT OUT WITH THE COVERED WAGON
LUCY SAYS PRAIRIE DOGS WENT OUT WITH THE COVERED WAGON
WE PRAIRIE DOGS ARE MAKING A COME BACK!
SCHULZ

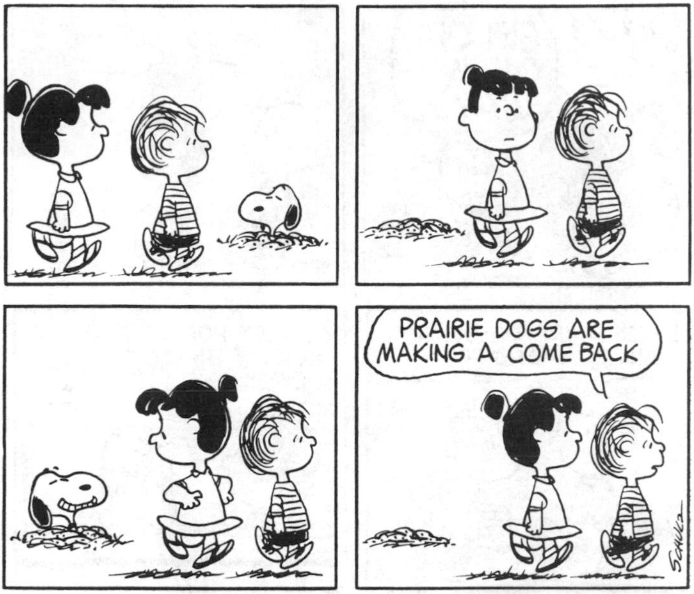
PRAIRIE DOGS ARE MAKING A COME BACK
SCHULZ

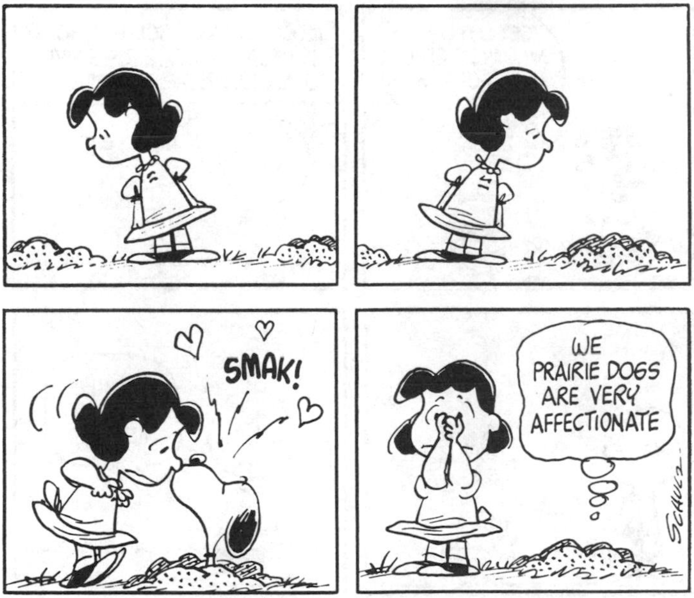
SMAK!
WE PRAIRIE DOGS ARE VERY AFFECTIONATE
SCHULZ

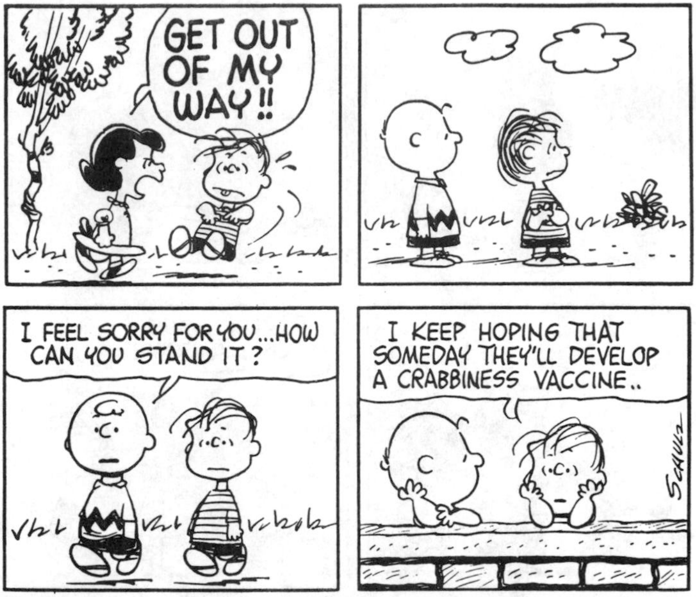
GET OUT OF MY WAY!!
I FEEL SORRY FOR YOU...HOW CAN YOU STAND IT?
I KEEP HOPING THAT SOMEDAY THEY'LL DEVELOP A CRABBINESS VACCINE..
SCHULZ

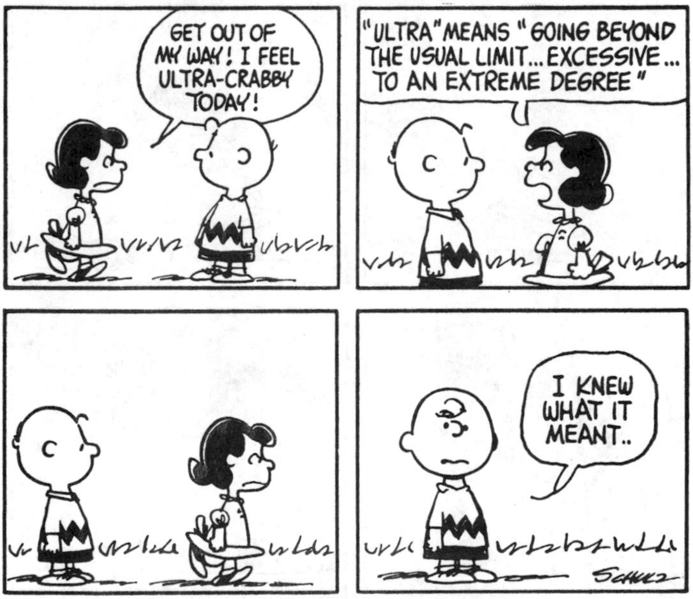
GET OUT OF MY WAY! I FEEL ULTRA-CRABBY TODAY!
"ULTRA" MEANS "GOING BEYOND THE USUAL LIMIT... EXCESSIVE... TO AN EXTREME DEGREE"
I KNEW WHAT IT MEANT..
SCHULZ

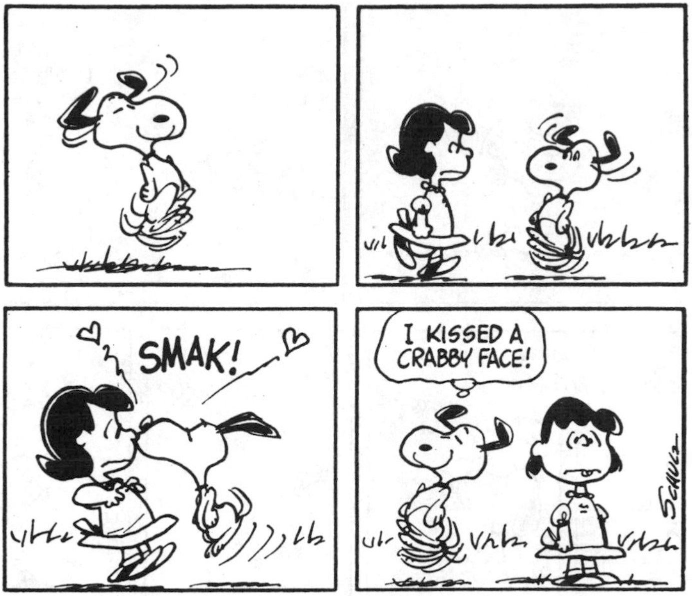
SMAK!
I KISSED A CRABBY FACE!

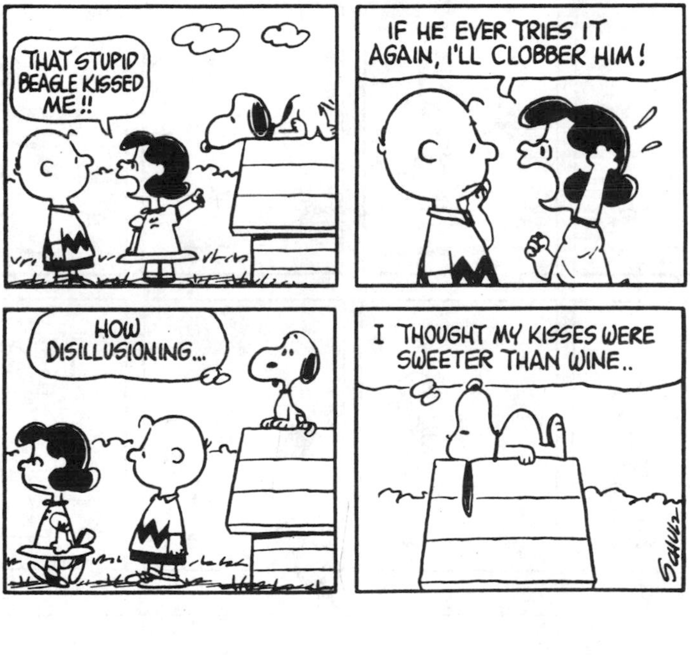
THAT STUPID BEAGLE KISSED ME!!
IF HE EVER TRIES IT AGAIN, I'LL CLOBBER HIM!
HOW DISILLUSIONING...
I THOUGHT MY KISSES WERE SWEETER THAN WINE..

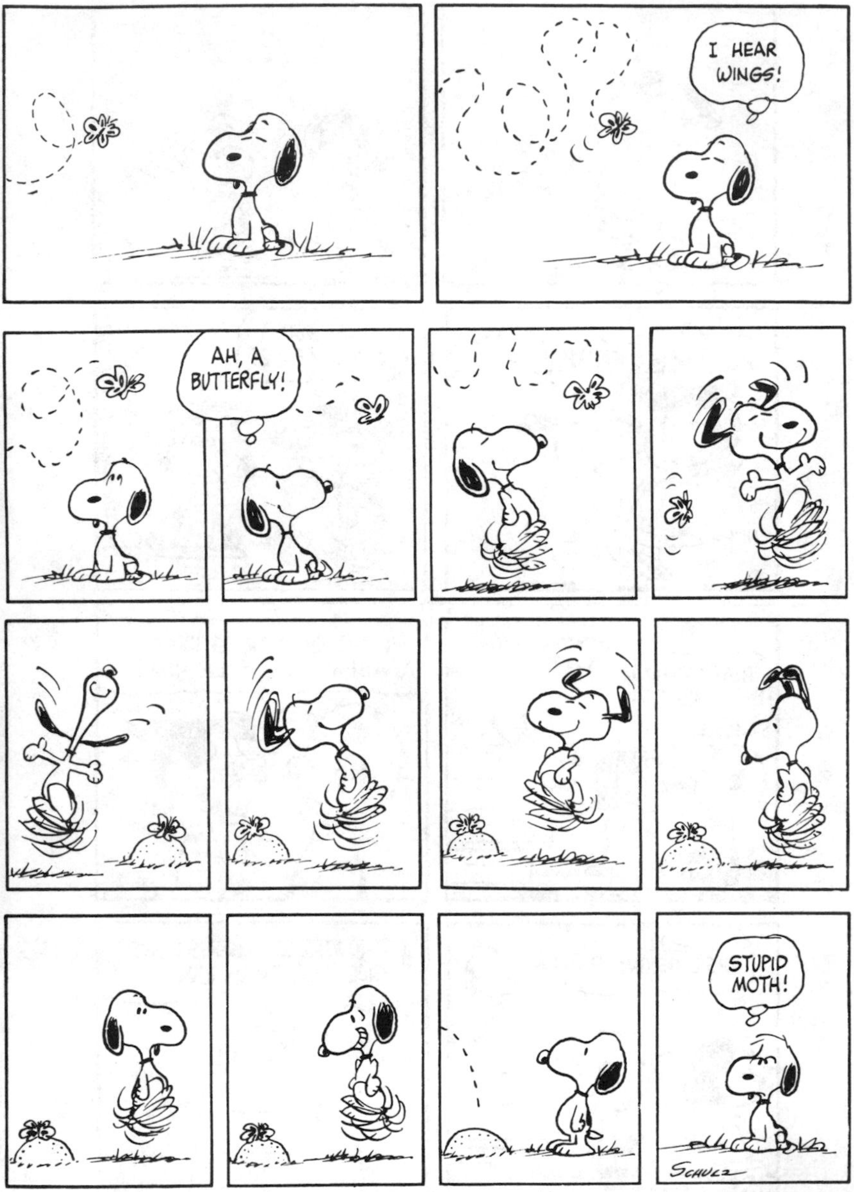
I HEAR WINGS!
AH, A BUTTERFLY!
STUPID MOTH!
SCHULZ

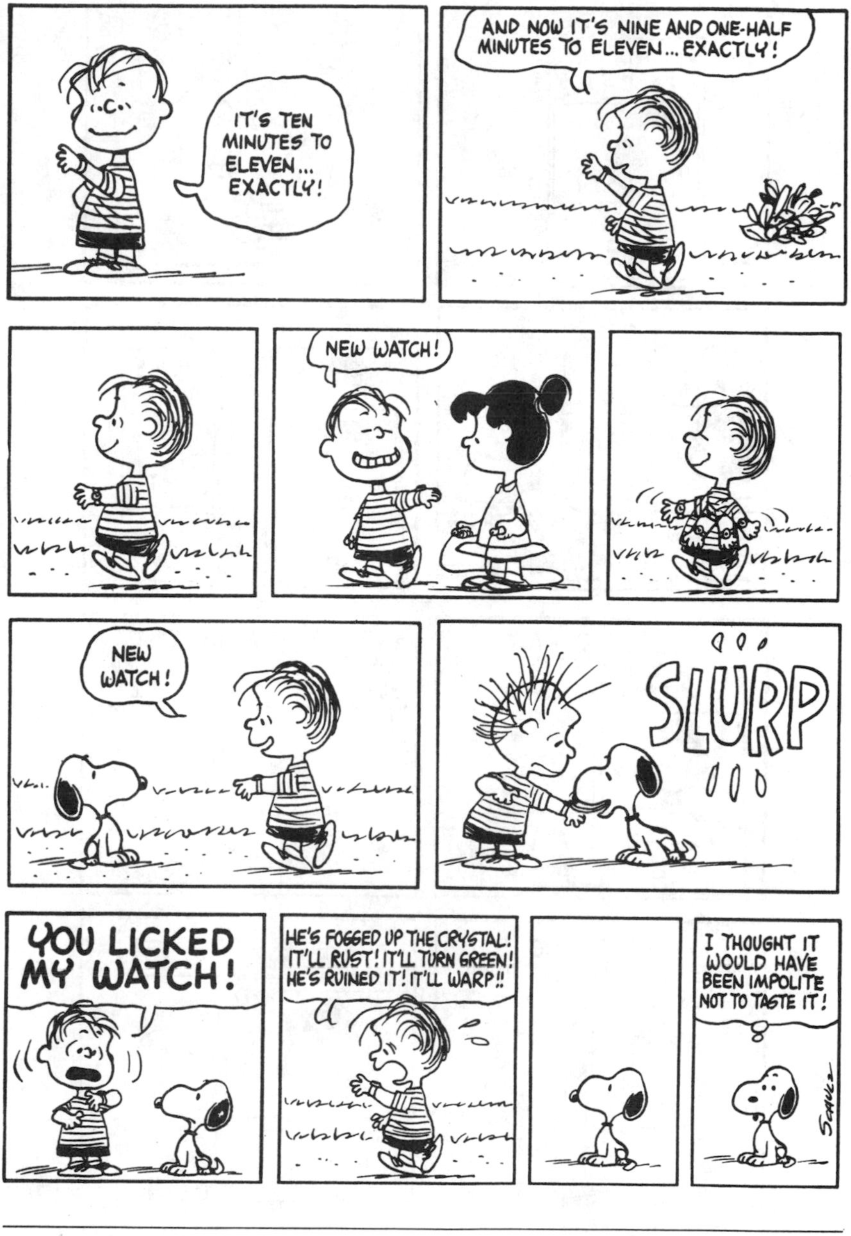

IT'S TEN MINUTES TO ELEVEN... EXACTLY!
AND NOW IT'S NINE AND ONE-HALF MINUTES TO ELEVEN... EXACTLY!
NEW WATCH!
NEW WATCH!
SLURP
YOU LICKED MY WATCH!
HE'S FOGGED UP THE CRYSTAL! IT'LL RUST! IT'LL TURN GREEN! HE'S RUINED IT! IT'LL WARP!!
I THOUGHT IT WOULD HAVE BEEN IMPOLITE NOT TO TASTE IT!
SCHULZ

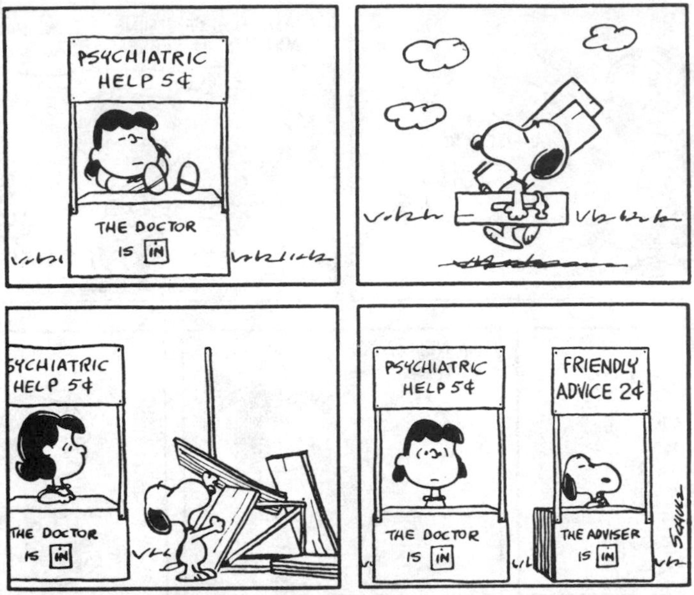
PSYCHIATRIC HELP 5¢
THE DOCTOR IS IN
FRIENDLY ADVICE 2¢
THE ADVISER IS IN
SCHULZ

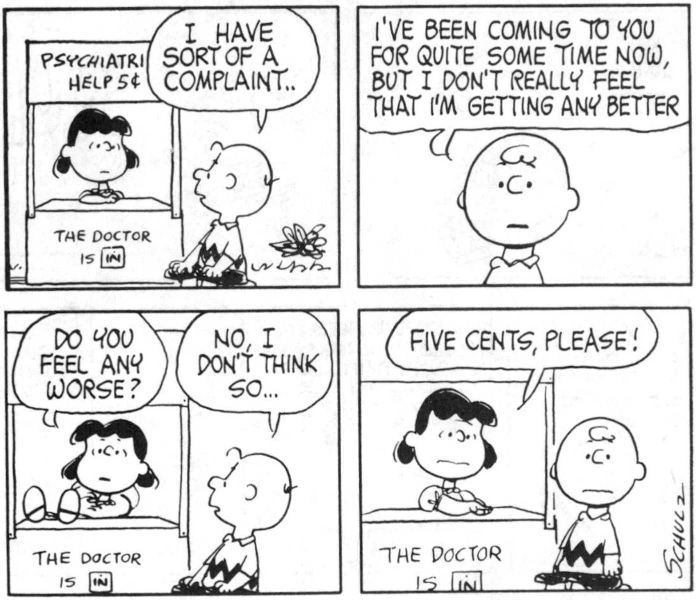
PSYCHIATRI HELP 5¢
I HAVE SORT OF A COMPLAINT..
THE DOCTOR IS IN
I'VE BEEN COMING TO YOU FOR QUITE SOME TIME NOW, BUT I DON'T REALLY FEEL THAT I'M GETTING ANY BETTER
DO YOU FEEL ANY WORSE?
NO, I DON'T THINK SO...
FIVE CENTS, PLEASE!
SCHULZ

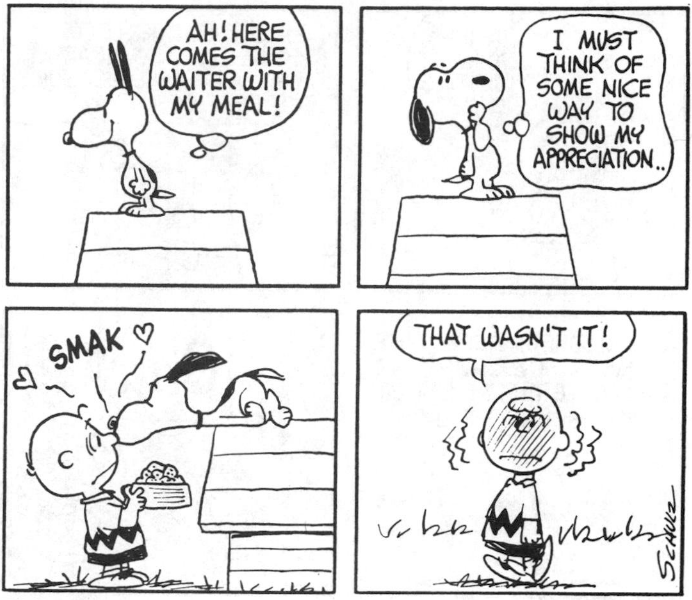
AH! HERE COMES THE WAITER WITH MY MEAL!
I MUST THINK OF SOME NICE WAY TO SHOW MY APPRECIATION..
SMAK
THAT WASN'T IT!
SCHULZ

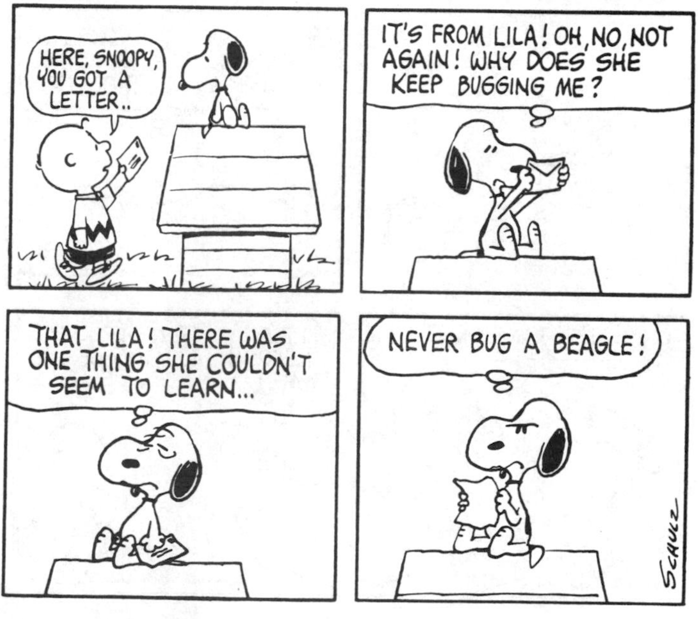
HERE, SNOOPY, YOU GOT A LETTER..
IT'S FROM LILA! OH, NO, NOT AGAIN! WHY DOES SHE KEEP BUGGING ME?
THAT LILA! THERE WAS ONE THING SHE COULDN'T SEEM TO LEARN...
NEVER BUG A BEAGLE!
SCHULZ

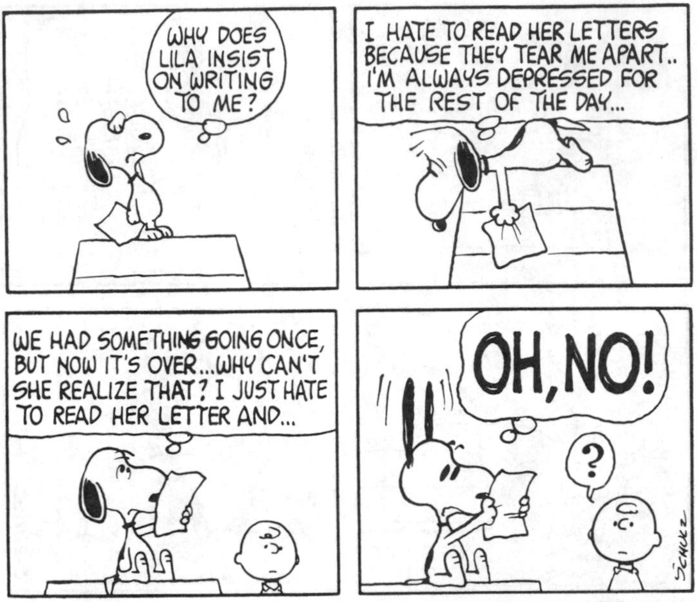
WHY DOES LILA INSIST ON WRITING TO ME?
I HATE TO READ HER LETTERS BECAUSE THEY TEAR ME APART.. I'M ALWAYS DEPRESSED FOR THE REST OF THE DAY...
WE HAD SOMETHING GOING ONCE, BUT NOW IT'S OVER...WHY CAN'T SHE REALIZE THAT? I JUST HATE TO READ HER LETTER AND...
OH, NO!
?
SCHULZ

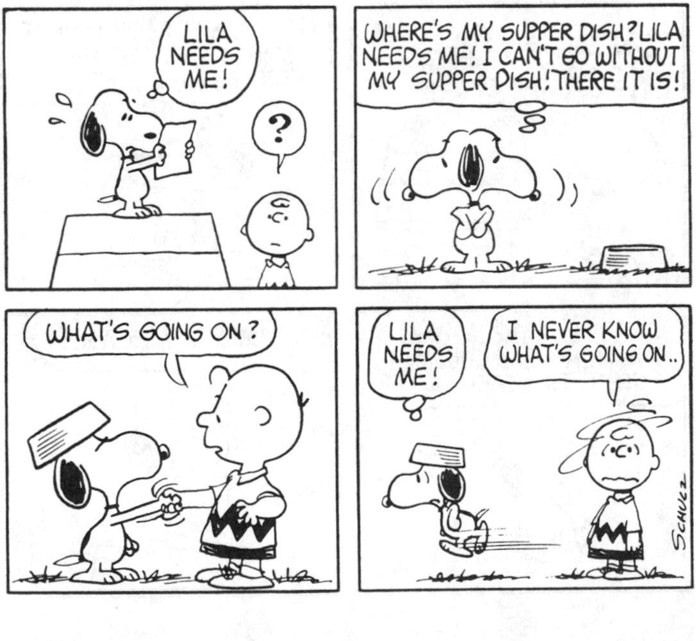
LILA NEEDS ME!
?
WHERE'S MY SUPPER DISH? LILA NEEDS ME! I CAN'T GO WITHOUT MY SUPPER DISH! THERE IT IS!
WHAT'S GOING ON?
LILA NEEDS ME!
I NEVER KNOW WHAT'S GOING ON..
SCHULZ

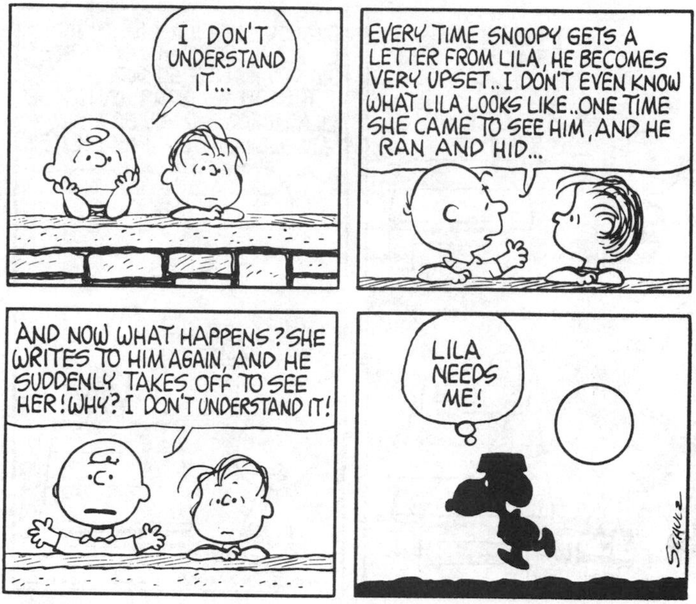
I DON'T UNDERSTAND IT...
EVERY TIME SNOOPY GETS A LETTER FROM LILA, HE BECOMES VERY UPSET.. I DON'T EVEN KNOW WHAT LILA LOOKS LIKE..ONE TIME SHE CAME TO SEE HIM, AND HE RAN AND HID...
AND NOW WHAT HAPPENS? SHE WRITES TO HIM AGAIN, AND HE SUDDENLY TAKES OFF TO SEE HER! WHY? I DON'T UNDERSTAND IT!
LILA NEEDS ME!
SCHULZ

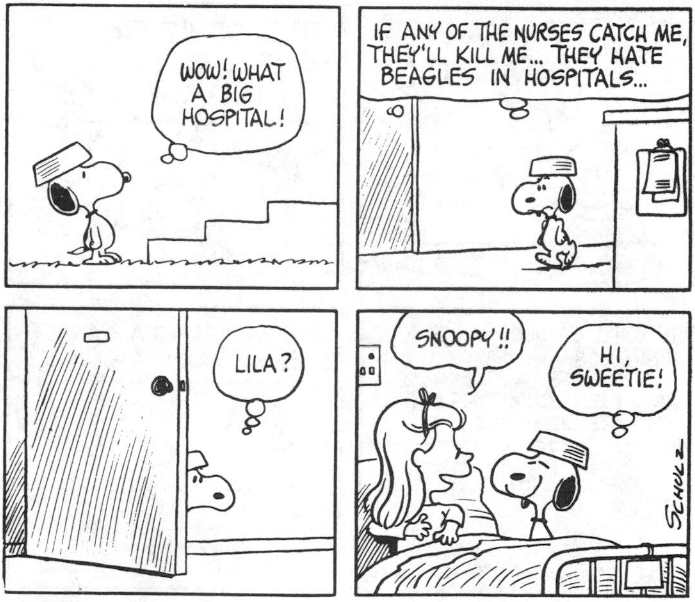
WOW! WHAT A BIG HOSPITAL!
IF ANY OF THE NURSES CATCH ME, THEY'LL KILL ME... THEY HATE BEAGLES IN HOSPITALS...
LILA?
SNOOPY!!
HI, SWEETIE!
SCHULZ

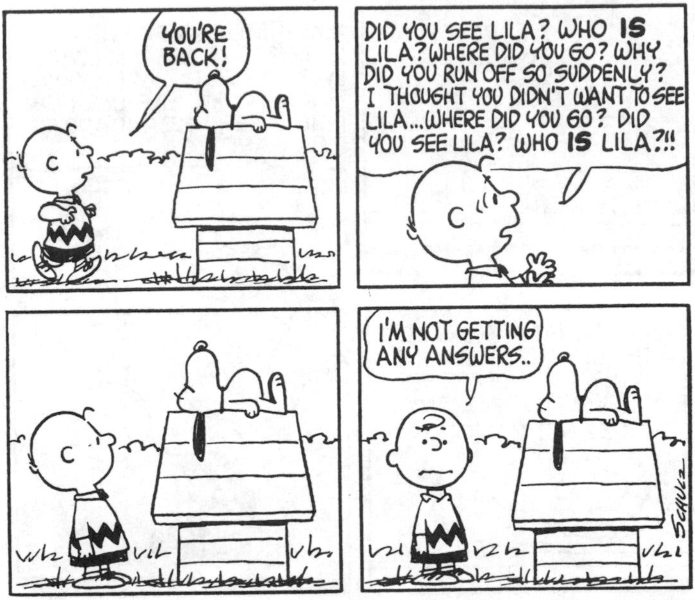
YOU'RE BACK!
DID YOU SEE LILA? WHO IS LILA? WHERE DID YOU GO? WHY DID YOU RUN OFF SO SUDDENLY? I THOUGHT YOU DIDN'T WANT TO SEE LILA...WHERE DID YOU GO? DID YOU SEE LILA? WHO IS LILA?!!
I'M NOT GETTING ANY ANSWERS..
SCHULZ

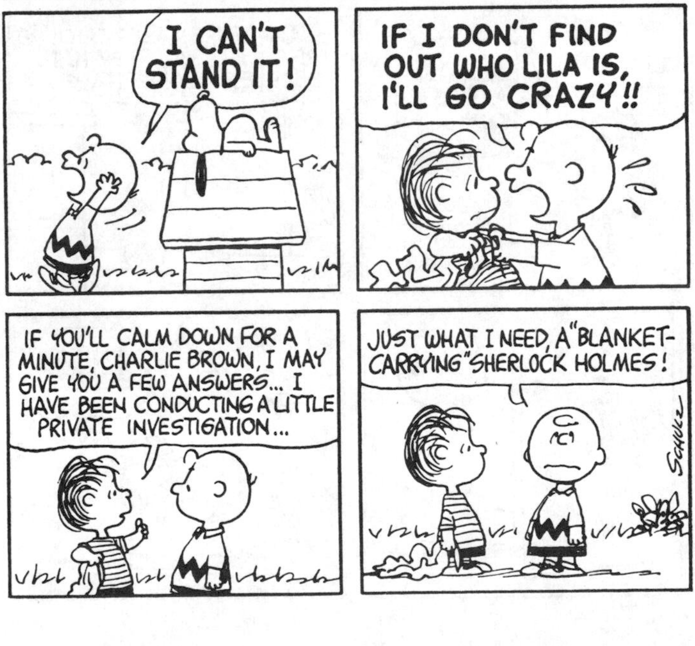
I CAN'T STAND IT!
IF I DON'T FIND OUT WHO LILA IS, I'LL GO CRAZY!!
IF YOU'LL CALM DOWN FOR A MINUTE, CHARLIE BROWN, I MAY GIVE YOU A FEW ANSWERS... I HAVE BEEN CONDUCTING A LITTLE PRIVATE INVESTIGATION...
JUST WHAT I NEED, A "BLANKET-CARRYING" SHERLOCK HOLMES!
SCHULZ

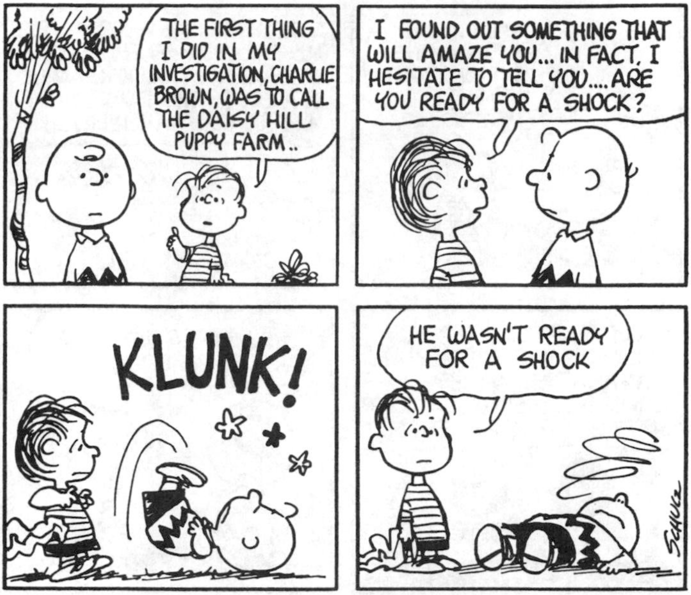
THE FIRST THING I DID IN MY INVESTIGATION, CHARLIE BROWN, WAS TO CALL THE DAISY HILL PUPPY FARM..
I FOUND OUT SOMETHING THAT WILL AMAZE YOU... IN FACT, I HESITATE TO TELL YOU.... ARE YOU READY FOR A SHOCK?
KLUNK!
HE WASN'T READY FOR A SHOCK
SCHULZ

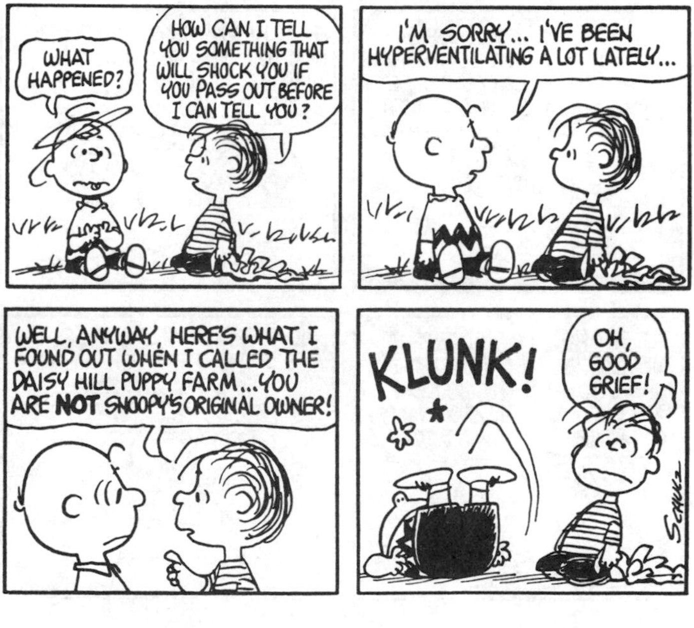
WHAT HAPPENED?
HOW CAN I TELL YOU SOMETHING THAT WILL SHOCK YOU IF YOU PASS OUT BEFORE I CAN TELL YOU?
I'M SORRY... I'VE BEEN HYPERVENTILATING A LOT LATELY...
WELL, ANYWAY, HERE'S WHAT I FOUND OUT WHEN I CALLED THE DAISY HILL PUPPY FARM...YOU ARE NOT SNOOPY'S ORIGINAL OWNER!
KLUNK!
OH, GOOD GRIEF!
SCHULZ

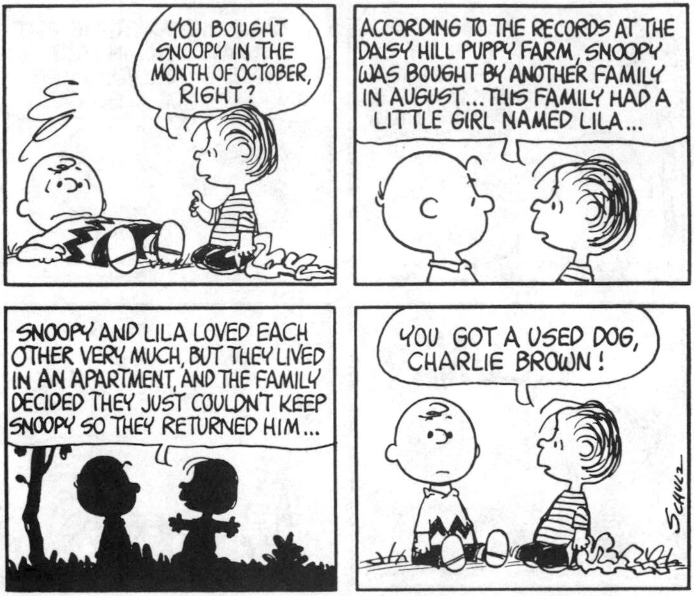
YOU BOUGHT SNOOPY IN THE MONTH OF OCTOBER, RIGHT?
ACCORDING TO THE RECORDS AT THE DAISY HILL PUPPY FARM, SNOOPY WAS BOUGHT BY ANOTHER FAMILY IN AUGUST...THIS FAMILY HAD A LITTLE GIRL NAMED LILA...
SNOOPY AND LILA LOVED EACH OTHER VERY MUCH, BUT THEY LIVED IN AN APARTMENT, AND THE FAMILY DECIDED THEY JUST COULDN'T KEEP SNOOPY SO THEY RETURNED HIM...
YOU GOT A USED DOG, CHARLIE BROWN!
SCHULZ

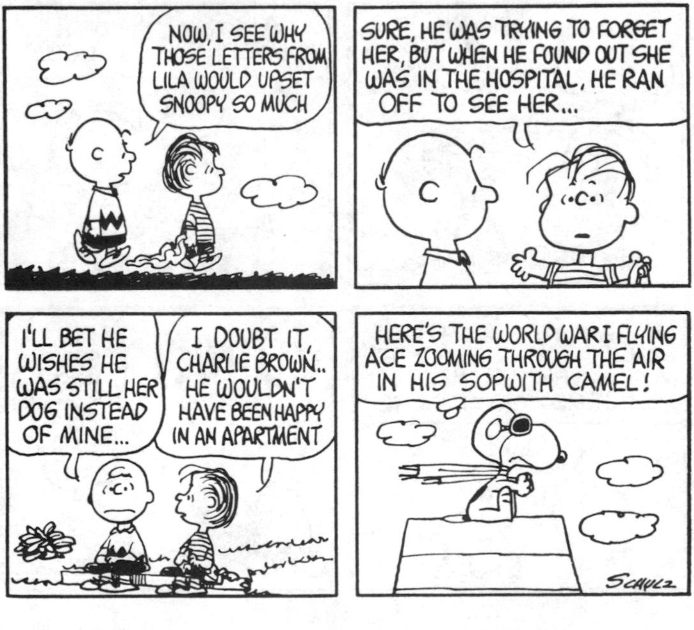
NOW, I SEE WHY THOSE LETTERS FROM LILA WOULD UPSET SNOOPY SO MUCH
SURE, HE WAS TRYING TO FORGET HER, BUT WHEN HE FOUND OUT SHE WAS IN THE HOSPITAL, HE RAN OFF TO SEE HER...
I'LL BET HE WISHES HE WAS STILL HER DOG INSTEAD OF MINE...
I DOUBT IT, CHARLIE BROWN.. HE WOULDN'T HAVE BEEN HAPPY IN AN APARTMENT
HERE'S THE WORLD WAR I FLYING ACE ZOOMING THROUGH THE AIR IN HIS SOPWITH CAMEL!
SCHULZ

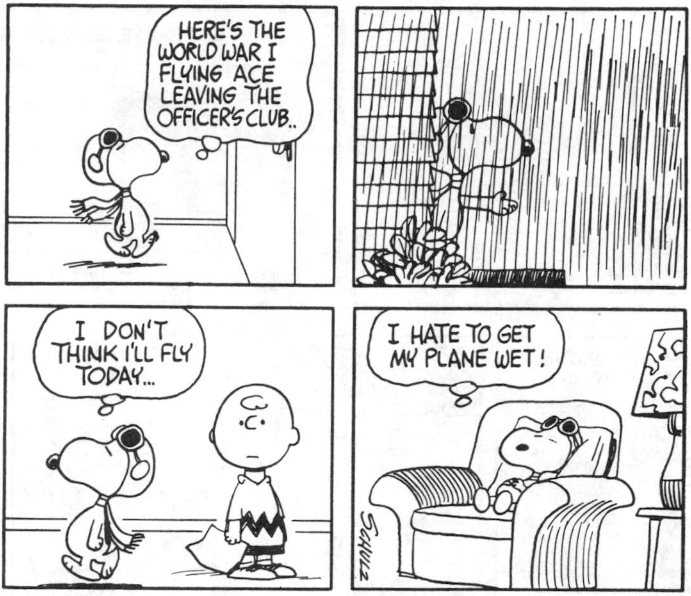
HERE'S THE WORLD WAR I FLYING ACE LEAVING THE OFFICER'S CLUB..
I DON'T THINK I'LL FLY TODAY...
I HATE TO GET MY PLANE WET!
SCHULZ

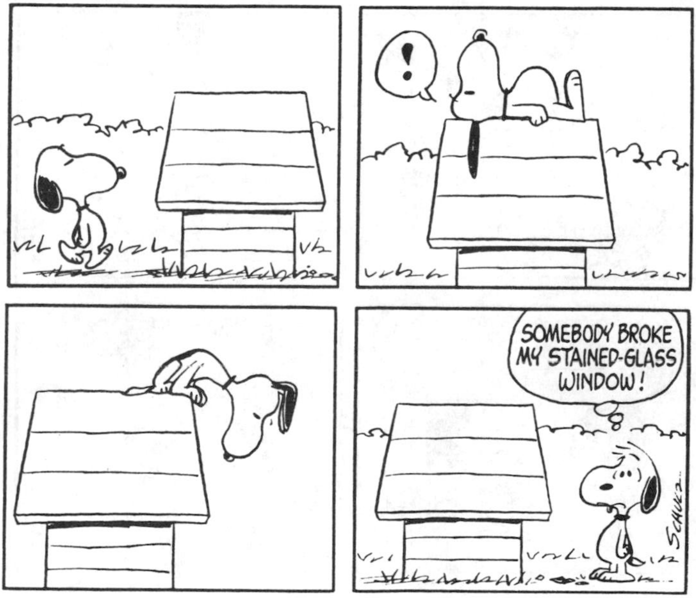
!
SOMEBODY BROKE MY STAINED-GLASS WINDOW!
SCHULZ

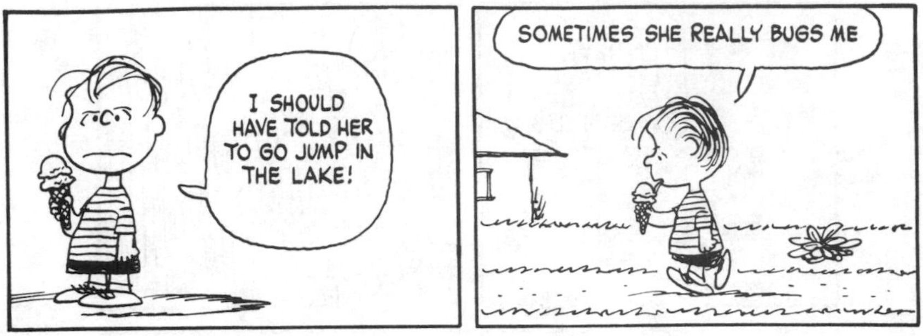
I SHOULD HAVE TOLD HER TO GO JUMP IN THE LAKE!
SOMETIMES SHE REALLY BUGS ME

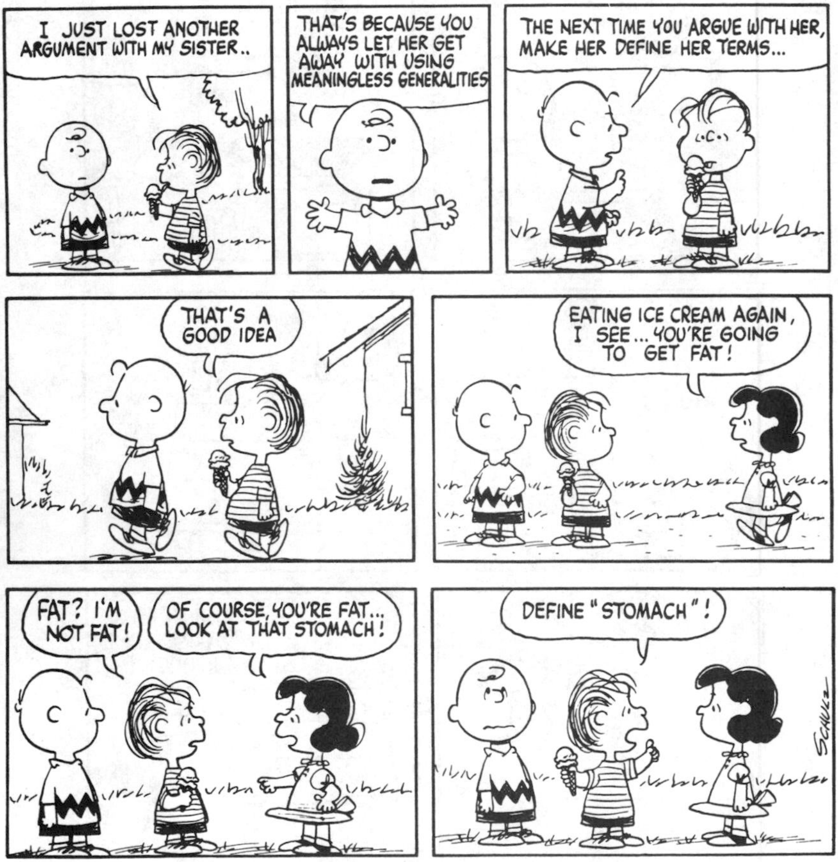
I JUST LOST ANOTHER ARGUMENT WITH MY SISTER..
THAT'S BECAUSE YOU ALWAYS LET HER GET AWAY WITH USING MEANINGLESS GENERALITIES
THE NEXT TIME YOU ARGUE WITH HER, MAKE HER DEFINE HER TERMS...
THAT'S A GOOD IDEA
EATING ICE CREAM AGAIN, I SEE... YOU'RE GOING TO GET FAT!
FAT? I'M NOT FAT!
OF COURSE, YOU'RE FAT... LOOK AT THAT STOMACH!
DEFINE "STOMACH"!
SCHULZ

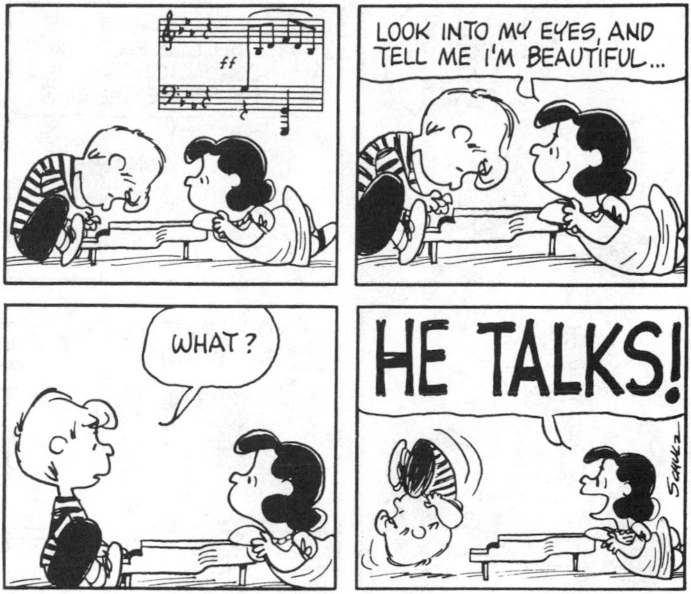
ff
LOOK INTO MY EYES, AND TELL ME I'M BEAUTIFUL...
WHAT?
HE TALKS!
SCHULZ

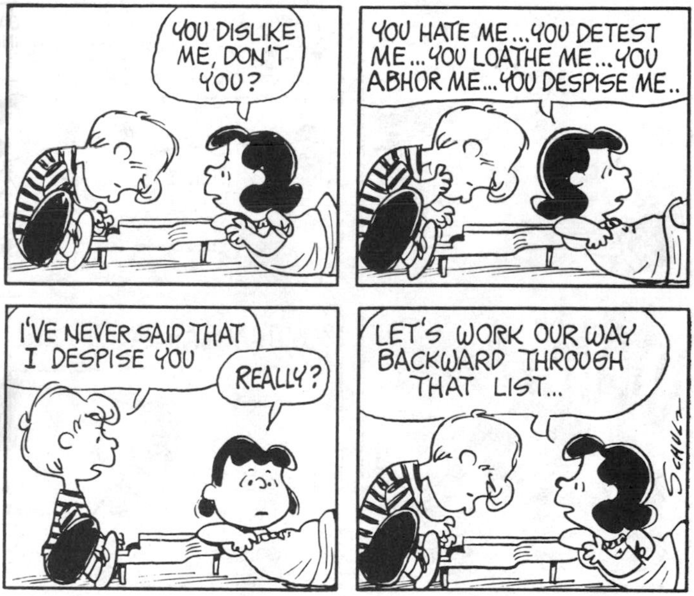
YOU DISLIKE ME, DON'T YOU?
YOU HATE ME...YOU DETEST ME...YOU LOATHE ME...YOU ABHOR ME...YOU DESPISE ME..
I'VE NEVER SAID THAT I DESPISE YOU
REALLY?
LET'S WORK OUR WAY BACKWARD THROUGH THAT LIST...
SCHULZ

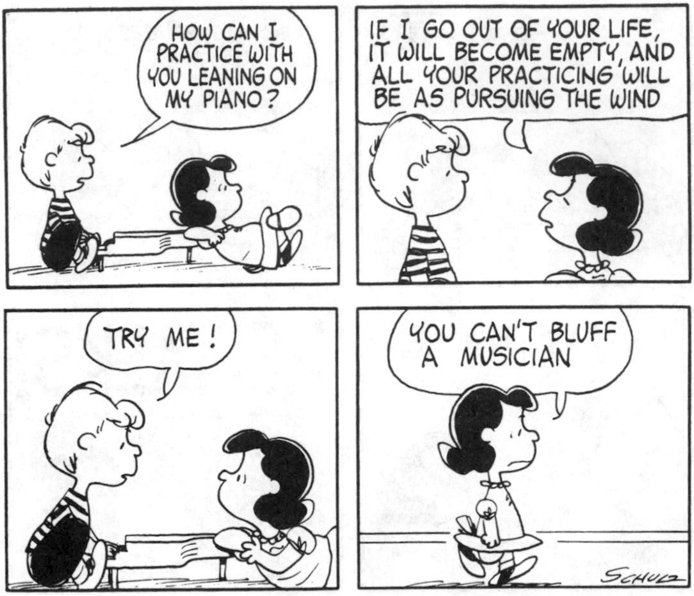
HOW CAN I PRACTICE WITH YOU LEANING ON MY PIANO?
IF I GO OUT OF YOUR LIFE, IT WILL BECOME EMPTY, AND ALL YOUR PRACTICING WILL BE AS PURSUING THE WIND
TRY ME!
YOU CAN'T BLUFF A MUSICIAN
SCHULZ

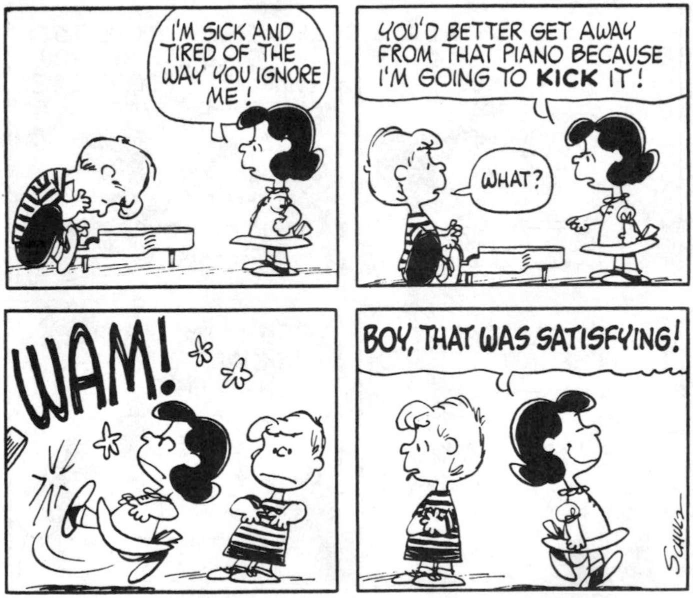
I'M SICK AND TIRED OF THE WAY YOU IGNORE ME!
YOU'D BETTER GET AWAY FROM THAT PIANO BECAUSE I'M GOING TO KICK IT!
WHAT?
WAM!
BOY, THAT WAS SATISFYING!
SCHULZ

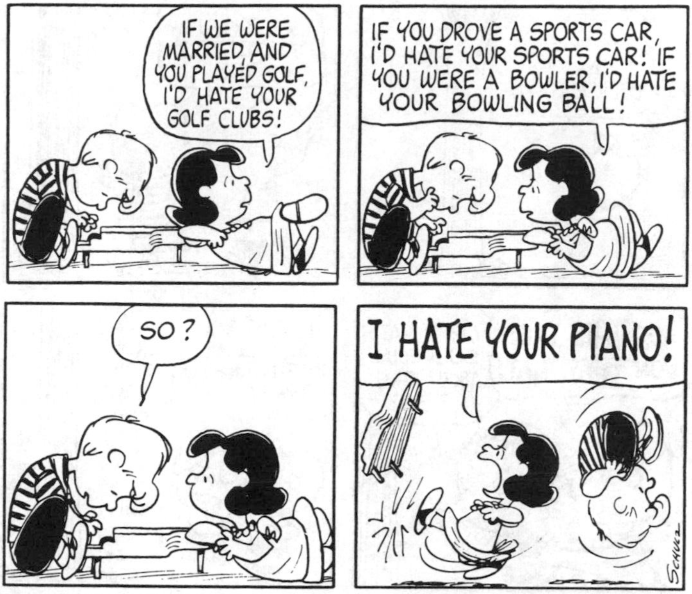
IF WE WERE MARRIED, AND YOU PLAYED GOLF, I'D HATE YOUR GOLF CLUBS!
IF YOU DROVE A SPORTS CAR, I'D HATE YOUR SPORTS CAR! IF YOU WERE A BOWLER, I'D HATE YOUR BOWLING BALL!
SO?
I HATE YOUR PIANO!
SCHULZ

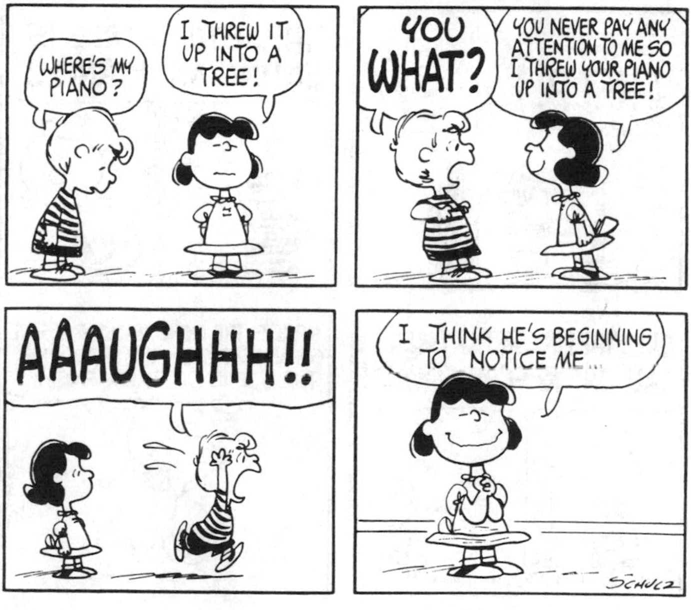
WHERE'S MY PIANO?
I THREW IT UP INTO A TREE!
YOU WHAT?
YOU NEVER PAY ANY ATTENTION TO ME SO I THREW YOUR PIANO UP INTO A TREE!
AAAUGHHH!!
I THINK HE'S BEGINNING TO NOTICE ME...
SCHULZ

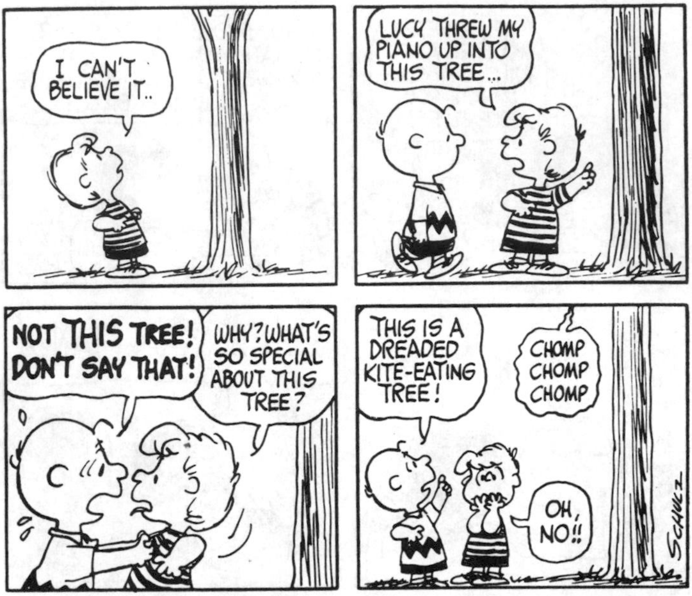
I CAN'T BELIEVE IT..
LUCY THREW MY PIANO UP INTO THIS TREE...
NOT THIS TREE! DON'T SAY THAT!
WHY? WHAT'S SO SPECIAL ABOUT THIS TREE?
THIS IS A DREADED KITE-EATING TREE!
CHOMP CHOMP CHOMP
OH, NO!!
SCHULZ

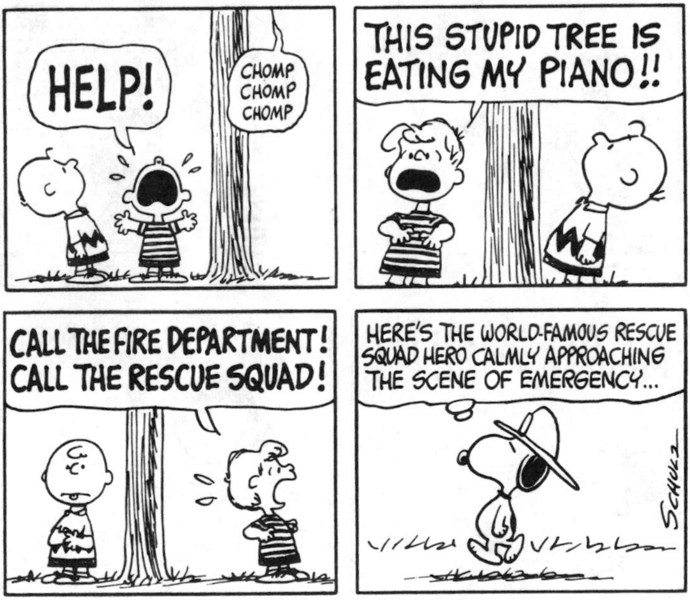
HELP!
CHOMP CHOMP CHOMP
THIS STUPID TREE IS EATING MY PIANO!!
CALL THE FIRE DEPARTMENT! CALL THE RESCUE SQUAD!
HERE'S THE WORLD-FAMOUS RESCUE SQUAD HERO CALMLY APPROACHING THE SCENE OF EMERGENCY...
SCHULZ

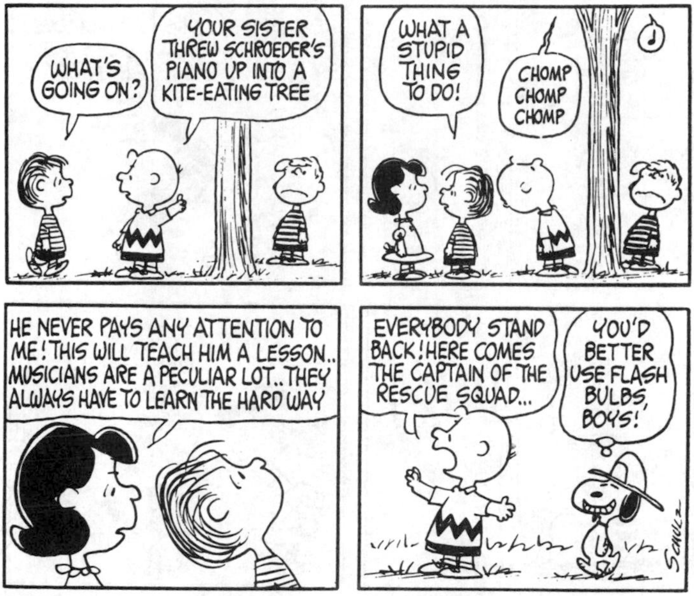
WHAT'S GOING ON?
YOUR SISTER THREW SCHROEDER'S PIANO UP INTO A KITE-EATING TREE
WHAT A STUPID THING TO DO!
CHOMP CHOMP CHOMP
HE NEVER PAYS ANY ATTENTION TO ME! THIS WILL TEACH HIM A LESSON.. MUSICIANS ARE A PECULIAR LOT.. THEY ALWAYS HAVE TO LEARN THE HARD WAY
EVERYBODY STAND BACK! HERE COMES THE CAPTAIN OF THE RESCUE SQUAD...
YOU'D BETTER USE FLASH BULBS, BOYS!
SCHULZ

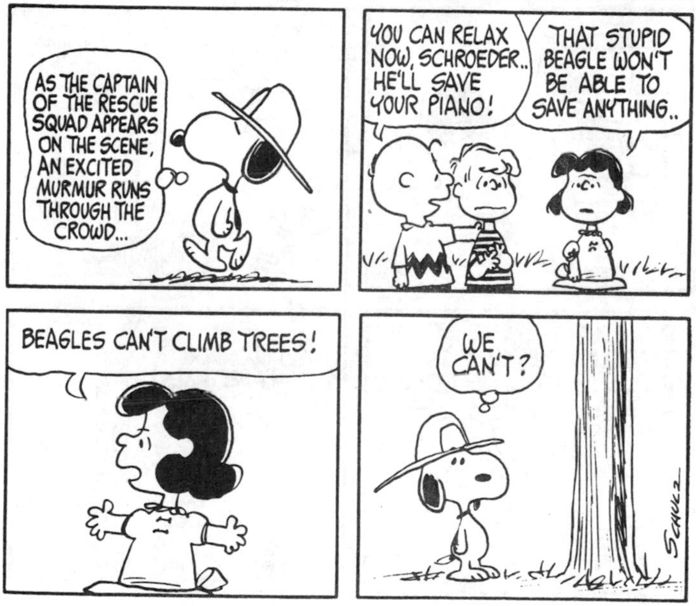
AS THE CAPTAIN OF THE RESCUE SQUAD APPEARS ON THE SCENE, AN EXCITED MURMUR RUNS THROUGH THE CROWD...
YOU CAN RELAX NOW, SCHROEDER.. HE'LL SAVE YOUR PIANO!
THAT STUPID BEAGLE WON'T BE ABLE TO SAVE ANYTHING..
BEAGLES CAN'T CLIMB TREES!
WE CAN'T?
SCHULZ

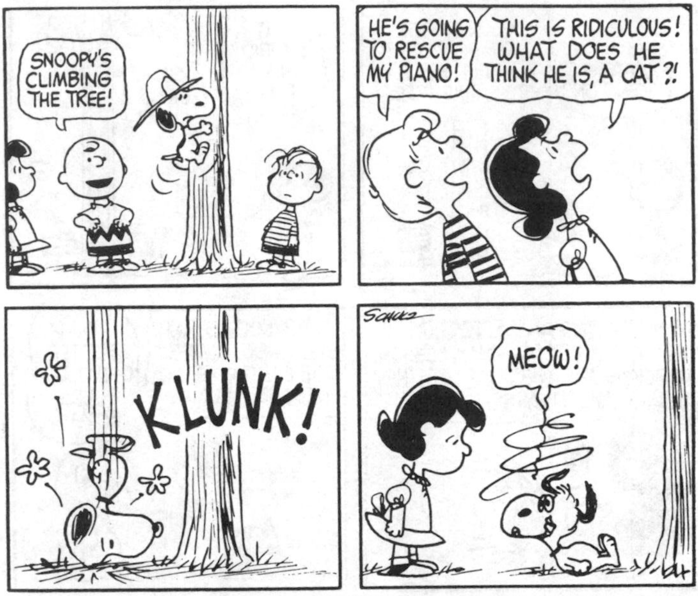
SNOOPY'S CLIMBING THE TREE!
HE'S GOING TO RESCUE MY PIANO!
THIS IS RIDICULOUS! WHAT DOES HE THINK HE IS, A CAT?!
KLUNK!
SCHULZ
MEOW!

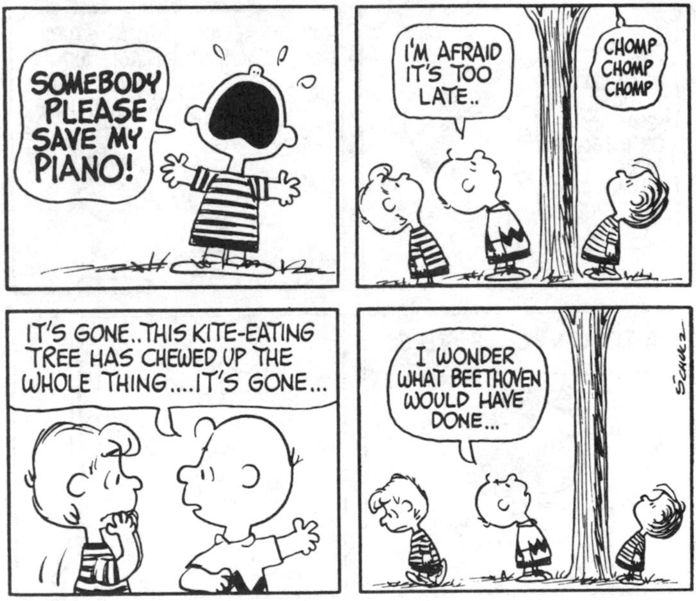
SOMEBODY PLEASE SAVE MY PIANO!
I'M AFRAID IT'S TOO LATE..
CHOMP CHOMP CHOMP
IT'S GONE..THIS KITE-EATING TREE HAS CHEWED UP THE WHOLE THING....IT'S GONE...
I WONDER WHAT BEETHOVEN WOULD HAVE DONE...
SCHULZ

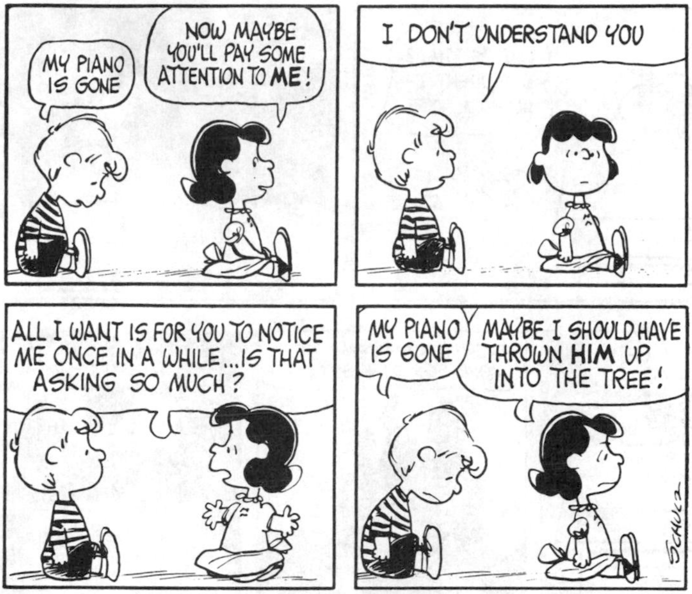

MY PIANO IS GONE
NOW MAYBE YOU'LL PAY SOME ATTENTION TO **ME**!
I DON'T UNDERSTAND YOU
ALL I WANT IS FOR YOU TO NOTICE ME ONCE IN A WHILE...IS THAT ASKING SO MUCH?
MY PIANO IS GONE
MAYBE I SHOULD HAVE THROWN **HIM** UP INTO THE TREE!
SCHULZ

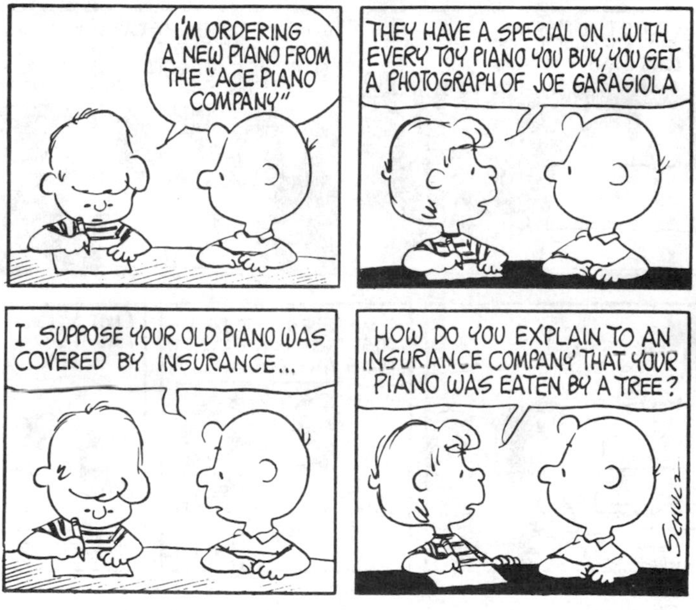

I'M ORDERING A NEW PIANO FROM THE "ACE PIANO COMPANY"
THEY HAVE A SPECIAL ON...WITH EVERY TOY PIANO YOU BUY, YOU GET A PHOTOGRAPH OF JOE GARAGIOLA
I SUPPOSE YOUR OLD PIANO WAS COVERED BY INSURANCE...
HOW DO YOU EXPLAIN TO AN INSURANCE COMPANY THAT YOUR PIANO WAS EATEN BY A TREE?
SCHULZ

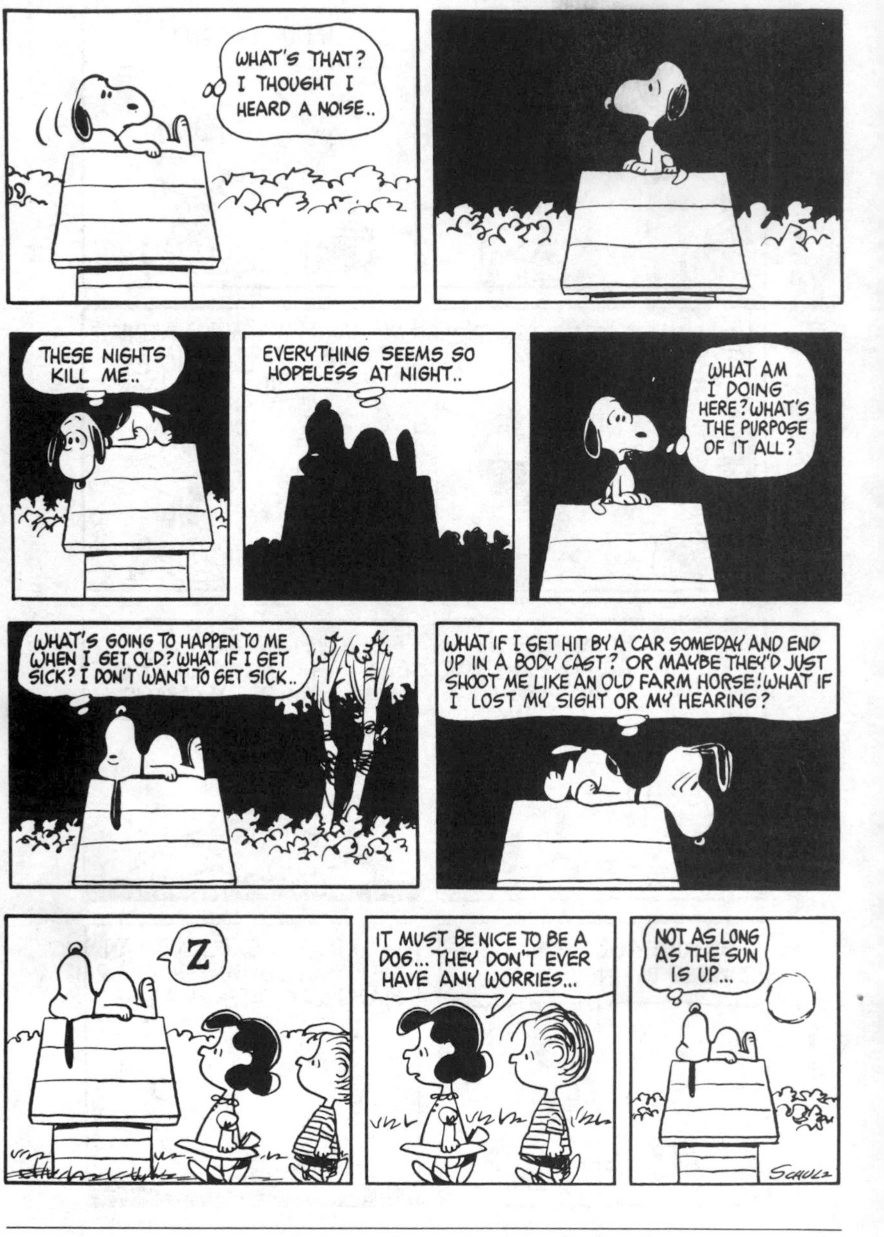

WHAT'S THAT? I THOUGHT I HEARD A NOISE..
THESE NIGHTS KILL ME..
EVERYTHING SEEMS SO HOPELESS AT NIGHT..
WHAT AM I DOING HERE? WHAT'S THE PURPOSE OF IT ALL?
WHAT'S GOING TO HAPPEN TO ME WHEN I GET OLD? WHAT IF I GET SICK? I DON'T WANT TO GET SICK..
WHAT IF I GET HIT BY A CAR SOMEDAY AND END UP IN A BODY CAST? OR MAYBE THEY'D JUST SHOOT ME LIKE AN OLD FARM HORSE! WHAT IF I LOST MY SIGHT OR MY HEARING?
Z
IT MUST BE NICE TO BE A DOG... THEY DON'T EVER HAVE ANY WORRIES...
NOT AS LONG AS THE SUN IS UP...
SCHULZ

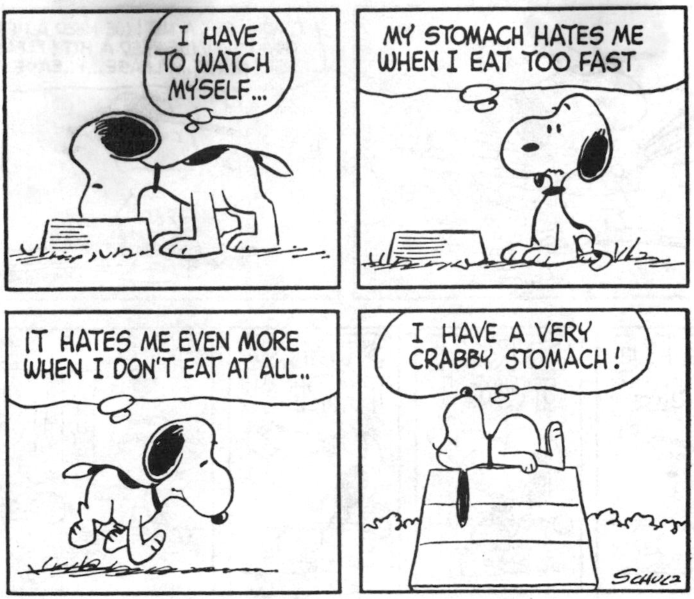
I HAVE TO WATCH MYSELF...
MY STOMACH HATES ME WHEN I EAT TOO FAST
IT HATES ME EVEN MORE WHEN I DON'T EAT AT ALL..
I HAVE A VERY CRABBY STOMACH!
SCHULZ

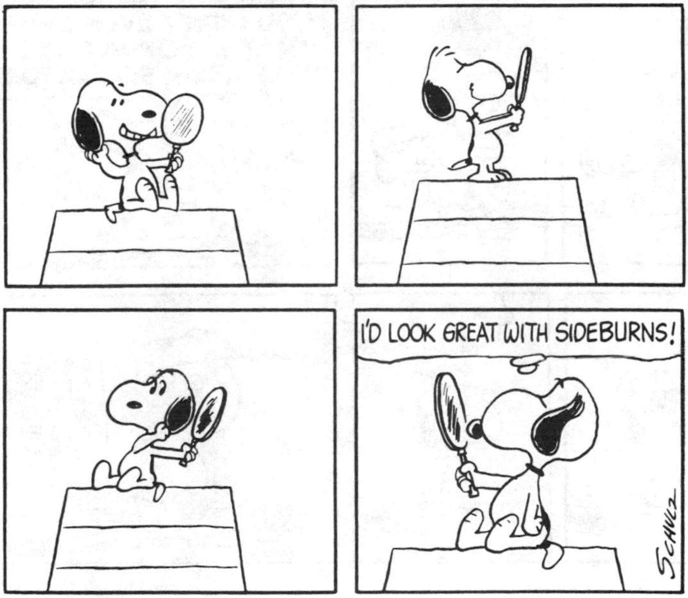
I'D LOOK GREAT WITH SIDEBURNS!
SCHULZ

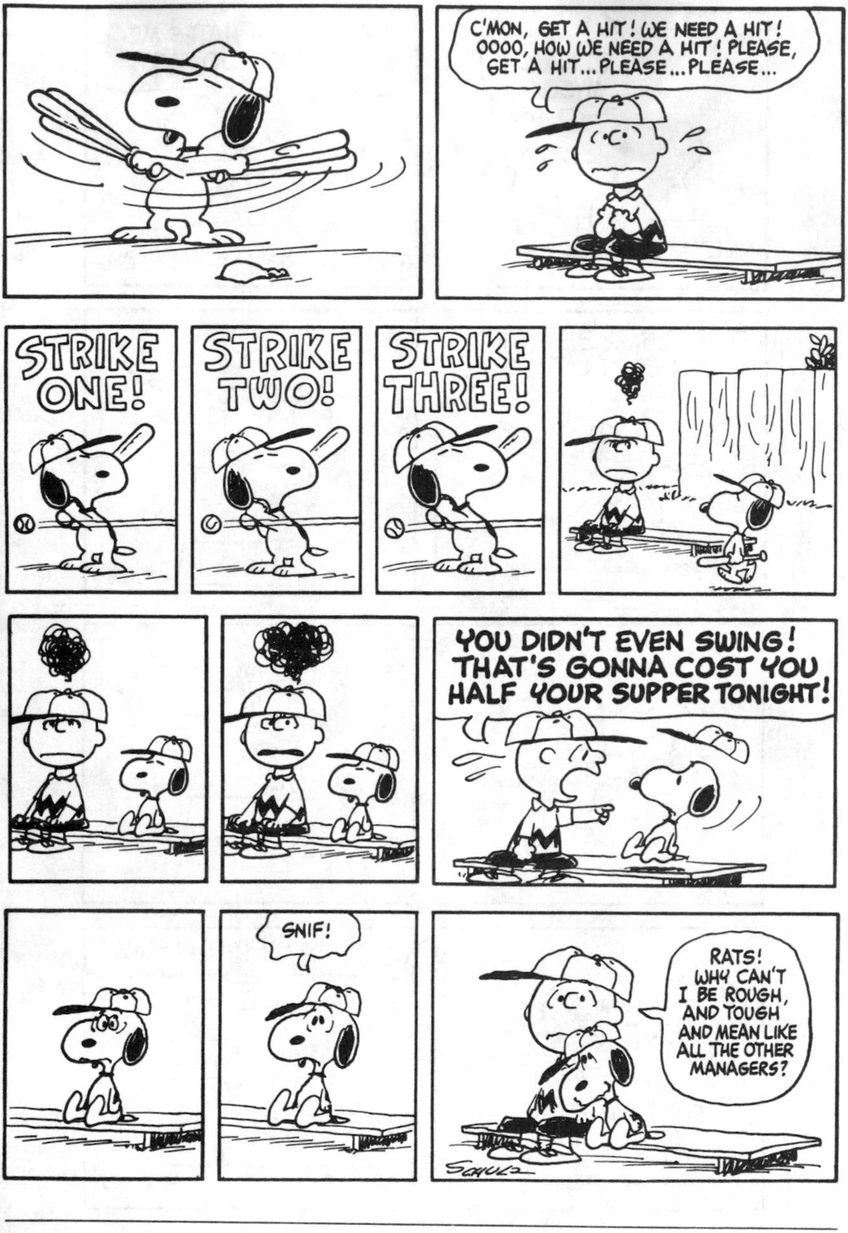
C'MON, GET A HIT! WE NEED A HIT! OOOO, HOW WE NEED A HIT! PLEASE, GET A HIT... PLEASE... PLEASE...
STRIKE ONE!
STRIKE TWO!
STRIKE THREE!
YOU DIDN'T EVEN SWING! THAT'S GONNA COST YOU HALF YOUR SUPPER TONIGHT!
SNIF!
RATS! WHY CAN'T I BE ROUGH, AND TOUGH AND MEAN LIKE ALL THE OTHER MANAGERS?
SCHULZ

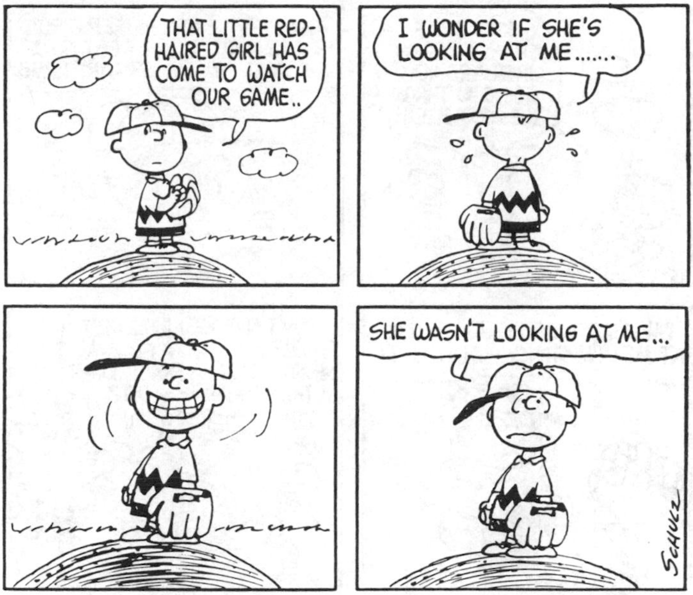
THAT LITTLE RED-HAIRED GIRL HAS COME TO WATCH OUR GAME..
I WONDER IF SHE'S LOOKING AT ME.......
SHE WASN'T LOOKING AT ME...
SCHULZ

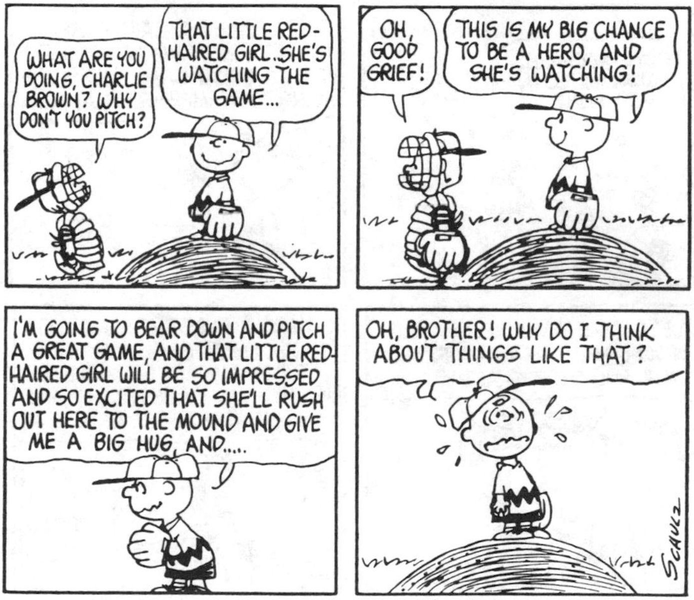
WHAT ARE YOU DOING, CHARLIE BROWN? WHY DON'T YOU PITCH?
THAT LITTLE RED-HAIRED GIRL..SHE'S WATCHING THE GAME...
OH, GOOD GRIEF!
THIS IS MY BIG CHANCE TO BE A HERO, AND SHE'S WATCHING!
I'M GOING TO BEAR DOWN AND PITCH A GREAT GAME, AND THAT LITTLE RED-HAIRED GIRL WILL BE SO IMPRESSED AND SO EXCITED THAT SHE'LL RUSH OUT HERE TO THE MOUND AND GIVE ME A BIG HUG, AND.....
OH, BROTHER! WHY DO I THINK ABOUT THINGS LIKE THAT?
SCHULZ

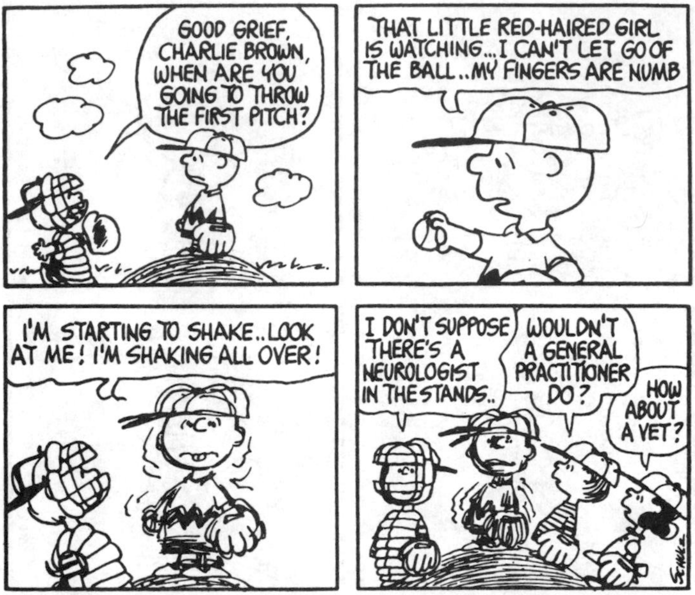
GOOD GRIEF, CHARLIE BROWN, WHEN ARE YOU GOING TO THROW THE FIRST PITCH?
THAT LITTLE RED-HAIRED GIRL IS WATCHING... I CAN'T LET GO OF THE BALL.. MY FINGERS ARE NUMB
I'M STARTING TO SHAKE.. LOOK AT ME! I'M SHAKING ALL OVER!
I DON'T SUPPOSE THERE'S A NEUROLOGIST IN THE STANDS..
WOULDN'T A GENERAL PRACTITIONER DO?
HOW ABOUT A VET?
SCHULZ

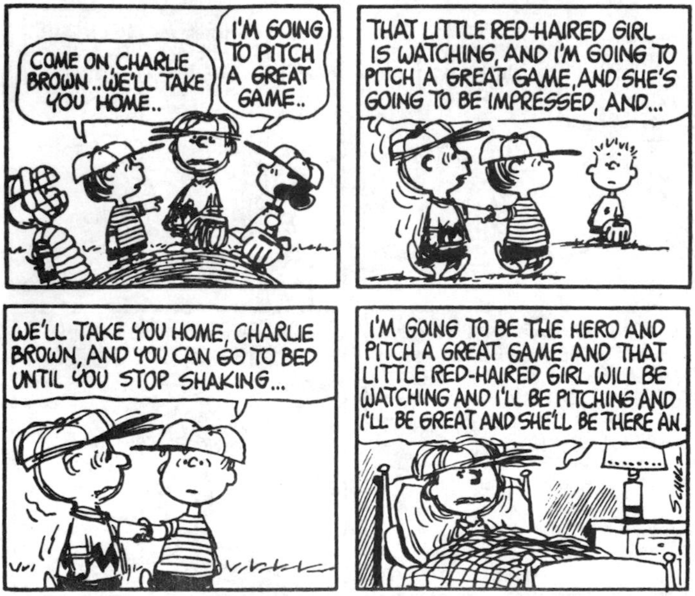
COME ON, CHARLIE BROWN.. WE'LL TAKE YOU HOME..
I'M GOING TO PITCH A GREAT GAME..
THAT LITTLE RED-HAIRED GIRL IS WATCHING, AND I'M GOING TO PITCH A GREAT GAME, AND SHE'S GOING TO BE IMPRESSED, AND...
WE'LL TAKE YOU HOME, CHARLIE BROWN, AND YOU CAN GO TO BED UNTIL YOU STOP SHAKING...
I'M GOING TO BE THE HERO AND PITCH A GREAT GAME AND THAT LITTLE RED-HAIRED GIRL WILL BE WATCHING AND I'LL BE PITCHING AND I'LL BE GREAT AND SHE'LL BE THERE AN
SCHULZ

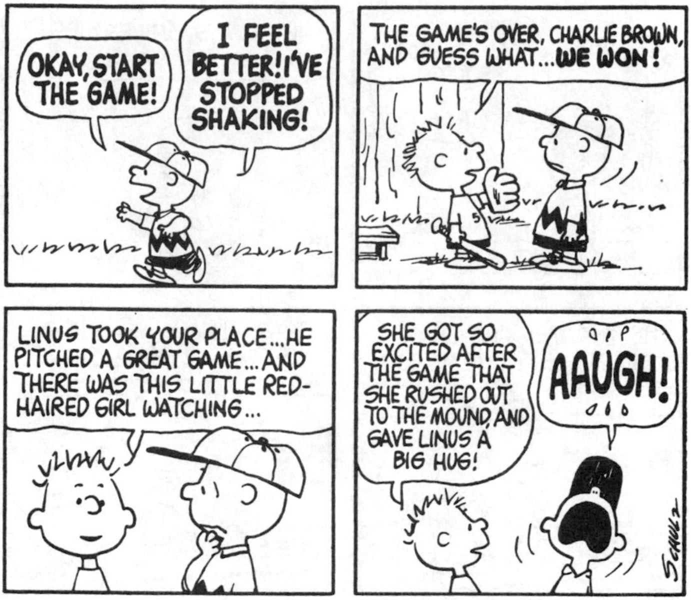
OKAY, START THE GAME!
I FEEL BETTER! I'VE STOPPED SHAKING!
THE GAME'S OVER, CHARLIE BROWN, AND GUESS WHAT...WE WON!
LINUS TOOK YOUR PLACE...HE PITCHED A GREAT GAME...AND THERE WAS THIS LITTLE RED-HAIRED GIRL WATCHING...
SHE GOT SO EXCITED AFTER THE GAME THAT SHE RUSHED OUT TO THE MOUND, AND GAVE LINUS A BIG HUG!
AAUGH!
SCHULZ

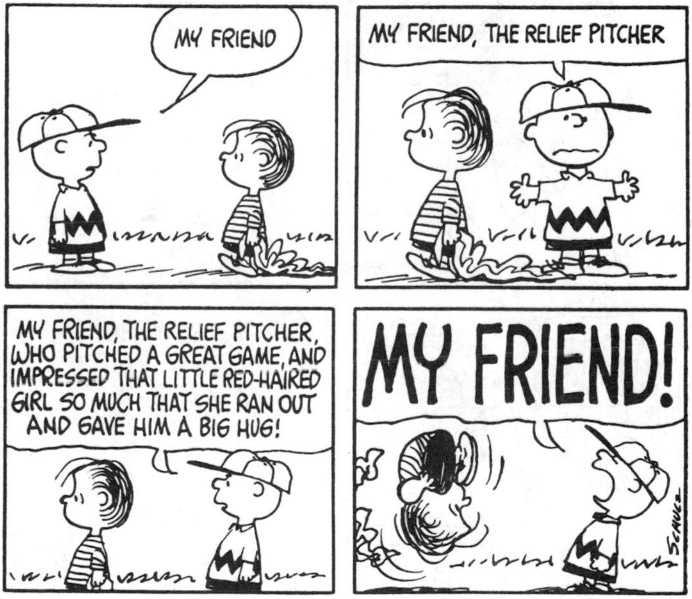
MY FRIEND
MY FRIEND, THE RELIEF PITCHER
MY FRIEND, THE RELIEF PITCHER, WHO PITCHED A GREAT GAME, AND IMPRESSED THAT LITTLE RED-HAIRED GIRL SO MUCH THAT SHE RAN OUT AND GAVE HIM A BIG HUG!
MY FRIEND!
SCHULZ

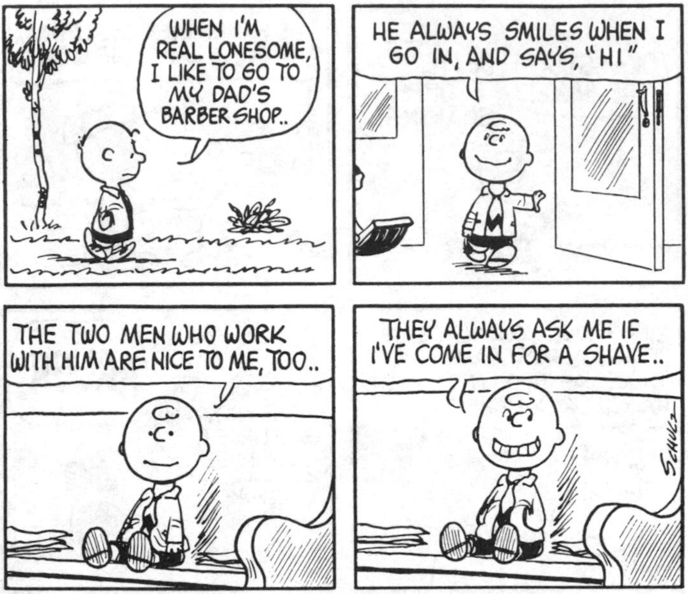
WHEN I'M REAL LONESOME, I LIKE TO GO TO MY DAD'S BARBER SHOP..
HE ALWAYS SMILES WHEN I GO IN, AND SAYS, "HI"
THE TWO MEN WHO WORK WITH HIM ARE NICE TO ME, TOO..
THEY ALWAYS ASK ME IF I'VE COME IN FOR A SHAVE..
SCHULZ

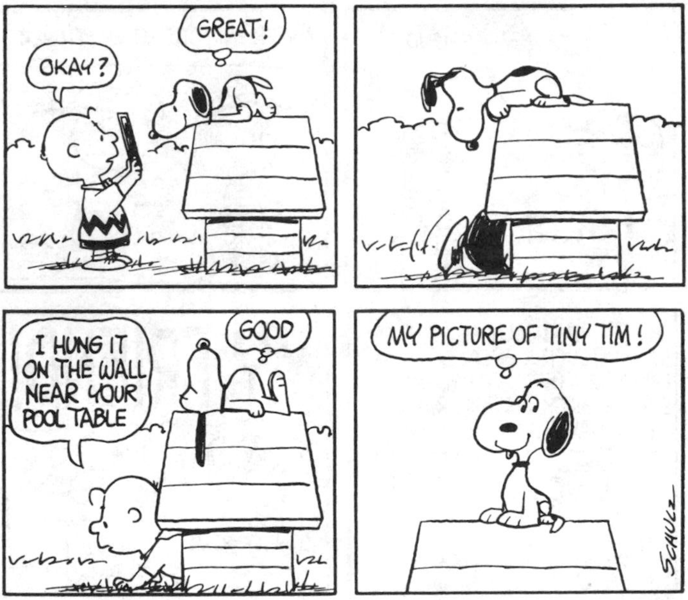
OKAY?
GREAT!
I HUNG IT ON THE WALL NEAR YOUR POOL TABLE
GOOD
MY PICTURE OF TINY TIM!
SCHULZ

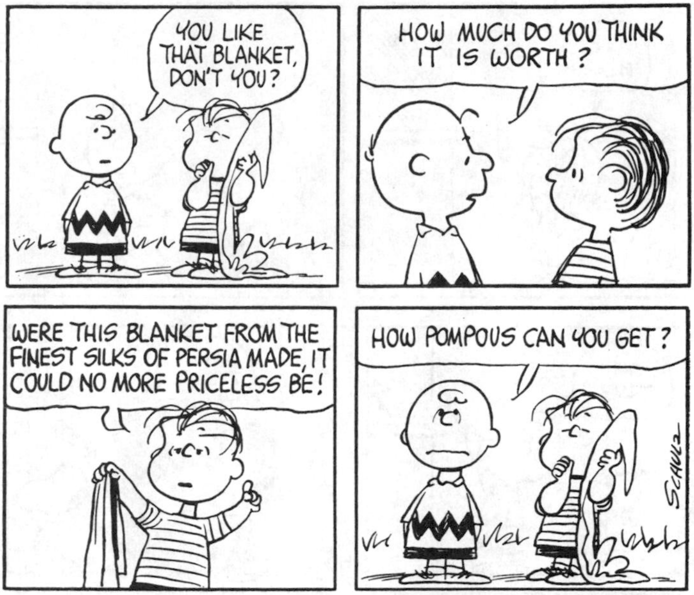
YOU LIKE THAT BLANKET, DON'T YOU?
HOW MUCH DO YOU THINK IT IS WORTH?
WERE THIS BLANKET FROM THE FINEST SILKS OF PERSIA MADE, IT COULD NO MORE PRICELESS BE!
HOW POMPOUS CAN YOU GET?
SCHULZ

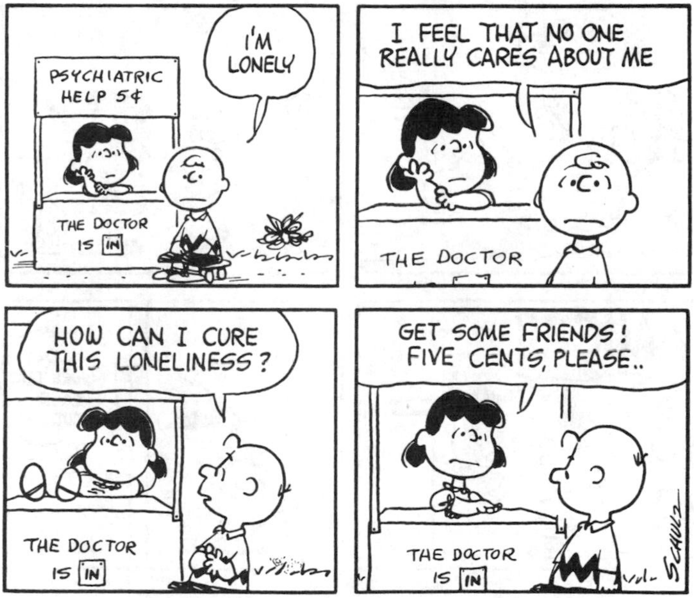
PSYCHIATRIC HELP 5¢
THE DOCTOR IS IN
I'M LONELY
I FEEL THAT NO ONE REALLY CARES ABOUT ME
THE DOCTOR
HOW CAN I CURE THIS LONELINESS?
THE DOCTOR IS IN
GET SOME FRIENDS! FIVE CENTS, PLEASE..
THE DOCTOR IS IN
SCHULZ

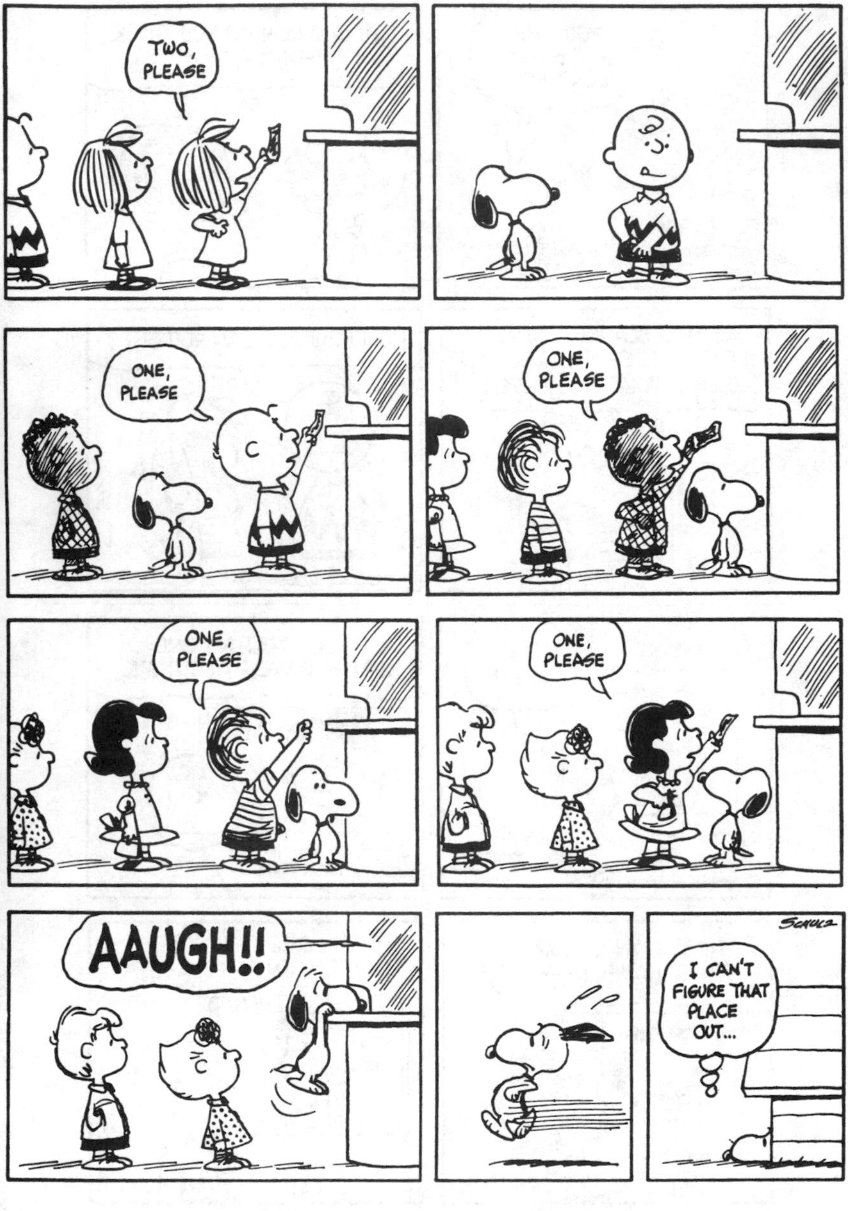
TWO, PLEASE
ONE, PLEASE
ONE, PLEASE
ONE, PLEASE
ONE, PLEASE
AAUGH!!
SCHULZ
I CAN'T FIGURE THAT PLACE OUT...

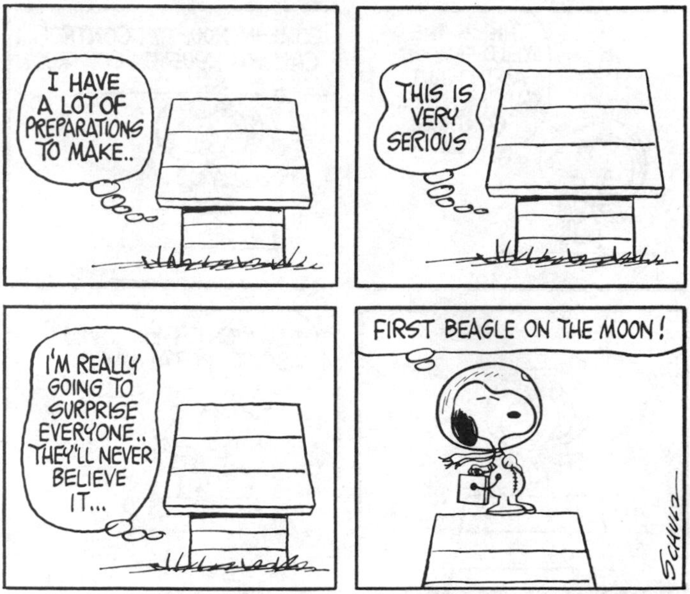
I HAVE A LOT OF PREPARATIONS TO MAKE..
THIS IS VERY SERIOUS
I'M REALLY GOING TO SURPRISE EVERYONE.. THEY'LL NEVER BELIEVE IT...
FIRST BEAGLE ON THE MOON!
SCHULZ

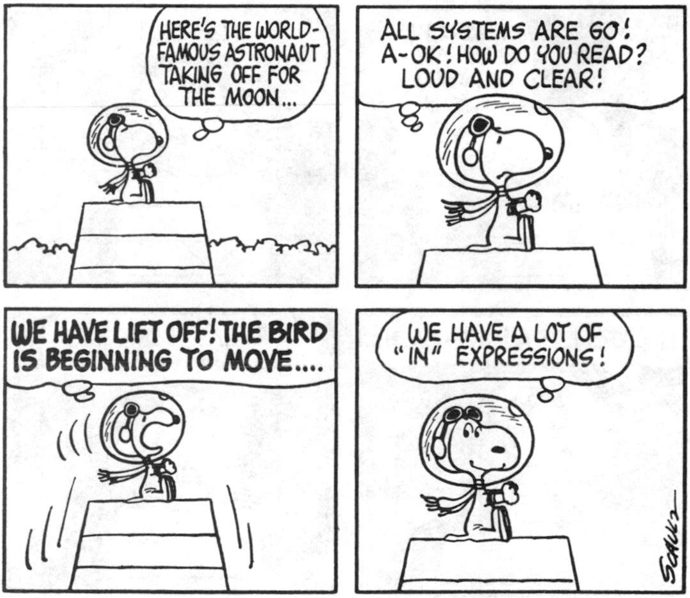
HERE'S THE WORLD-FAMOUS ASTRONAUT TAKING OFF FOR THE MOON...
ALL SYSTEMS ARE GO! A-OK! HOW DO YOU READ? LOUD AND CLEAR!
WE HAVE LIFT OFF! THE BIRD IS BEGINNING TO MOVE....
WE HAVE A LOT OF "IN" EXPRESSIONS!
SCHULZ

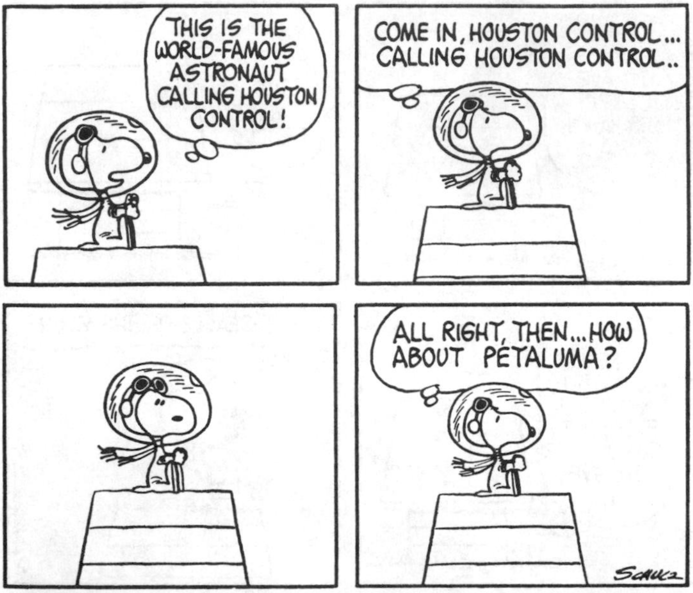
THIS IS THE WORLD-FAMOUS ASTRONAUT CALLING HOUSTON CONTROL!
COME IN, HOUSTON CONTROL... CALLING HOUSTON CONTROL..
ALL RIGHT, THEN...HOW ABOUT PETALUMA?
SCHULZ

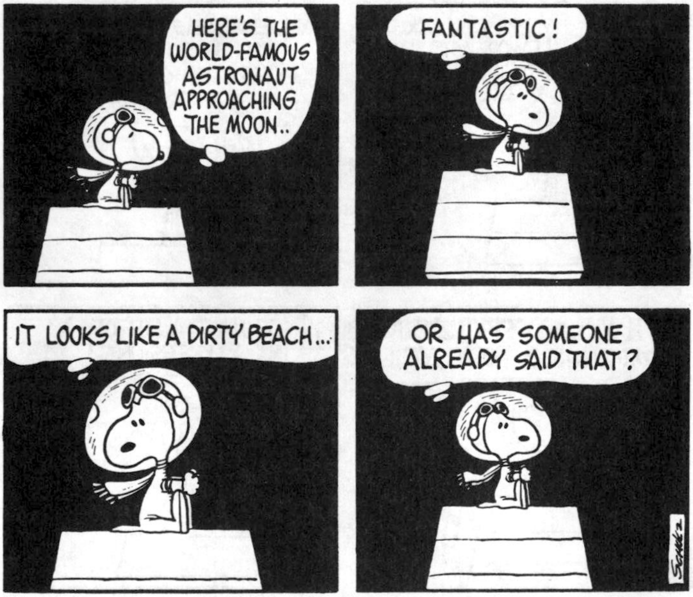
HERE'S THE WORLD-FAMOUS ASTRONAUT APPROACHING THE MOON..
FANTASTIC!
IT LOOKS LIKE A DIRTY BEACH...
OR HAS SOMEONE ALREADY SAID THAT?
SCHULZ

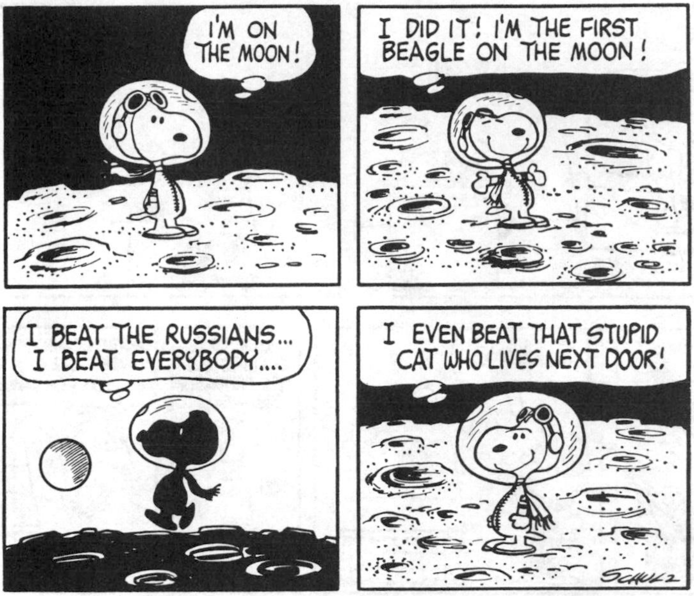
I'M ON THE MOON!
I DID IT! I'M THE FIRST BEAGLE ON THE MOON!
I BEAT THE RUSSIANS... I BEAT EVERYBODY....
I EVEN BEAT THAT STUPID CAT WHO LIVES NEXT DOOR!
SCHULZ

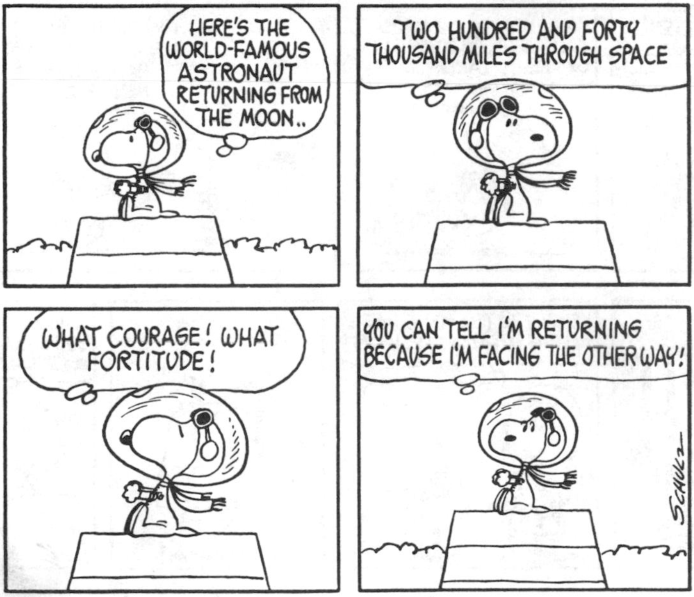
HERE'S THE WORLD-FAMOUS ASTRONAUT RETURNING FROM THE MOON..
TWO HUNDRED AND FORTY THOUSAND MILES THROUGH SPACE
WHAT COURAGE! WHAT FORTITUDE!
YOU CAN TELL I'M RETURNING BECAUSE I'M FACING THE OTHER WAY!
SCHULZ

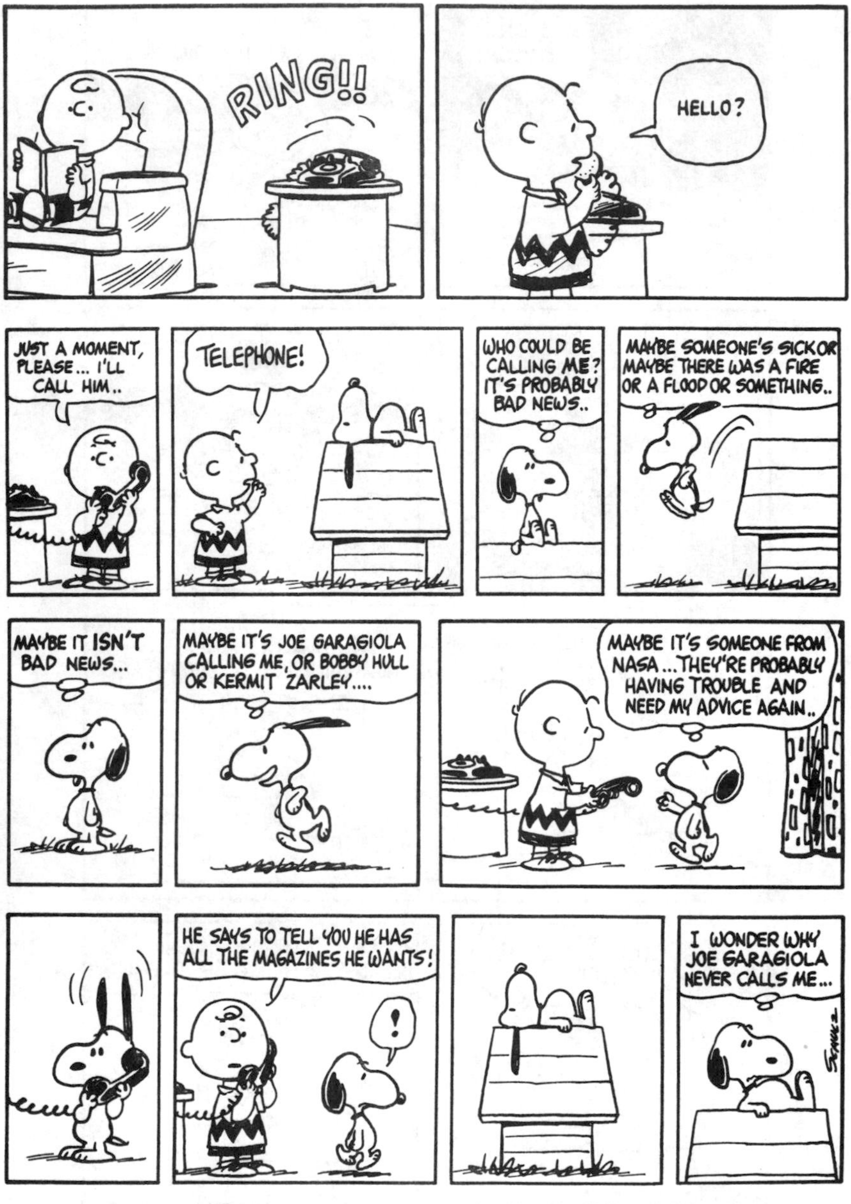
RING!!
HELLO?
JUST A MOMENT, PLEASE... I'LL CALL HIM..
TELEPHONE!
WHO COULD BE CALLING ME? IT'S PROBABLY BAD NEWS..
MAYBE SOMEONE'S SICK OR MAYBE THERE WAS A FIRE OR A FLOOD OR SOMETHING..
MAYBE IT ISN'T BAD NEWS...
MAYBE IT'S JOE GARAGIOLA CALLING ME, OR BOBBY HULL OR KERMIT ZARLEY....
MAYBE IT'S SOMEONE FROM NASA...THEY'RE PROBABLY HAVING TROUBLE AND NEED MY ADVICE AGAIN..
HE SAYS TO TELL YOU HE HAS ALL THE MAGAZINES HE WANTS!
!
I WONDER WHY JOE GARAGIOLA NEVER CALLS ME...

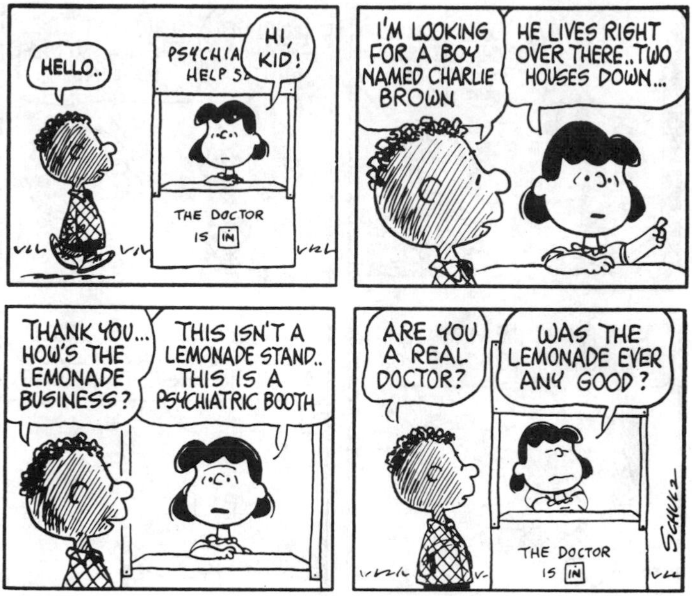
HELLO..
HI, KID!
THE DOCTOR IS IN
I'M LOOKING FOR A BOY NAMED CHARLIE BROWN
HE LIVES RIGHT OVER THERE..TWO HOUSES DOWN...
THANK YOU... HOW'S THE LEMONADE BUSINESS?
THIS ISN'T A LEMONADE STAND.. THIS IS A PSYCHIATRIC BOOTH
ARE YOU A REAL DOCTOR?
WAS THE LEMONADE EVER ANY GOOD?
THE DOCTOR IS IN
SCHULZ

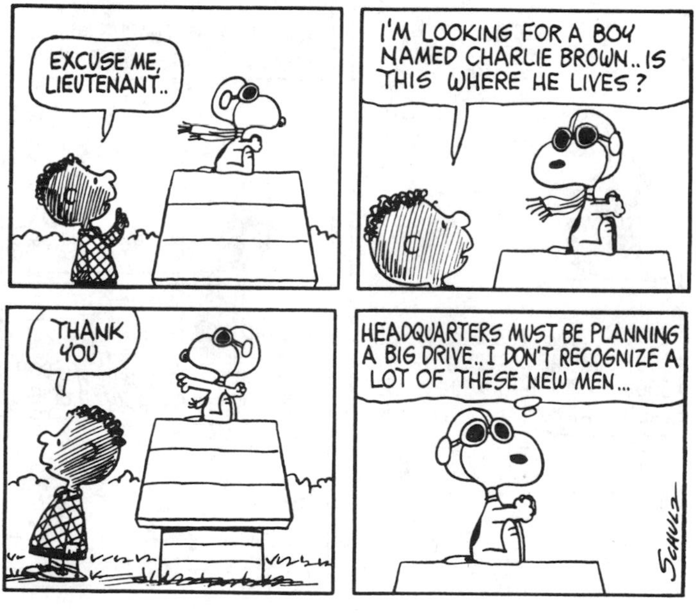
EXCUSE ME, LIEUTENANT..
I'M LOOKING FOR A BOY NAMED CHARLIE BROWN.. IS THIS WHERE HE LIVES?
THANK YOU
HEADQUARTERS MUST BE PLANNING A BIG DRIVE.. I DON'T RECOGNIZE A LOT OF THESE NEW MEN...
SCHULZ

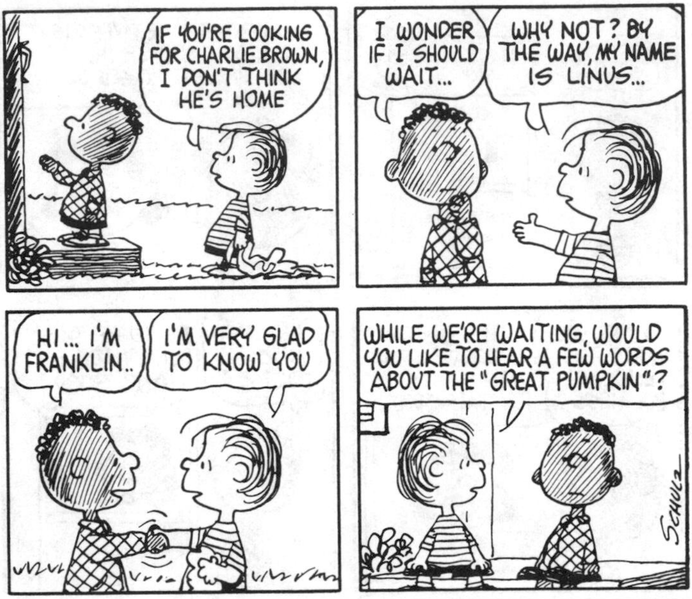

IF YOU'RE LOOKING FOR CHARLIE BROWN, I DON'T THINK HE'S HOME
I WONDER IF I SHOULD WAIT...
WHY NOT? BY THE WAY, MY NAME IS LINUS...
HI... I'M FRANKLIN..
I'M VERY GLAD TO KNOW YOU
WHILE WE'RE WAITING, WOULD YOU LIKE TO HEAR A FEW WORDS ABOUT THE "GREAT PUMPKIN"?
SCHULZ

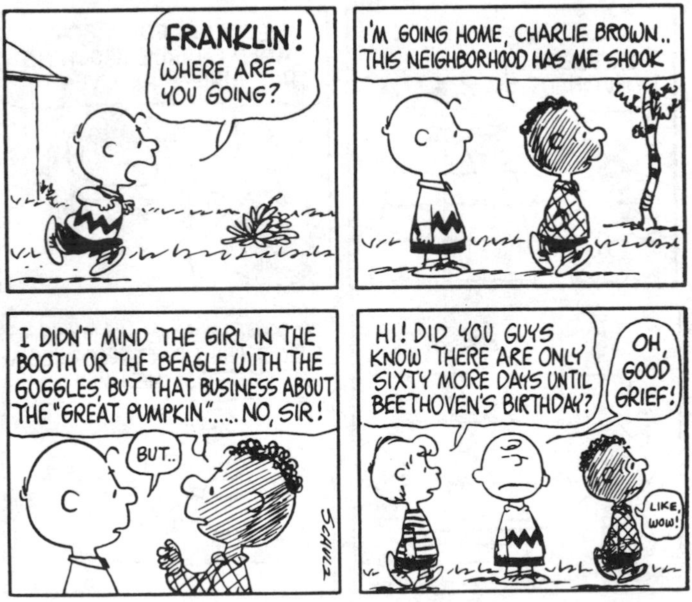

FRANKLIN! WHERE ARE YOU GOING?
I'M GOING HOME, CHARLIE BROWN.. THIS NEIGHBORHOOD HAS ME SHOOK
I DIDN'T MIND THE GIRL IN THE BOOTH OR THE BEAGLE WITH THE GOGGLES, BUT THAT BUSINESS ABOUT THE "GREAT PUMPKIN"..... NO, SIR!
BUT..
SCHULZ
HI! DID YOU GUYS KNOW THERE ARE ONLY SIXTY MORE DAYS UNTIL BEETHOVEN'S BIRTHDAY?
OH, GOOD GRIEF!
LIKE, WOW!

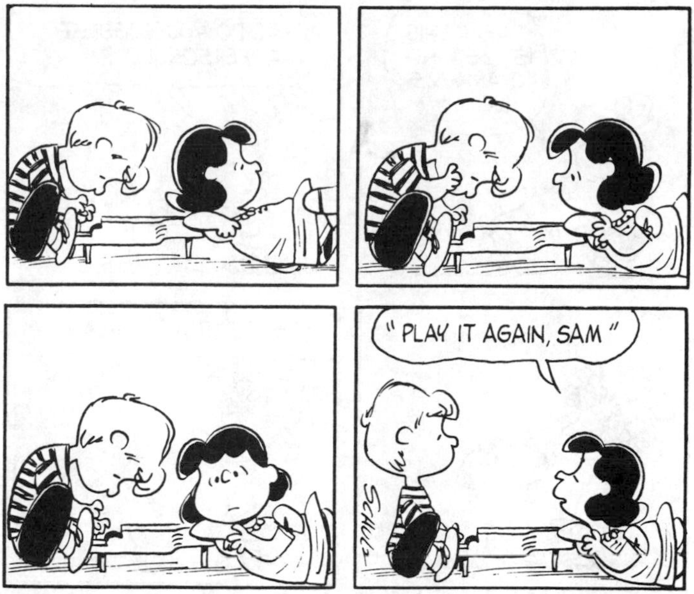
" PLAY IT AGAIN, SAM "
SCHULZ

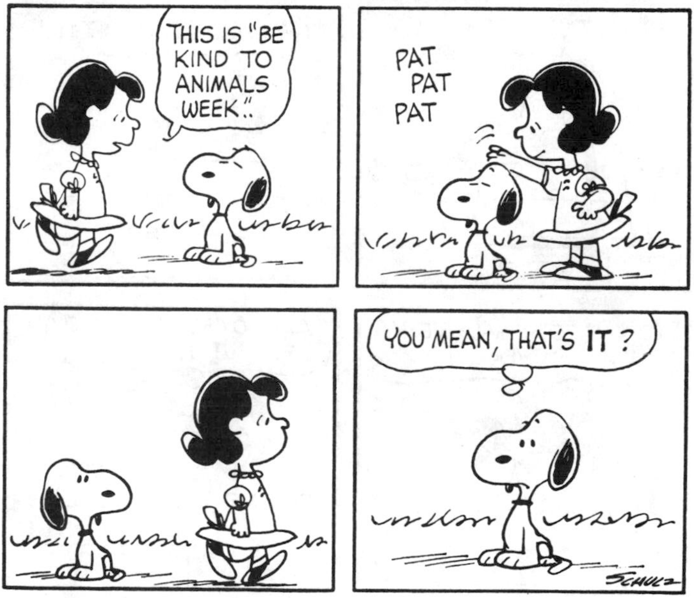
THIS IS "BE KIND TO ANIMALS WEEK."
PAT
PAT
PAT
YOU MEAN, THAT'S IT ?
SCHULZ

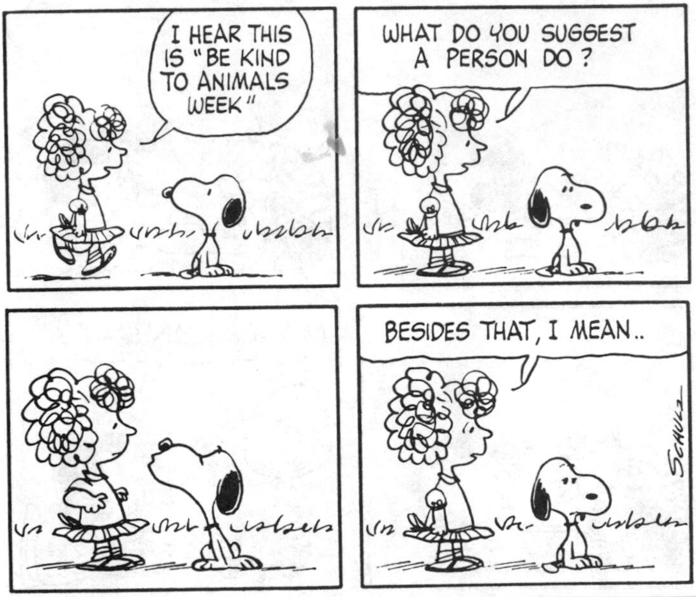

I HEAR THIS IS "BE KIND TO ANIMALS WEEK"
WHAT DO YOU SUGGEST A PERSON DO?
BESIDES THAT, I MEAN..
SCHULZ

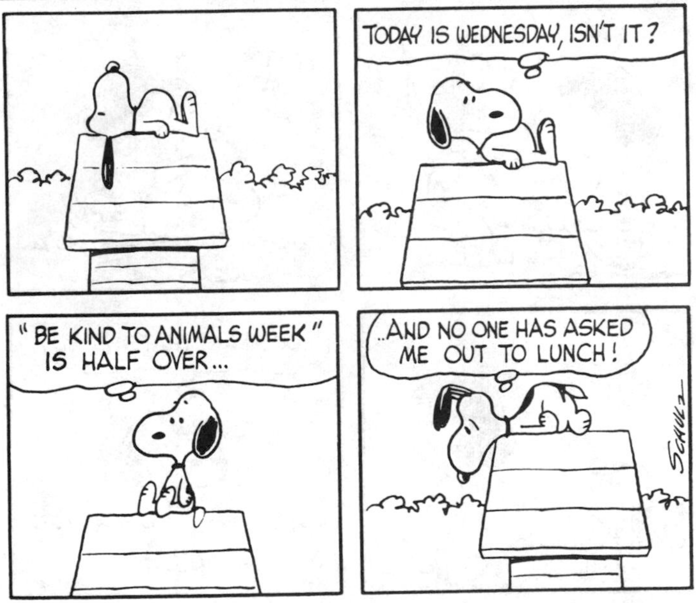

TODAY IS WEDNESDAY, ISN'T IT?
"BE KIND TO ANIMALS WEEK" IS HALF OVER...
..AND NO ONE HAS ASKED ME OUT TO LUNCH!
SCHULZ

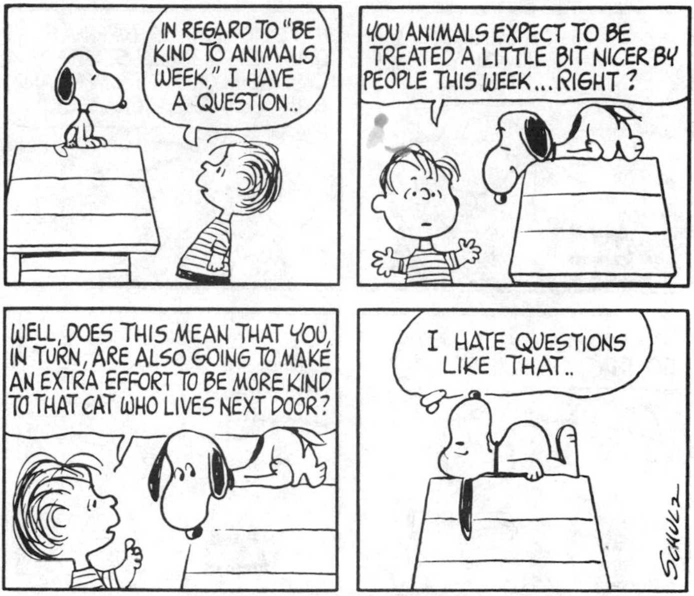
IN REGARD TO "BE KIND TO ANIMALS WEEK," I HAVE A QUESTION..
YOU ANIMALS EXPECT TO BE TREATED A LITTLE BIT NICER BY PEOPLE THIS WEEK... RIGHT?
WELL, DOES THIS MEAN THAT YOU, IN TURN, ARE ALSO GOING TO MAKE AN EXTRA EFFORT TO BE MORE KIND TO THAT CAT WHO LIVES NEXT DOOR?
I HATE QUESTIONS LIKE THAT..
SCHULZ

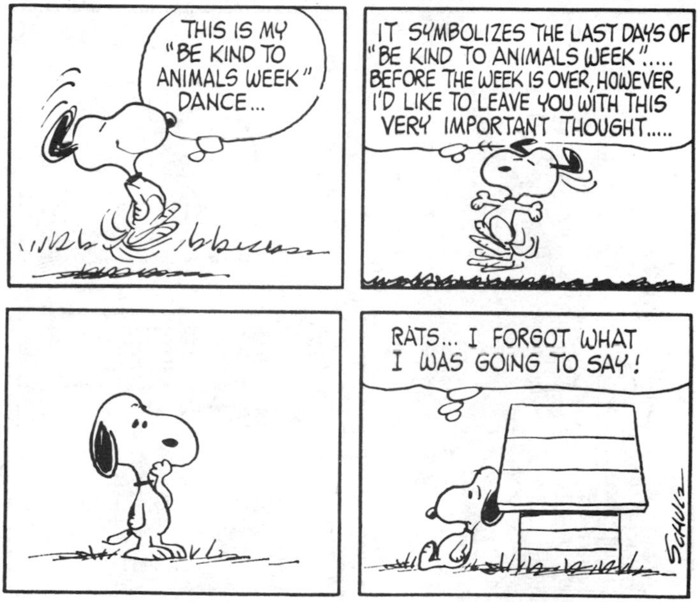
THIS IS MY "BE KIND TO ANIMALS WEEK" DANCE...
IT SYMBOLIZES THE LAST DAYS OF "BE KIND TO ANIMALS WEEK"..... BEFORE THE WEEK IS OVER, HOWEVER, I'D LIKE TO LEAVE YOU WITH THIS VERY IMPORTANT THOUGHT.....
RATS... I FORGOT WHAT I WAS GOING TO SAY!
SCHULZ

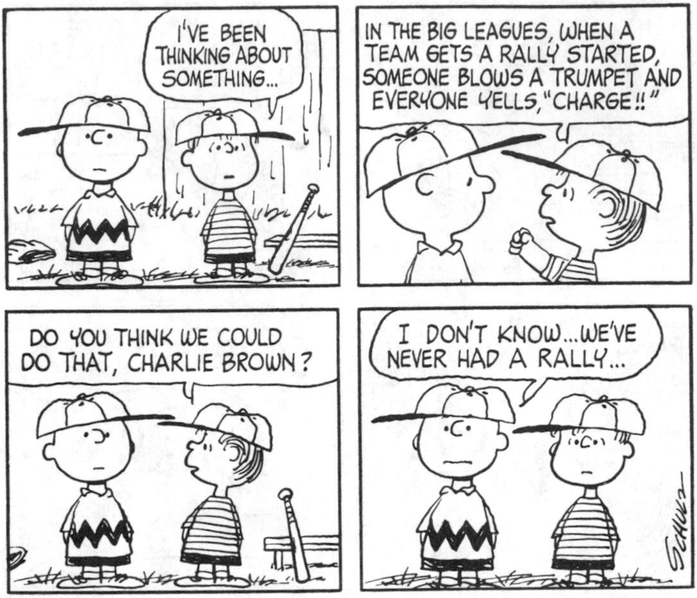
I'VE BEEN THINKING ABOUT SOMETHING...
IN THE BIG LEAGUES, WHEN A TEAM GETS A RALLY STARTED, SOMEONE BLOWS A TRUMPET AND EVERYONE YELLS, "CHARGE!!"
DO YOU THINK WE COULD DO THAT, CHARLIE BROWN?
I DON'T KNOW...WE'VE NEVER HAD A RALLY...

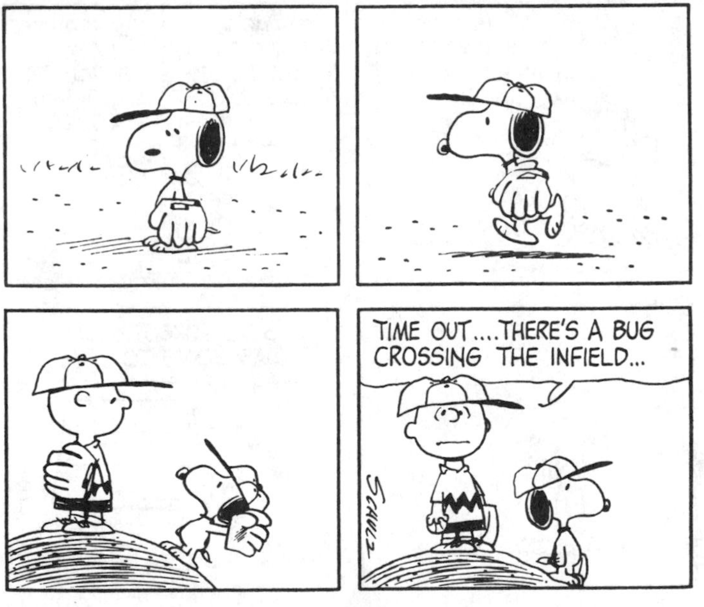
TIME OUT....THERE'S A BUG CROSSING THE INFIELD...

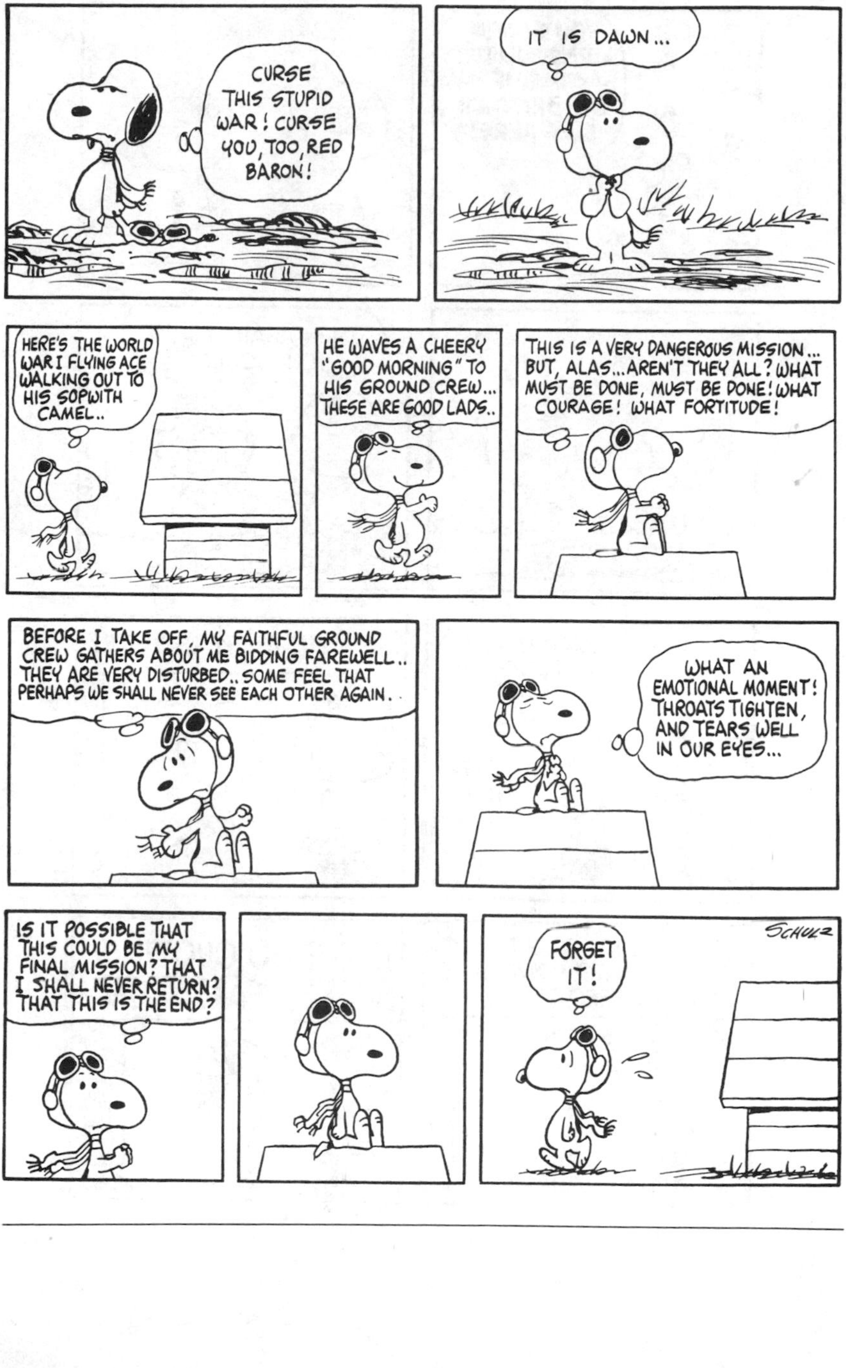
CURSE THIS STUPID WAR! CURSE YOU, TOO, RED BARON!
IT IS DAWN...
HERE'S THE WORLD WAR I FLYING ACE WALKING OUT TO HIS SOPWITH CAMEL..
HE WAVES A CHEERY "GOOD MORNING" TO HIS GROUND CREW... THESE ARE GOOD LADS..
THIS IS A VERY DANGEROUS MISSION... BUT, ALAS...AREN'T THEY ALL? WHAT MUST BE DONE, MUST BE DONE! WHAT COURAGE! WHAT FORTITUDE!
BEFORE I TAKE OFF, MY FAITHFUL GROUND CREW GATHERS ABOUT ME BIDDING FAREWELL.. THEY ARE VERY DISTURBED.. SOME FEEL THAT PERHAPS WE SHALL NEVER SEE EACH OTHER AGAIN..
WHAT AN EMOTIONAL MOMENT! THROATS TIGHTEN, AND TEARS WELL IN OUR EYES...
IS IT POSSIBLE THAT THIS COULD BE MY FINAL MISSION? THAT I SHALL NEVER RETURN? THAT THIS IS THE END?
SCHULZ
FORGET IT!

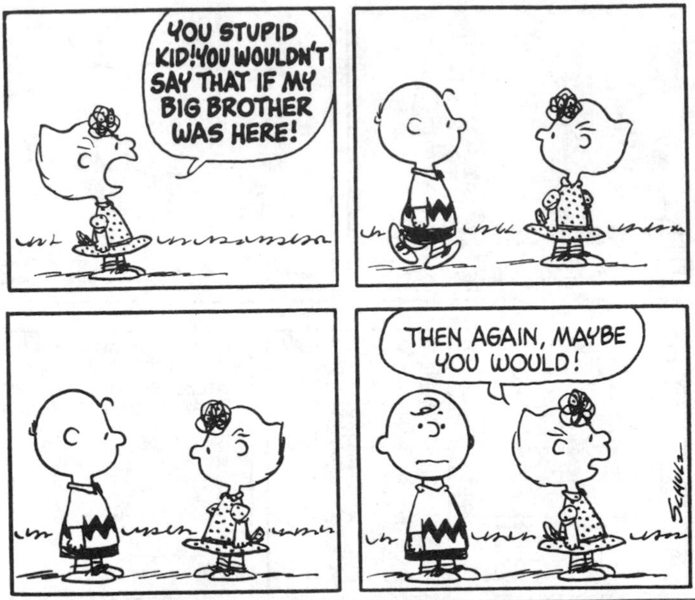
YOU STUPID KID! YOU WOULDN'T SAY THAT IF MY BIG BROTHER WAS HERE!
THEN AGAIN, MAYBE YOU WOULD!
SCHULZ

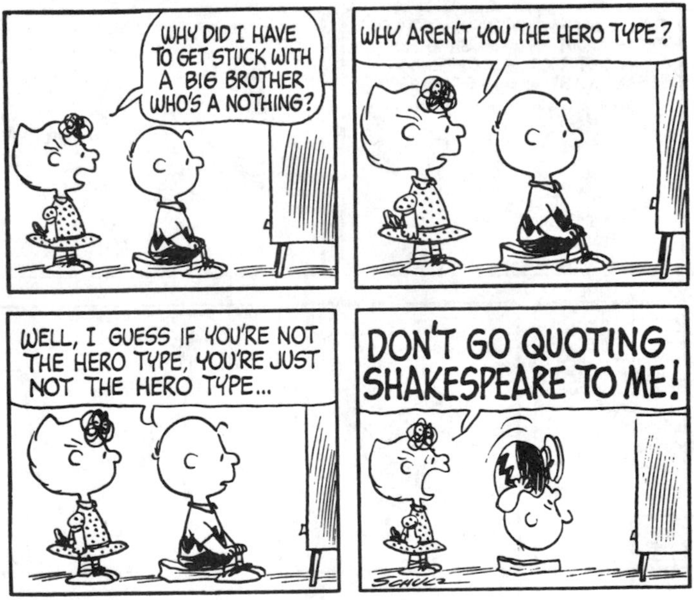
WHY DID I HAVE TO GET STUCK WITH A BIG BROTHER WHO'S A NOTHING?
WHY AREN'T YOU THE HERO TYPE?
WELL, I GUESS IF YOU'RE NOT THE HERO TYPE, YOU'RE JUST NOT THE HERO TYPE...
DON'T GO QUOTING SHAKESPEARE TO ME!
SCHULZ

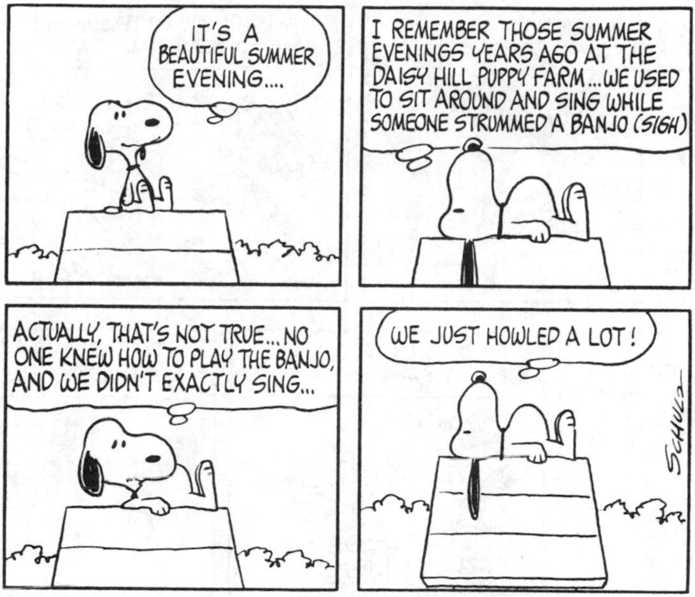
IT'S A BEAUTIFUL SUMMER EVENING....
I REMEMBER THOSE SUMMER EVENINGS YEARS AGO AT THE DAISY HILL PUPPY FARM...WE USED TO SIT AROUND AND SING WHILE SOMEONE STRUMMED A BANJO (SIGH)
ACTUALLY, THAT'S NOT TRUE... NO ONE KNEW HOW TO PLAY THE BANJO, AND WE DIDN'T EXACTLY SING...
WE JUST HOWLED A LOT!
SCHULZ

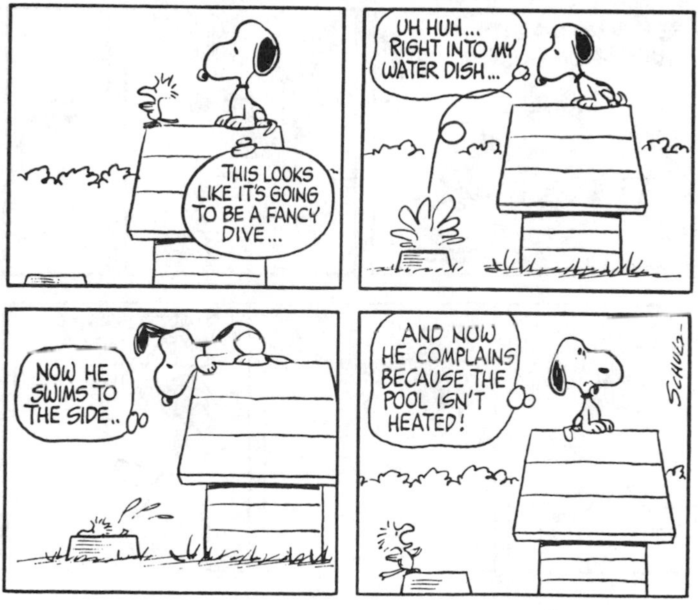
THIS LOOKS LIKE IT'S GOING TO BE A FANCY DIVE...
UH HUH... RIGHT INTO MY WATER DISH...
NOW HE SWIMS TO THE SIDE..
AND NOW HE COMPLAINS BECAUSE THE POOL ISN'T HEATED!
SCHULZ

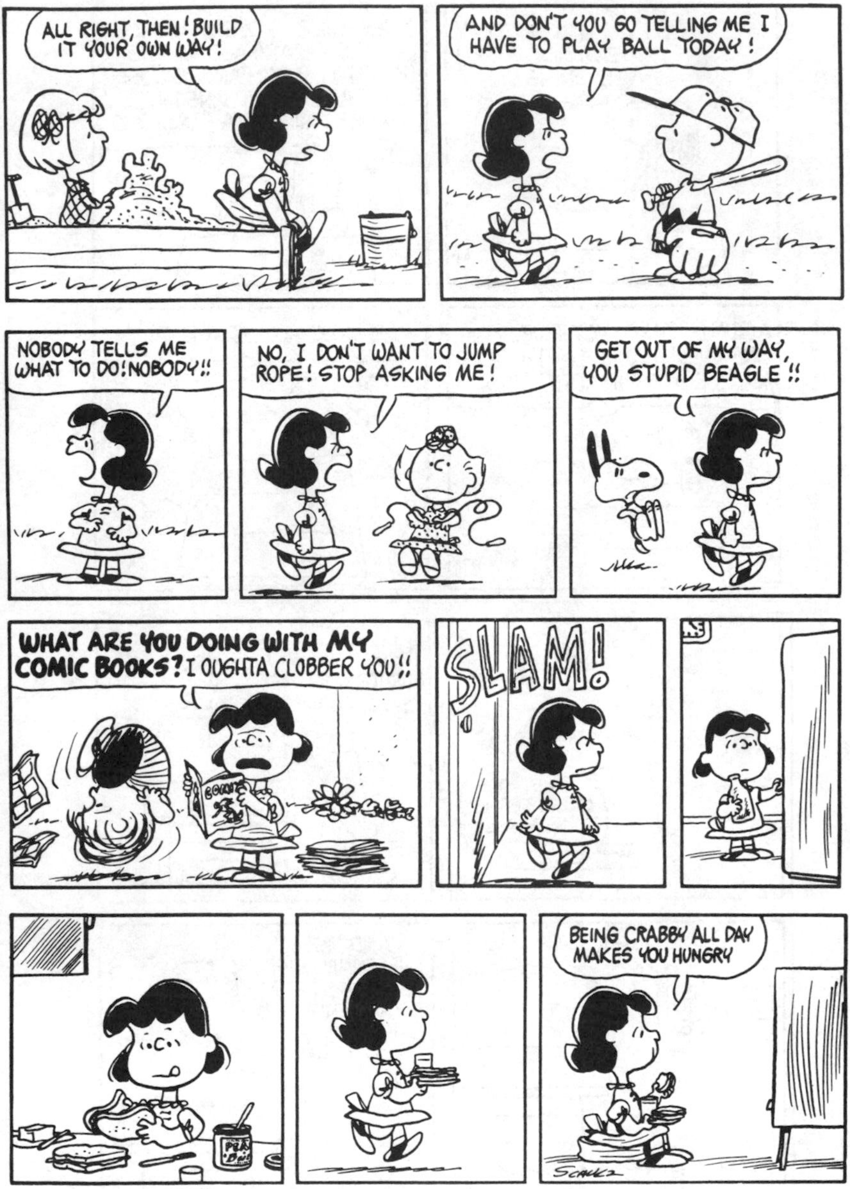

ALL RIGHT, THEN! BUILD IT YOUR OWN WAY!
AND DON'T YOU GO TELLING ME I HAVE TO PLAY BALL TODAY!
NOBODY TELLS ME WHAT TO DO! NOBODY!!
NO, I DON'T WANT TO JUMP ROPE! STOP ASKING ME!
GET OUT OF MY WAY, YOU STUPID BEAGLE!!
WHAT ARE YOU DOING WITH MY COMIC BOOKS? I OUGHTA CLOBBER YOU!!
SLAM!
BEING CRABBY ALL DAY MAKES YOU HUNGRY
SCHULZ

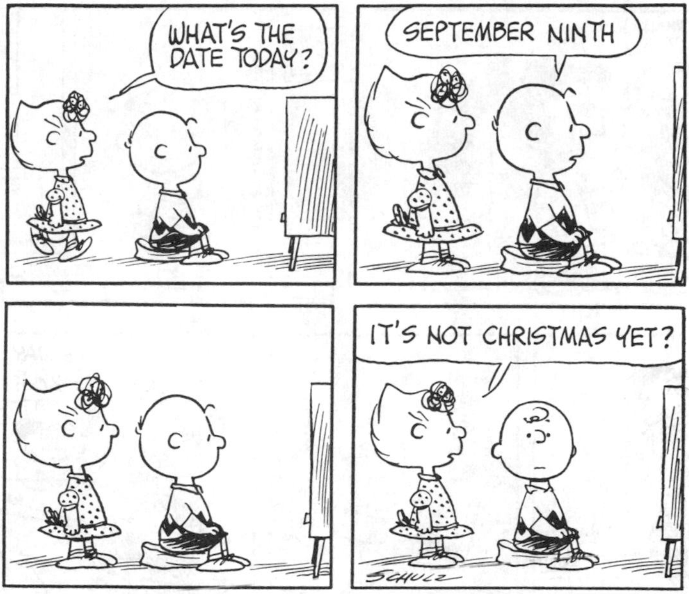
WHAT'S THE DATE TODAY?
SEPTEMBER NINTH
IT'S NOT CHRISTMAS YET?
SCHULZ

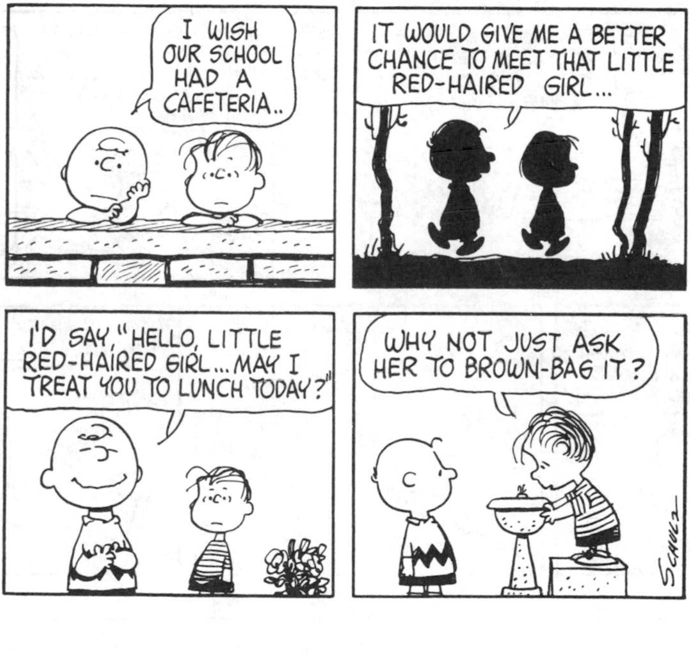
I WISH OUR SCHOOL HAD A CAFETERIA..
IT WOULD GIVE ME A BETTER CHANCE TO MEET THAT LITTLE RED-HAIRED GIRL...
I'D SAY, "HELLO, LITTLE RED-HAIRED GIRL... MAY I TREAT YOU TO LUNCH TODAY?"
WHY NOT JUST ASK HER TO BROWN-BAG IT?
SCHULZ

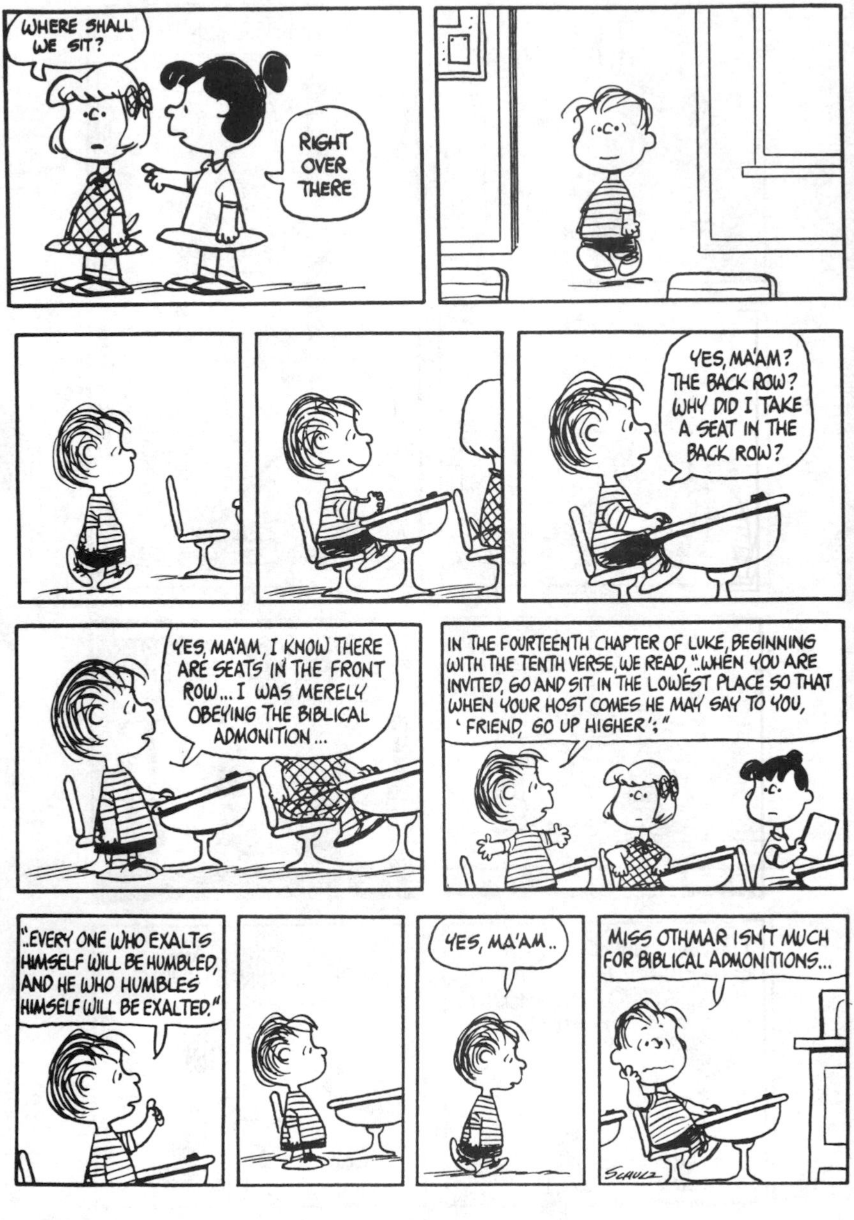
WHERE SHALL WE SIT?
RIGHT OVER THERE
YES, MA'AM? THE BACK ROW? WHY DID I TAKE A SEAT IN THE BACK ROW?
YES, MA'AM, I KNOW THERE ARE SEATS IN THE FRONT ROW... I WAS MERELY OBEYING THE BIBLICAL ADMONITION...
IN THE FOURTEENTH CHAPTER OF LUKE, BEGINNING WITH THE TENTH VERSE, WE READ, "...WHEN YOU ARE INVITED, GO AND SIT IN THE LOWEST PLACE SO THAT WHEN YOUR HOST COMES HE MAY SAY TO YOU, 'FRIEND, GO UP HIGHER';"
"...EVERY ONE WHO EXALTS HIMSELF WILL BE HUMBLED, AND HE WHO HUMBLES HIMSELF WILL BE EXALTED."
YES, MA'AM..
MISS OTHMAR ISN'T MUCH FOR BIBLICAL ADMONITIONS...
SCHULZ

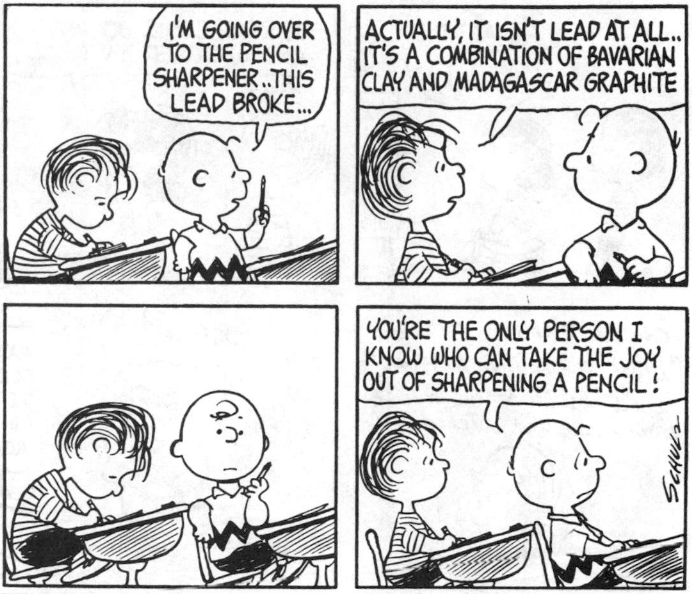
I'M GOING OVER TO THE PENCIL SHARPENER..THIS LEAD BROKE...
ACTUALLY, IT ISN'T LEAD AT ALL.. IT'S A COMBINATION OF BAVARIAN CLAY AND MADAGASCAR GRAPHITE
YOU'RE THE ONLY PERSON I KNOW WHO CAN TAKE THE JOY OUT OF SHARPENING A PENCIL!

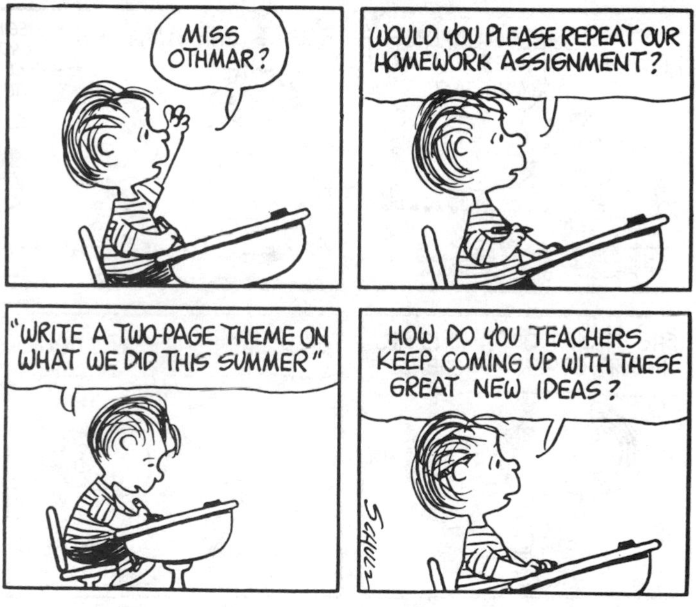
MISS OTHMAR?
WOULD YOU PLEASE REPEAT OUR HOMEWORK ASSIGNMENT?
"WRITE A TWO-PAGE THEME ON WHAT WE DID THIS SUMMER"
HOW DO YOU TEACHERS KEEP COMING UP WITH THESE GREAT NEW IDEAS?

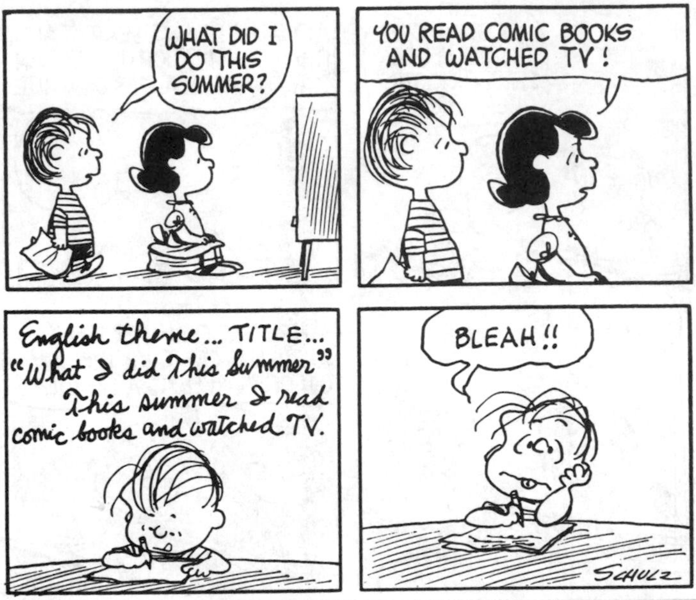
WHAT DID I DO THIS SUMMER?
YOU READ COMIC BOOKS AND WATCHED TV!
English theme... TITLE... "What I did This Summer" This summer I read comic books and watched TV.
BLEAH!!

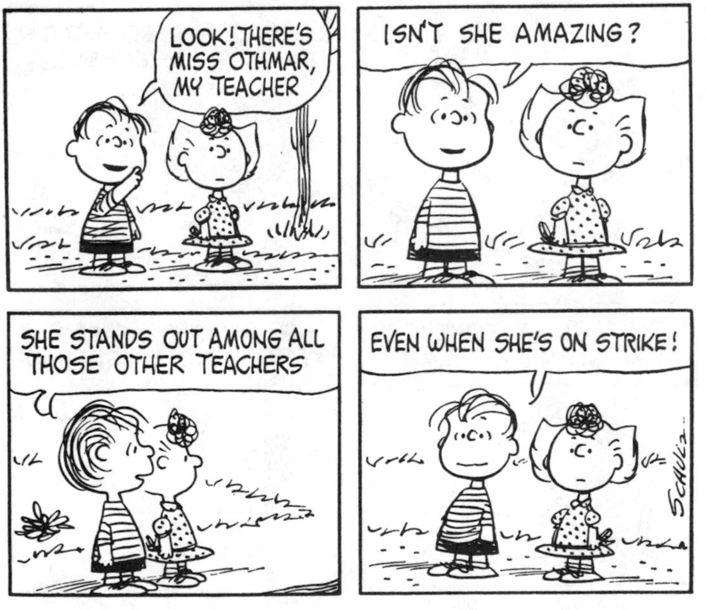
LOOK! THERE'S MISS OTHMAR, MY TEACHER
ISN'T SHE AMAZING?
SHE STANDS OUT AMONG ALL THOSE OTHER TEACHERS
EVEN WHEN SHE'S ON STRIKE!

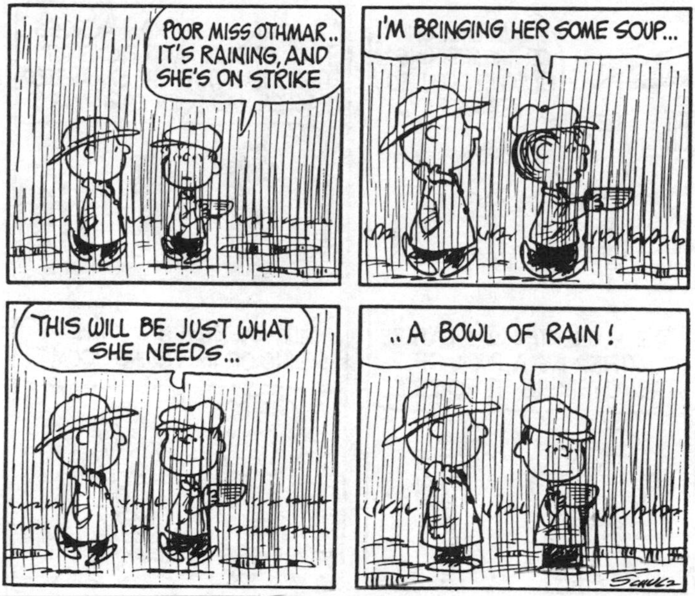
POOR MISS OTHMAR.. IT'S RAINING, AND SHE'S ON STRIKE
I'M BRINGING HER SOME SOUP...
THIS WILL BE JUST WHAT SHE NEEDS...
..A BOWL OF RAIN!
SCHULZ

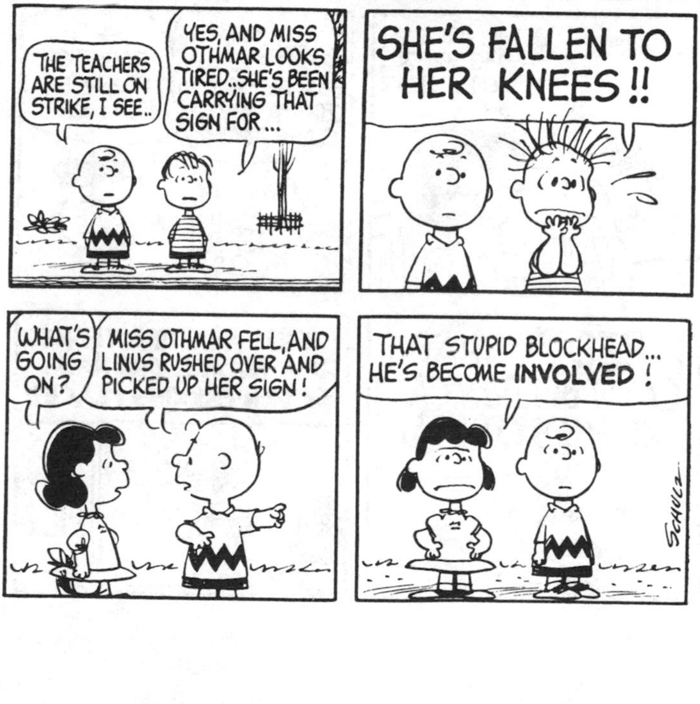
THE TEACHERS ARE STILL ON STRIKE, I SEE..
YES, AND MISS OTHMAR LOOKS TIRED..SHE'S BEEN CARRYING THAT SIGN FOR...
SHE'S FALLEN TO HER KNEES!!
WHAT'S GOING ON?
MISS OTHMAR FELL, AND LINUS RUSHED OVER AND PICKED UP HER SIGN!
THAT STUPID BLOCKHEAD... HE'S BECOME **INVOLVED**!
SCHULZ

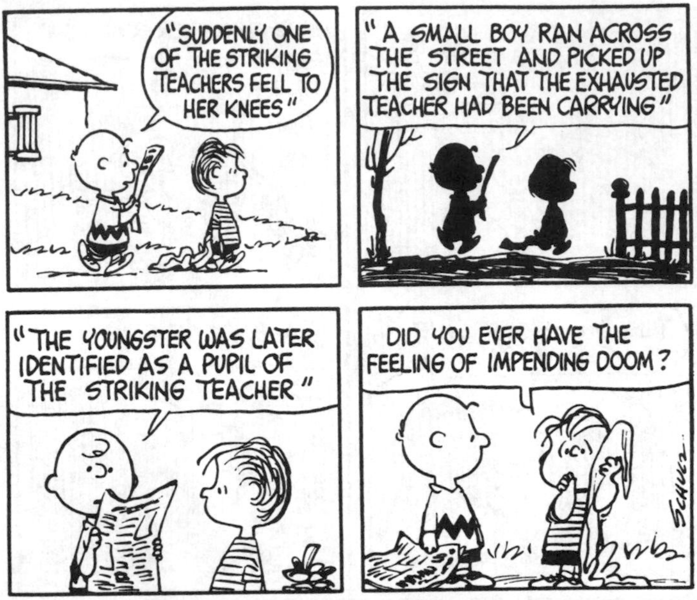
"SUDDENLY ONE OF THE STRIKING TEACHERS FELL TO HER KNEES"
"A SMALL BOY RAN ACROSS THE STREET AND PICKED UP THE SIGN THAT THE EXHAUSTED TEACHER HAD BEEN CARRYING"
"THE YOUNGSTER WAS LATER IDENTIFIED AS A PUPIL OF THE STRIKING TEACHER"
DID YOU EVER HAVE THE FEELING OF IMPENDING DOOM?
SCHULZ

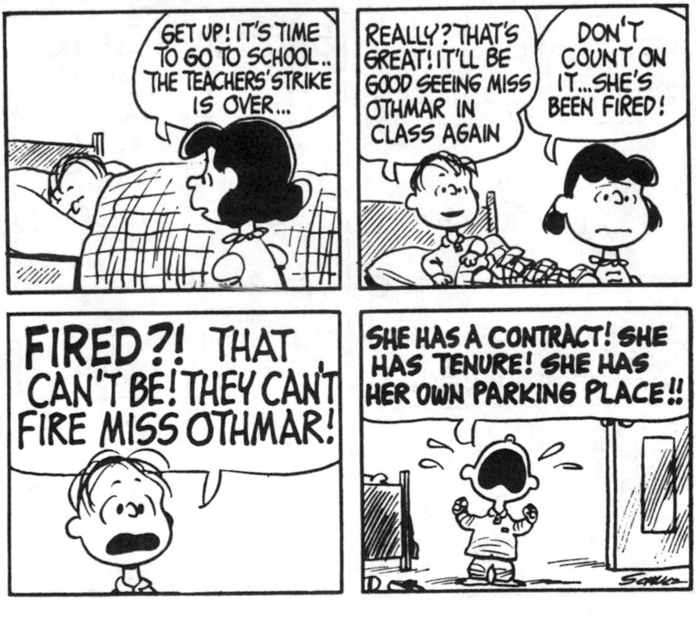
GET UP! IT'S TIME TO GO TO SCHOOL.. THE TEACHERS' STRIKE IS OVER...
REALLY? THAT'S GREAT! IT'LL BE GOOD SEEING MISS OTHMAR IN CLASS AGAIN
DON'T COUNT ON IT...SHE'S BEEN FIRED!
FIRED?! THAT CAN'T BE! THEY CAN'T FIRE MISS OTHMAR!
SHE HAS A CONTRACT! SHE HAS TENURE! SHE HAS HER OWN PARKING PLACE!!
SCHULZ

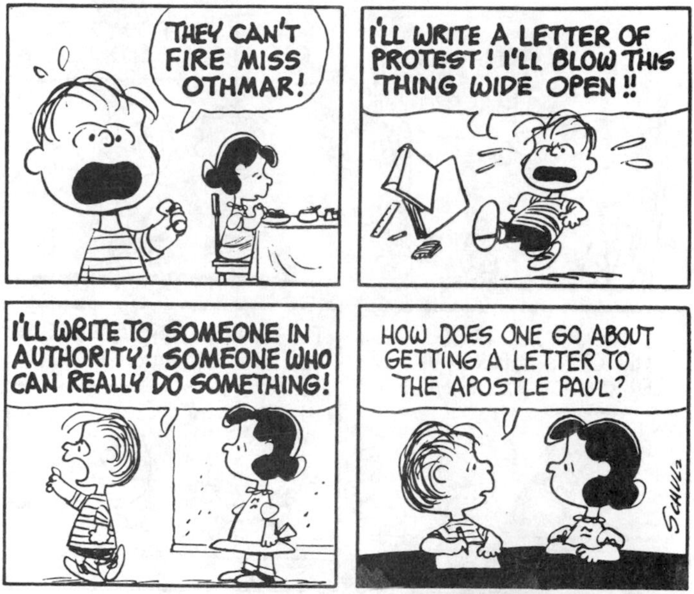
THEY CAN'T FIRE MISS OTHMAR!
I'LL WRITE A LETTER OF PROTEST! I'LL BLOW THIS THING WIDE OPEN!!
I'LL WRITE TO SOMEONE IN AUTHORITY! SOMEONE WHO CAN REALLY DO SOMETHING!
HOW DOES ONE GO ABOUT GETTING A LETTER TO THE APOSTLE PAUL?
SCHULZ

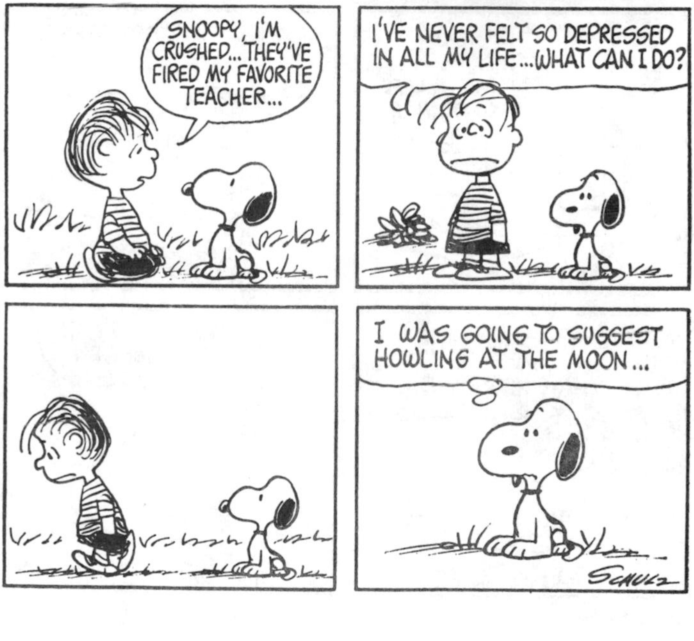
SNOOPY, I'M CRUSHED... THEY'VE FIRED MY FAVORITE TEACHER...
I'VE NEVER FELT SO DEPRESSED IN ALL MY LIFE... WHAT CAN I DO?
I WAS GOING TO SUGGEST HOWLING AT THE MOON...
SCHULZ

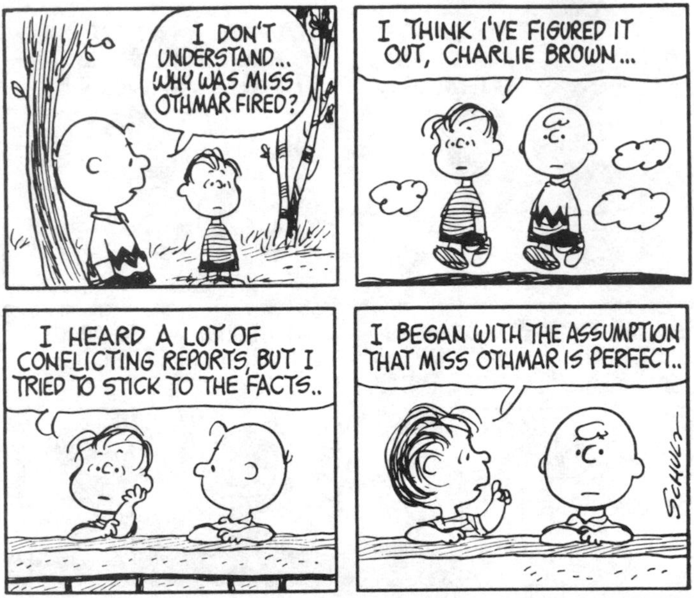
I DON'T UNDERSTAND... WHY WAS MISS OTHMAR FIRED?
I THINK I'VE FIGURED IT OUT, CHARLIE BROWN...
I HEARD A LOT OF CONFLICTING REPORTS, BUT I TRIED TO STICK TO THE FACTS..
I BEGAN WITH THE ASSUMPTION THAT MISS OTHMAR IS PERFECT..
SCHULZ

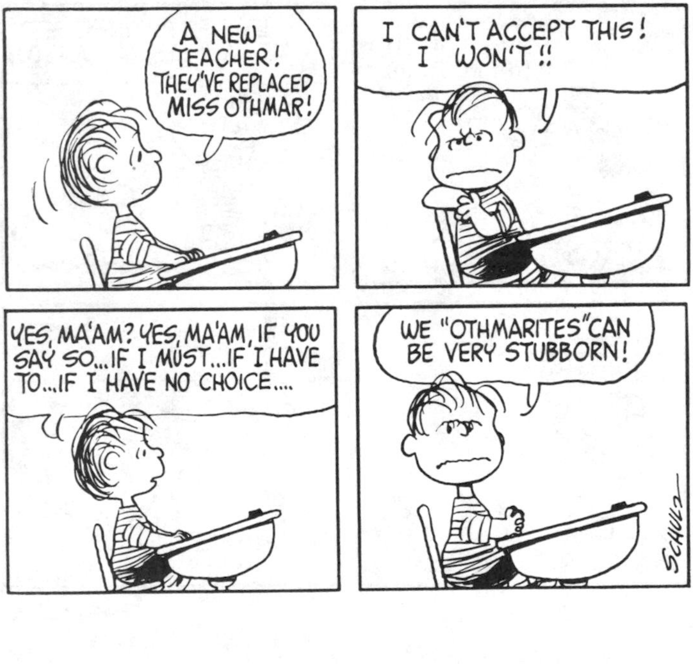
A NEW TEACHER! THEY'VE REPLACED MISS OTHMAR!
I CAN'T ACCEPT THIS! I WON'T!!
YES, MA'AM? YES, MA'AM, IF YOU SAY SO...IF I MUST...IF I HAVE TO...IF I HAVE NO CHOICE....
WE "OTHMARITES" CAN BE VERY STUBBORN!
SCHULZ

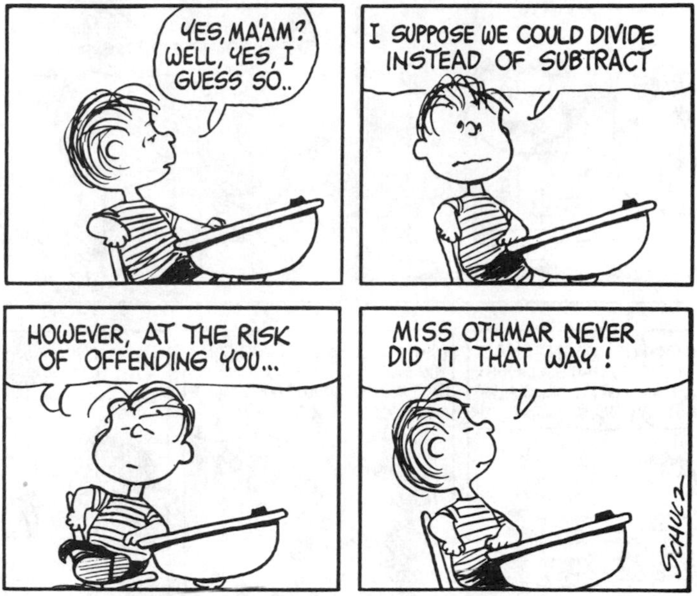
YES, MA'AM? WELL, YES, I GUESS SO..
I SUPPOSE WE COULD DIVIDE INSTEAD OF SUBTRACT
HOWEVER, AT THE RISK OF OFFENDING YOU...
MISS OTHMAR NEVER DID IT THAT WAY!
SCHULZ

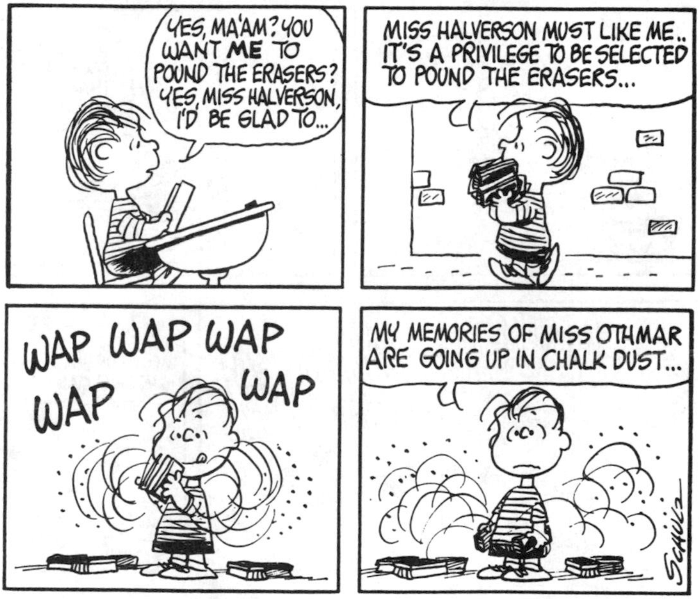
YES, MA'AM? YOU WANT ME TO POUND THE ERASERS? YES, MISS HALVERSON, I'D BE GLAD TO...
MISS HALVERSON MUST LIKE ME.. IT'S A PRIVILEGE TO BE SELECTED TO POUND THE ERASERS...
WAP WAP WAP WAP WAP
MY MEMORIES OF MISS OTHMAR ARE GOING UP IN CHALK DUST...
SCHULZ

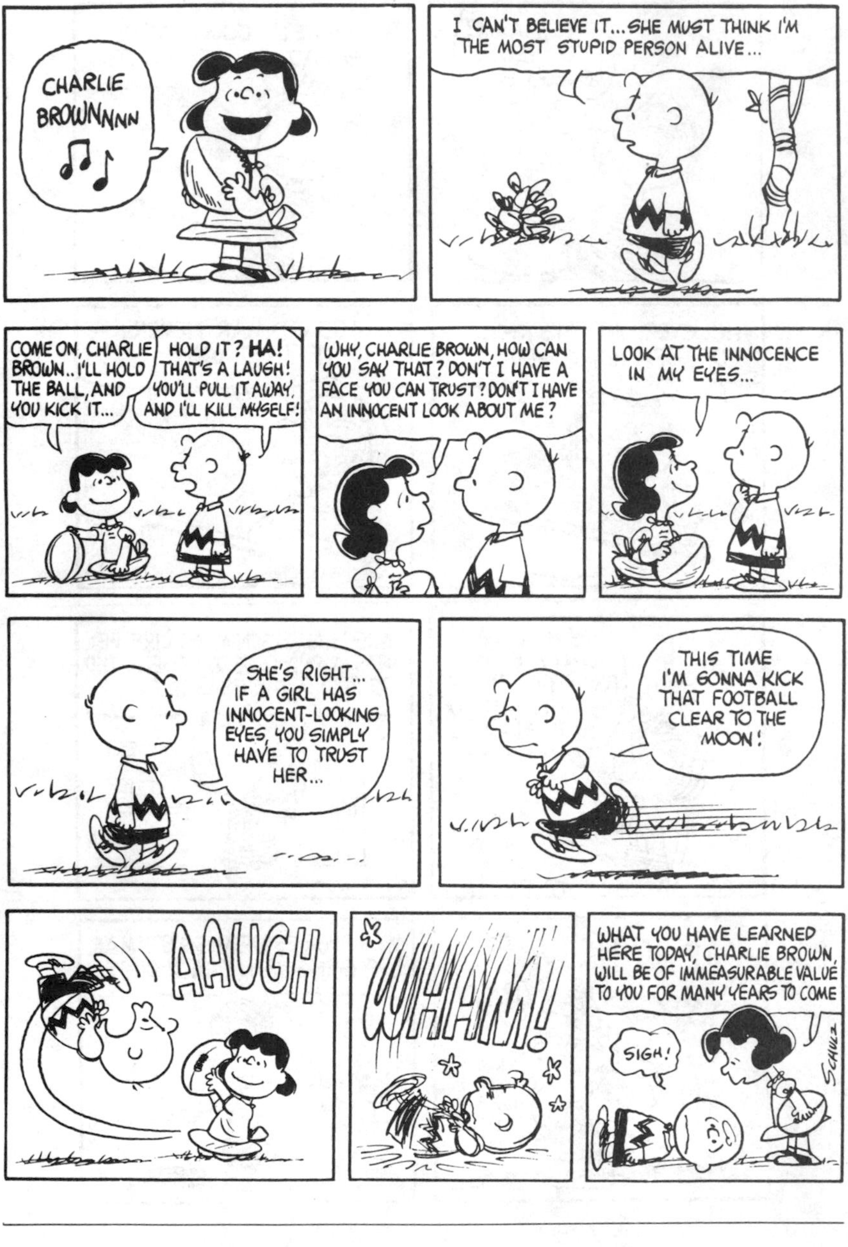
CHARLIE BROWNNNN
I CAN'T BELIEVE IT...SHE MUST THINK I'M THE MOST STUPID PERSON ALIVE...
COME ON, CHARLIE BROWN.. I'LL HOLD THE BALL, AND YOU KICK IT...
HOLD IT? HA! THAT'S A LAUGH! YOU'LL PULL IT AWAY, AND I'LL KILL MYSELF!
WHY, CHARLIE BROWN, HOW CAN YOU SAY THAT? DON'T I HAVE A FACE YOU CAN TRUST? DON'T I HAVE AN INNOCENT LOOK ABOUT ME?
LOOK AT THE INNOCENCE IN MY EYES...
SHE'S RIGHT... IF A GIRL HAS INNOCENT-LOOKING EYES, YOU SIMPLY HAVE TO TRUST HER...
THIS TIME I'M GONNA KICK THAT FOOTBALL CLEAR TO THE MOON!
AAUGH
WHAM!
WHAT YOU HAVE LEARNED HERE TODAY, CHARLIE BROWN, WILL BE OF IMMEASURABLE VALUE TO YOU FOR MANY YEARS TO COME
SIGH!
SCHULZ

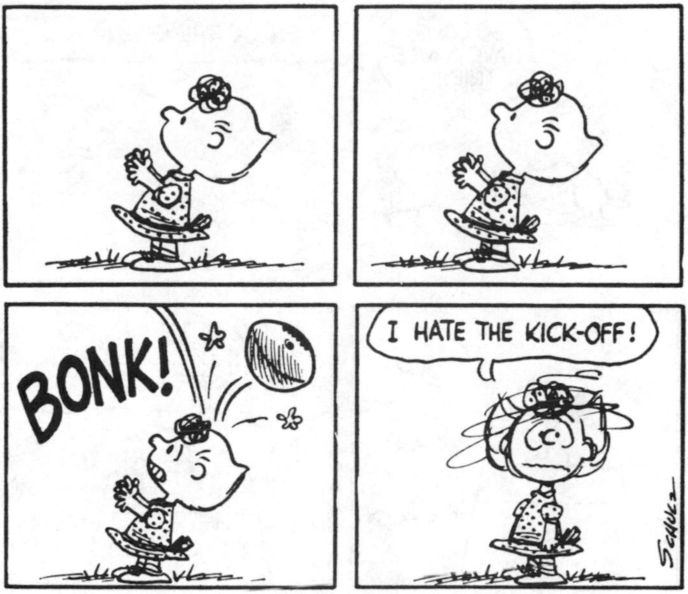
BONK!
I HATE THE KICK-OFF!
SCHULZ

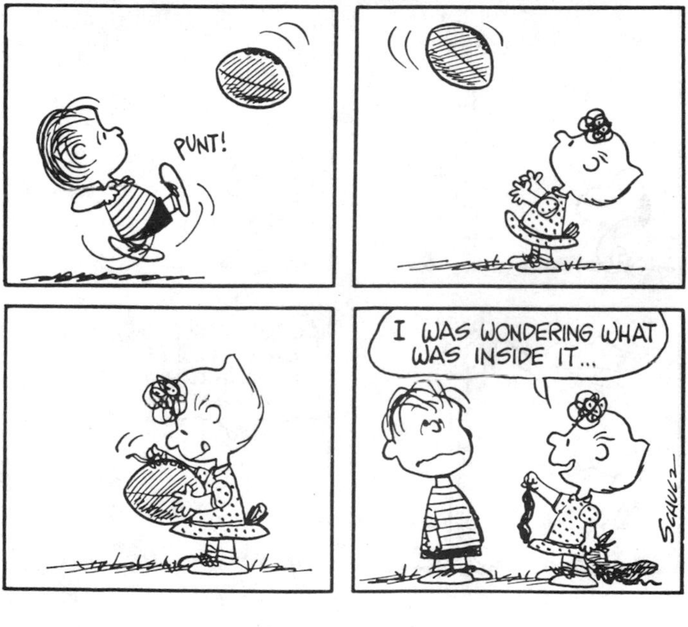
PUNT!
I WAS WONDERING WHAT WAS INSIDE IT...
SCHULZ

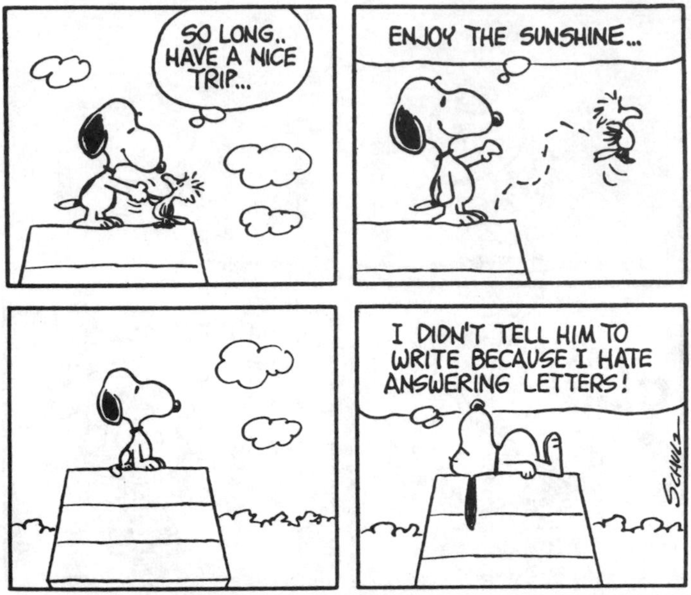
SO LONG..
HAVE A NICE
TRIP...
ENJOY THE SUNSHINE...
I DIDN'T TELL HIM TO
WRITE BECAUSE I HATE
ANSWERING LETTERS!
SCHULZ

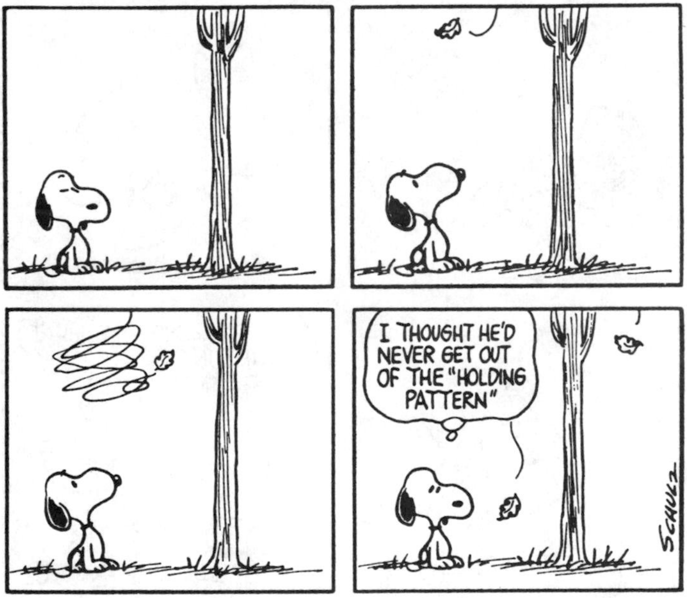
I THOUGHT HE'D
NEVER GET OUT
OF THE "HOLDING
PATTERN"
SCHULZ

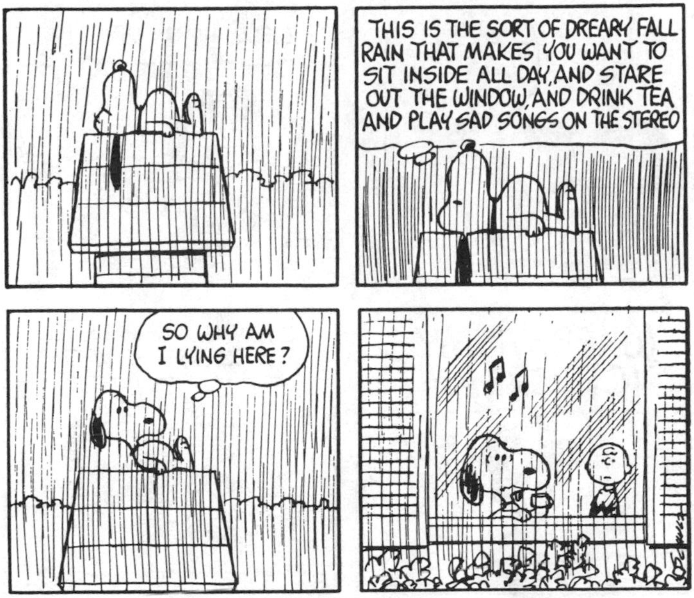
THIS IS THE SORT OF DREARY FALL RAIN THAT MAKES YOU WANT TO SIT INSIDE ALL DAY, AND STARE OUT THE WINDOW, AND DRINK TEA AND PLAY SAD SONGS ON THE STEREO
SO WHY AM I LYING HERE?

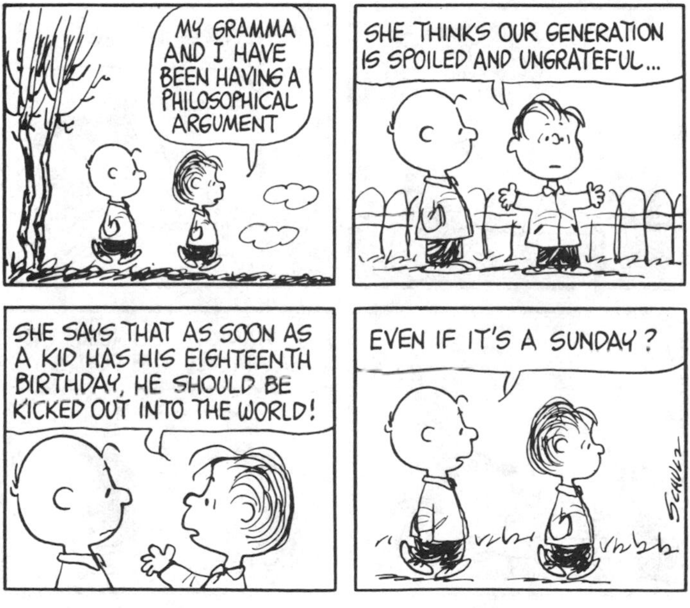
MY GRAMMA AND I HAVE BEEN HAVING A PHILOSOPHICAL ARGUMENT
SHE THINKS OUR GENERATION IS SPOILED AND UNGRATEFUL...
SHE SAYS THAT AS SOON AS A KID HAS HIS EIGHTEENTH BIRTHDAY, HE SHOULD BE KICKED OUT INTO THE WORLD!
EVEN IF IT'S A SUNDAY?

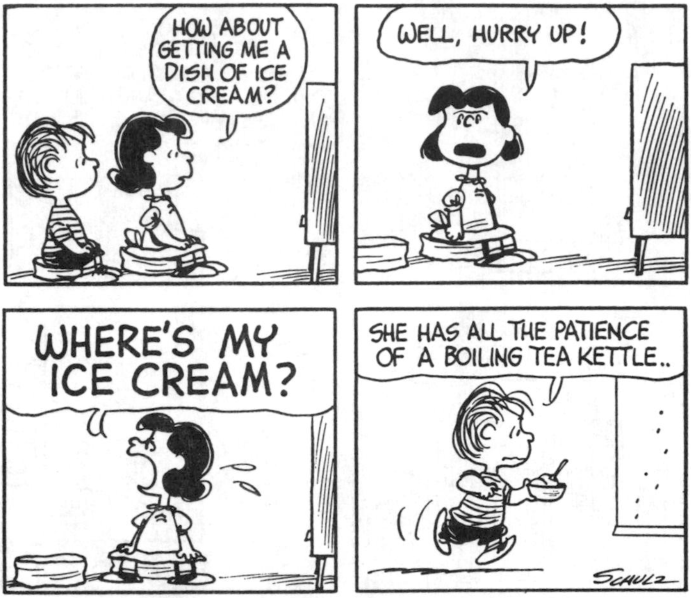
HOW ABOUT GETTING ME A DISH OF ICE CREAM?
WELL, HURRY UP!
WHERE'S MY ICE CREAM?
SHE HAS ALL THE PATIENCE OF A BOILING TEA KETTLE..

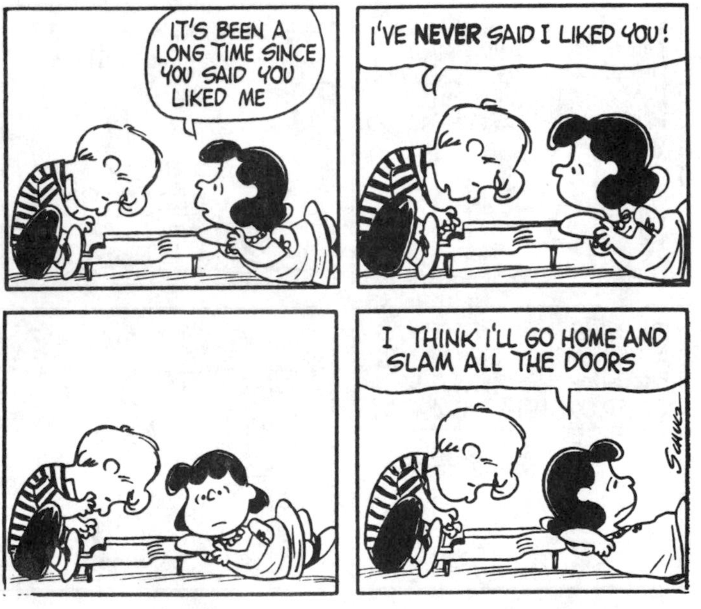
IT'S BEEN A LONG TIME SINCE YOU SAID YOU LIKED ME
I'VE **NEVER** SAID I LIKED YOU!
I THINK I'LL GO HOME AND SLAM ALL THE DOORS

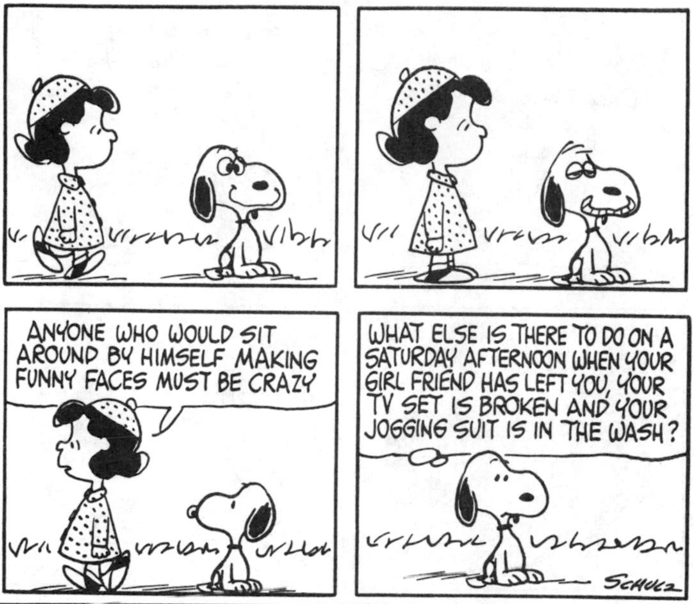
ANYONE WHO WOULD SIT AROUND BY HIMSELF MAKING FUNNY FACES MUST BE CRAZY
WHAT ELSE IS THERE TO DO ON A SATURDAY AFTERNOON WHEN YOUR GIRL FRIEND HAS LEFT YOU, YOUR TV SET IS BROKEN AND YOUR JOGGING SUIT IS IN THE WASH?
SCHULZ

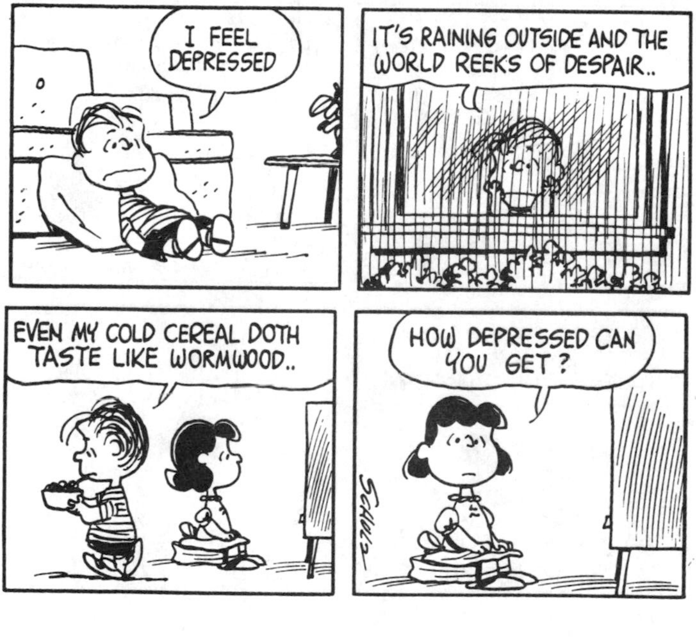
I FEEL DEPRESSED
IT'S RAINING OUTSIDE AND THE WORLD REEKS OF DESPAIR..
EVEN MY COLD CEREAL DOTH TASTE LIKE WORMWOOD..
HOW DEPRESSED CAN YOU GET?
SCHULZ

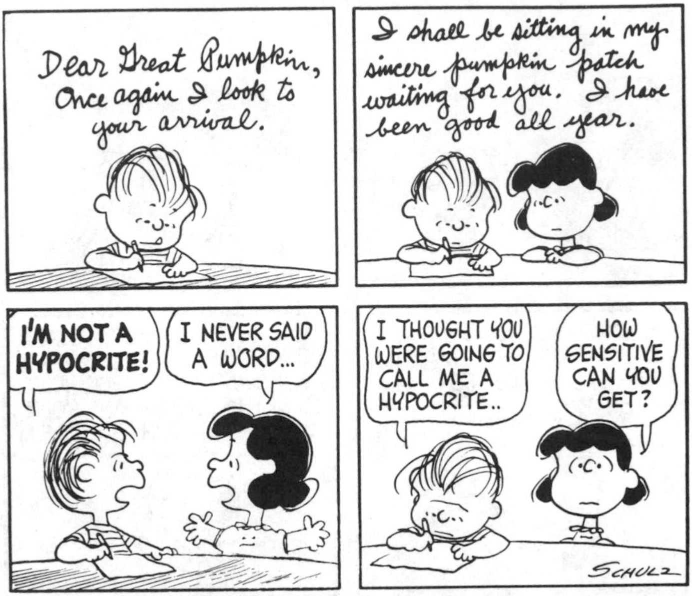
Dear Great Pumpkin, Once again I look to your arrival.
I shall be sitting in my sincere pumpkin patch waiting for you. I have been good all year.
I'M NOT A HYPOCRITE!
I NEVER SAID A WORD...
I THOUGHT YOU WERE GOING TO CALL ME A HYPOCRITE..
HOW SENSITIVE CAN YOU GET?
SCHULZ

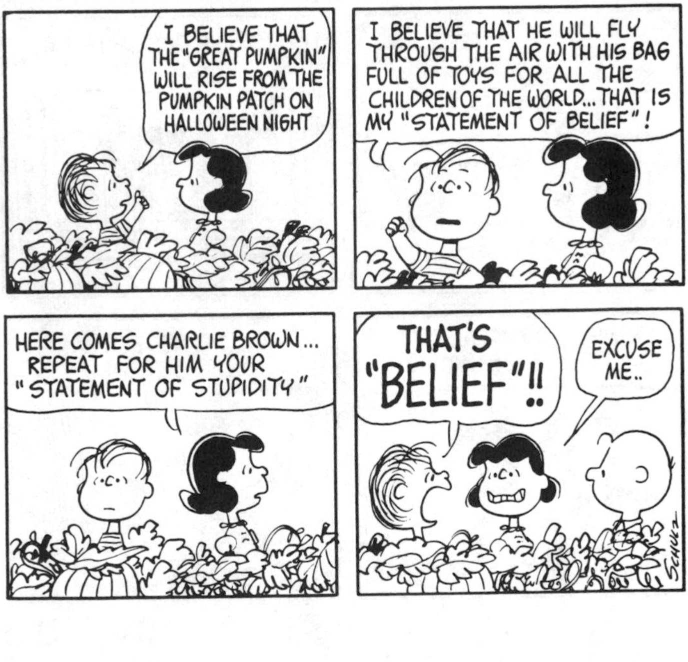
I BELIEVE THAT THE "GREAT PUMPKIN" WILL RISE FROM THE PUMPKIN PATCH ON HALLOWEEN NIGHT
I BELIEVE THAT HE WILL FLY THROUGH THE AIR WITH HIS BAG FULL OF TOYS FOR ALL THE CHILDREN OF THE WORLD...THAT IS MY "STATEMENT OF BELIEF"!
HERE COMES CHARLIE BROWN... REPEAT FOR HIM YOUR "STATEMENT OF STUPIDITY"
THAT'S "BELIEF"!!
EXCUSE ME..
SCHULZ

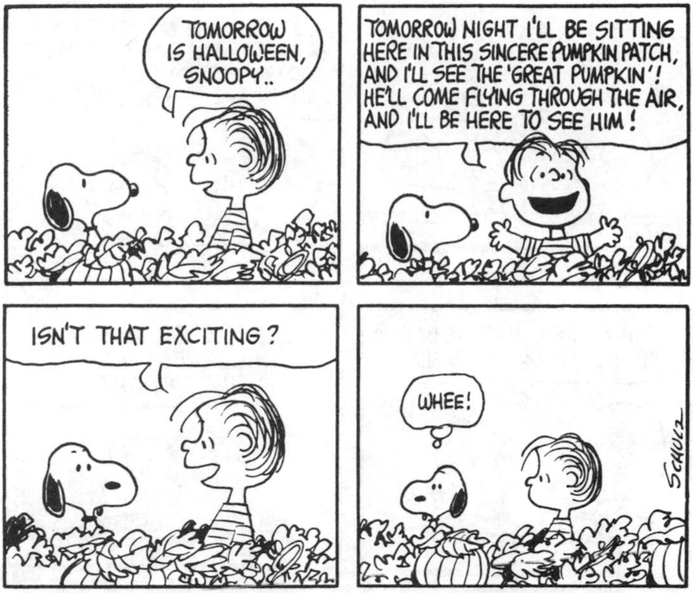
TOMORROW IS HALLOWEEN, SNOOPY..
TOMORROW NIGHT I'LL BE SITTING HERE IN THIS SINCERE PUMPKIN PATCH, AND I'LL SEE THE 'GREAT PUMPKIN'! HE'LL COME FLYING THROUGH THE AIR, AND I'LL BE HERE TO SEE HIM!
ISN'T THAT EXCITING?
WHEE!
SCHULZ

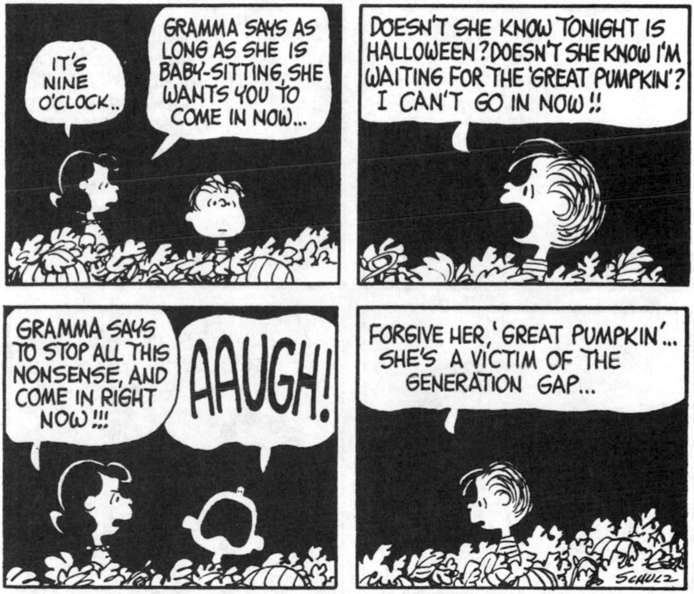
IT'S NINE O'CLOCK..
GRAMMA SAYS AS LONG AS SHE IS BABY-SITTING, SHE WANTS YOU TO COME IN NOW...
DOESN'T SHE KNOW TONIGHT IS HALLOWEEN? DOESN'T SHE KNOW I'M WAITING FOR THE 'GREAT PUMPKIN'? I CAN'T GO IN NOW!!
GRAMMA SAYS TO STOP ALL THIS NONSENSE, AND COME IN RIGHT NOW!!!
AAUGH!
FORGIVE HER, 'GREAT PUMPKIN'... SHE'S A VICTIM OF THE GENERATION GAP...
SCHULZ

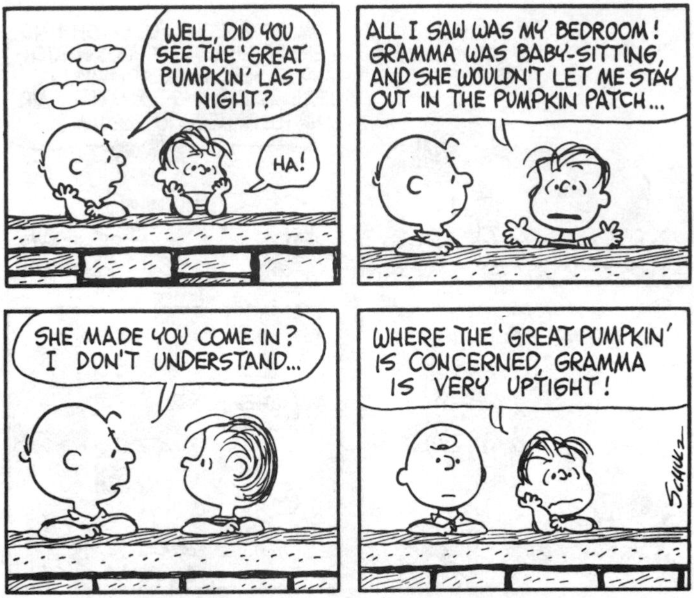
WELL, DID YOU SEE THE 'GREAT PUMPKIN' LAST NIGHT?
HA!
ALL I SAW WAS MY BEDROOM! GRAMMA WAS BABY-SITTING, AND SHE WOULDN'T LET ME STAY OUT IN THE PUMPKIN PATCH...
SHE MADE YOU COME IN? I DON'T UNDERSTAND...
WHERE THE 'GREAT PUMPKIN' IS CONCERNED, GRAMMA IS VERY UPTIGHT!
SCHULZ

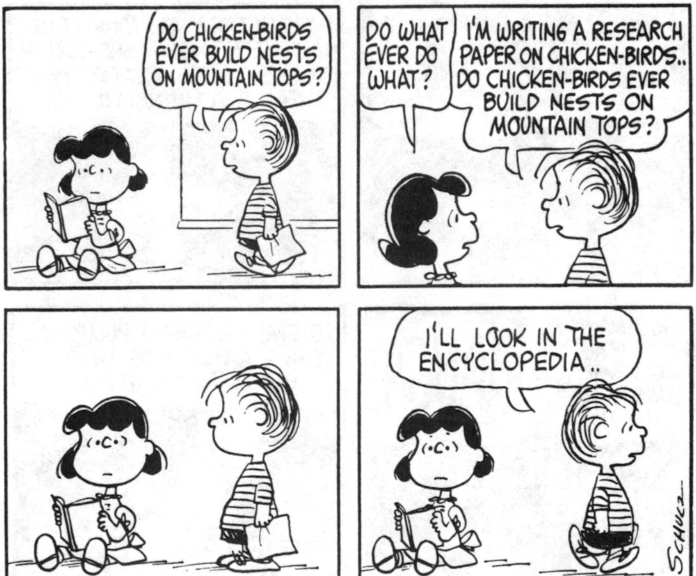
DO CHICKEN-BIRDS EVER BUILD NESTS ON MOUNTAIN TOPS?
DO WHAT EVER DO WHAT?
I'M WRITING A RESEARCH PAPER ON CHICKEN-BIRDS.. DO CHICKEN-BIRDS EVER BUILD NESTS ON MOUNTAIN TOPS?
I'LL LOOK IN THE ENCYCLOPEDIA..
SCHULZ

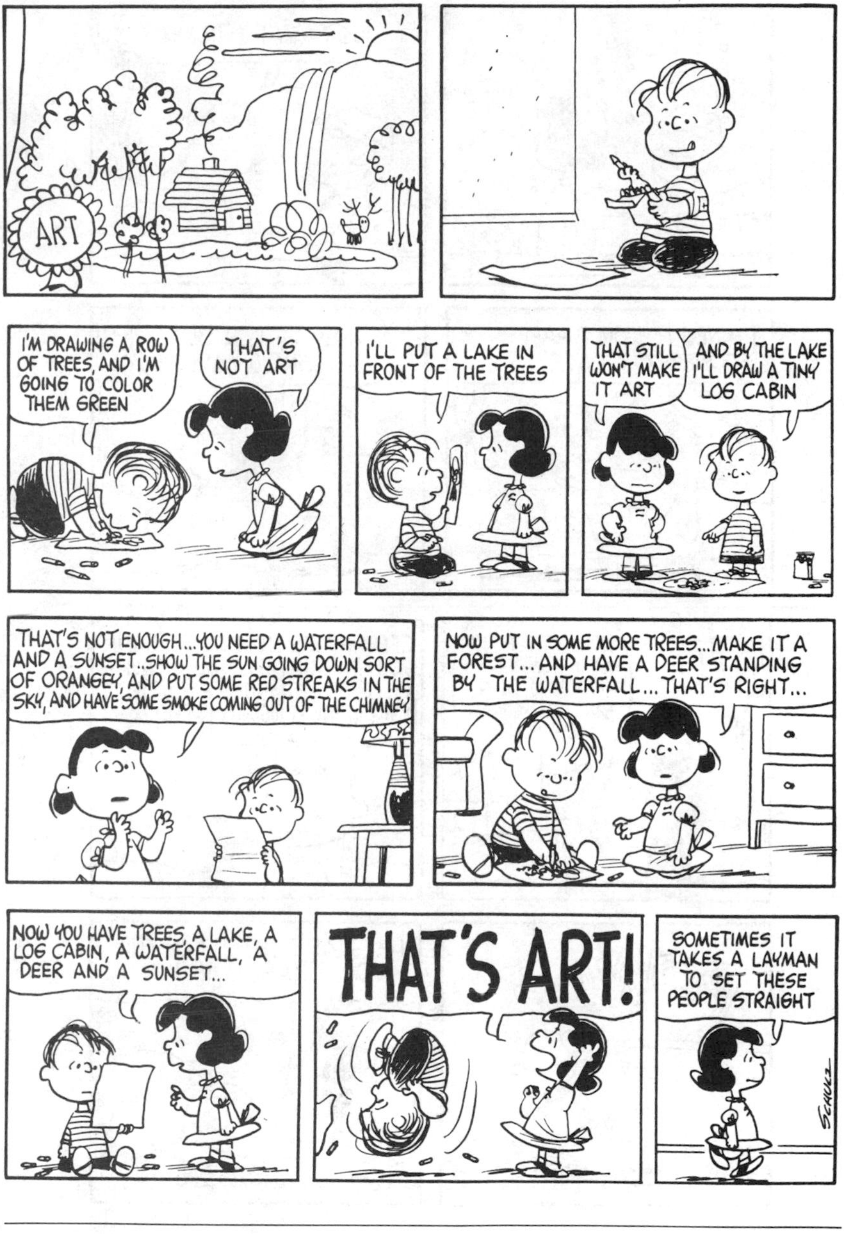
ART
I'M DRAWING A ROW OF TREES, AND I'M GOING TO COLOR THEM GREEN
THAT'S NOT ART
I'LL PUT A LAKE IN FRONT OF THE TREES
THAT STILL WON'T MAKE IT ART
AND BY THE LAKE I'LL DRAW A TINY LOG CABIN
THAT'S NOT ENOUGH...YOU NEED A WATERFALL AND A SUNSET..SHOW THE SUN GOING DOWN SORT OF ORANGEY, AND PUT SOME RED STREAKS IN THE SKY, AND HAVE SOME SMOKE COMING OUT OF THE CHIMNEY
NOW PUT IN SOME MORE TREES...MAKE IT A FOREST...AND HAVE A DEER STANDING BY THE WATERFALL...THAT'S RIGHT...
NOW YOU HAVE TREES, A LAKE, A LOG CABIN, A WATERFALL, A DEER AND A SUNSET...
THAT'S ART!
SOMETIMES IT TAKES A LAYMAN TO SET THESE PEOPLE STRAIGHT
SCHULZ

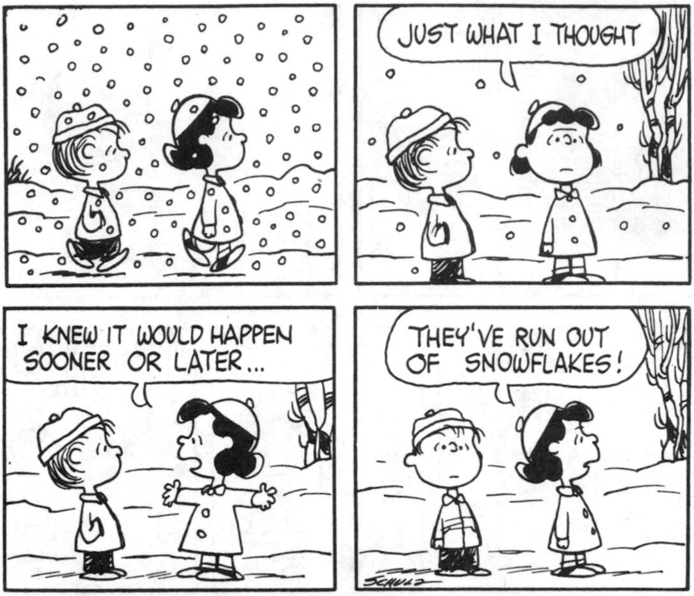
JUST WHAT I THOUGHT
I KNEW IT WOULD HAPPEN SOONER OR LATER...
THEY'VE RUN OUT OF SNOWFLAKES!

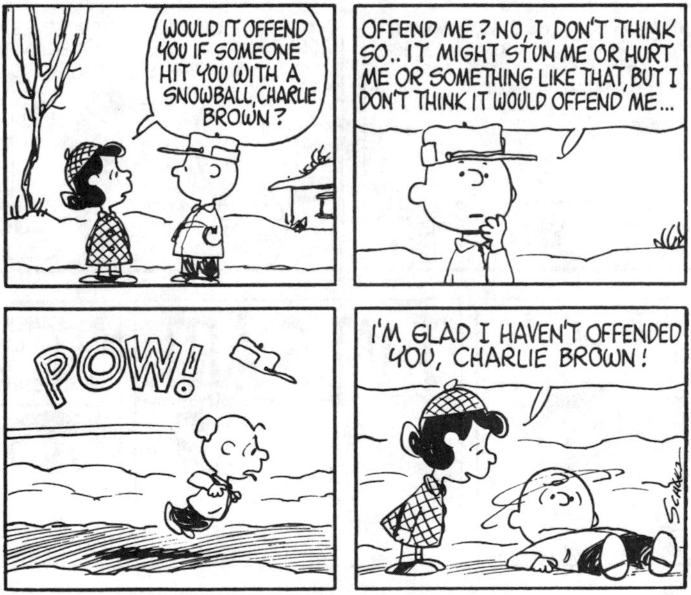
WOULD IT OFFEND YOU IF SOMEONE HIT YOU WITH A SNOWBALL, CHARLIE BROWN?
OFFEND ME? NO, I DON'T THINK SO.. IT MIGHT STUN ME OR HURT ME OR SOMETHING LIKE THAT, BUT I DON'T THINK IT WOULD OFFEND ME...
POW!
I'M GLAD I HAVEN'T OFFENDED YOU, CHARLIE BROWN!

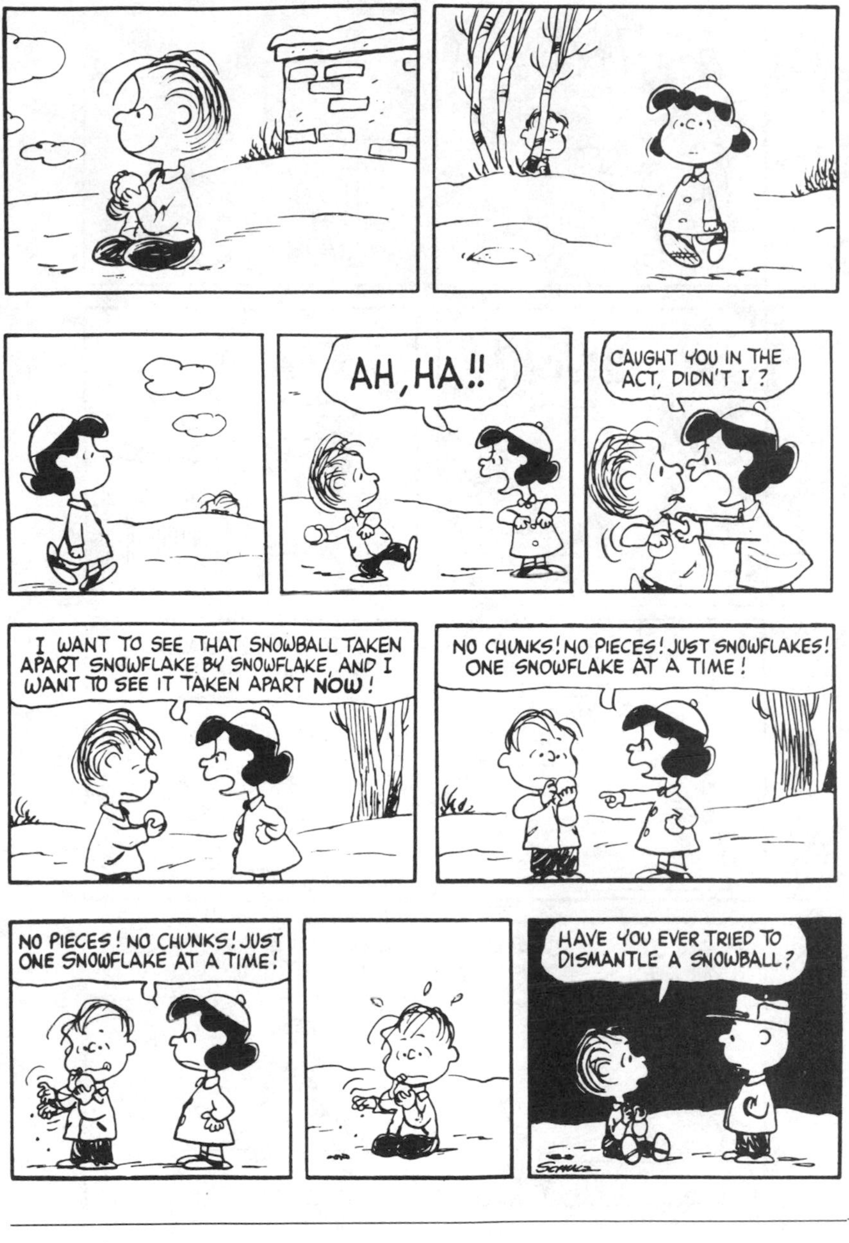
AH, HA!!
CAUGHT YOU IN THE ACT, DIDN'T I ?
I WANT TO SEE THAT SNOWBALL TAKEN APART SNOWFLAKE BY SNOWFLAKE, AND I WANT TO SEE IT TAKEN APART NOW !
NO CHUNKS! NO PIECES! JUST SNOWFLAKES! ONE SNOWFLAKE AT A TIME !
NO PIECES! NO CHUNKS! JUST ONE SNOWFLAKE AT A TIME!
HAVE YOU EVER TRIED TO DISMANTLE A SNOWBALL?
SCHULZ

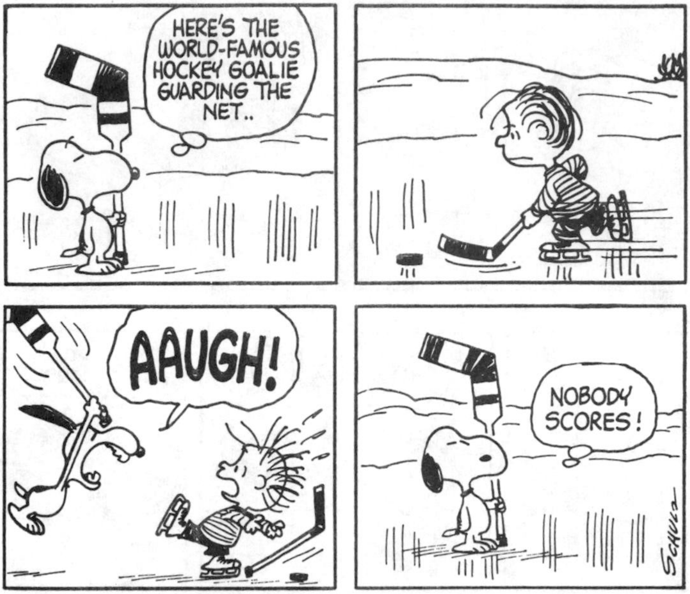
HERE'S THE WORLD-FAMOUS HOCKEY GOALIE GUARDING THE NET..
AAUGH!
NOBODY SCORES!
SCHULZ

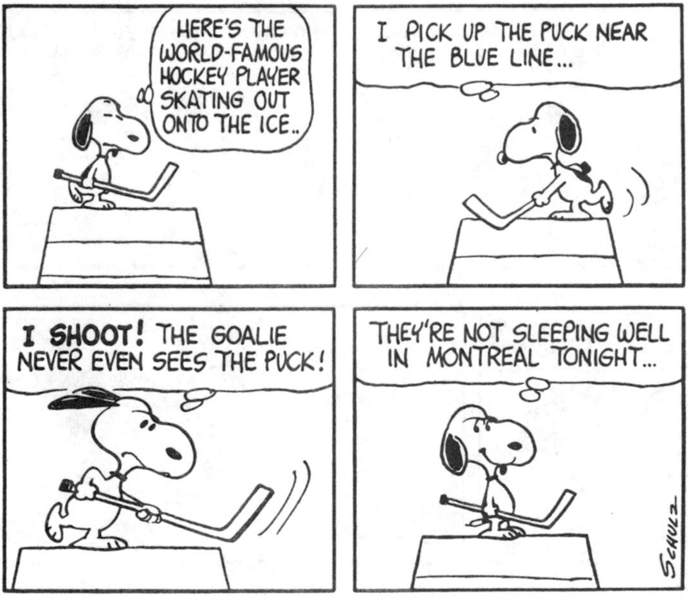
HERE'S THE WORLD-FAMOUS HOCKEY PLAYER SKATING OUT ONTO THE ICE..
I PICK UP THE PUCK NEAR THE BLUE LINE...
I SHOOT! THE GOALIE NEVER EVEN SEES THE PUCK!
THEY'RE NOT SLEEPING WELL IN MONTREAL TONIGHT...
SCHULZ

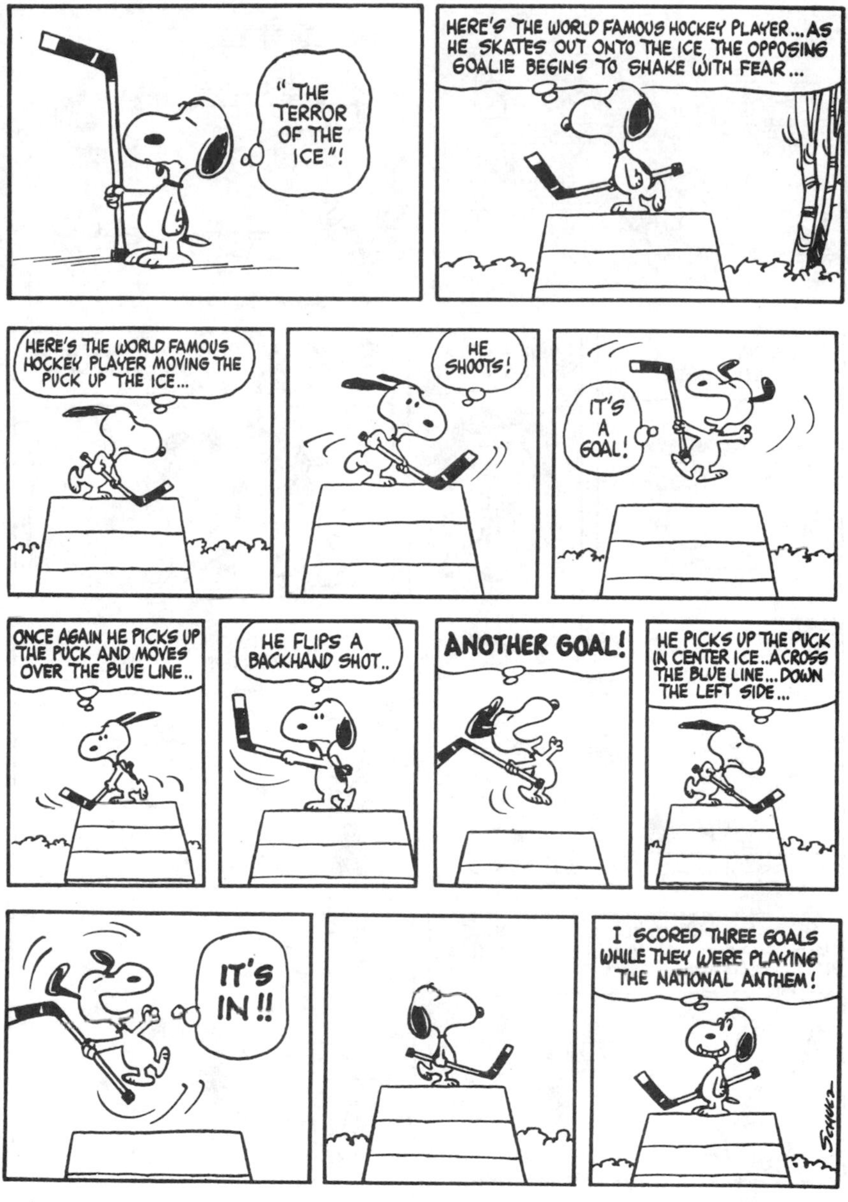
"THE TERROR OF THE ICE"!
HERE'S THE WORLD FAMOUS HOCKEY PLAYER...AS HE SKATES OUT ONTO THE ICE, THE OPPOSING GOALIE BEGINS TO SHAKE WITH FEAR...
HERE'S THE WORLD FAMOUS HOCKEY PLAYER MOVING THE PUCK UP THE ICE...
HE SHOOTS!
IT'S A GOAL!
ONCE AGAIN HE PICKS UP THE PUCK AND MOVES OVER THE BLUE LINE..
HE FLIPS A BACKHAND SHOT..
ANOTHER GOAL!
HE PICKS UP THE PUCK IN CENTER ICE..ACROSS THE BLUE LINE...DOWN THE LEFT SIDE...
IT'S IN!!
I SCORED THREE GOALS WHILE THEY WERE PLAYING THE NATIONAL ANTHEM!
SCHULZ

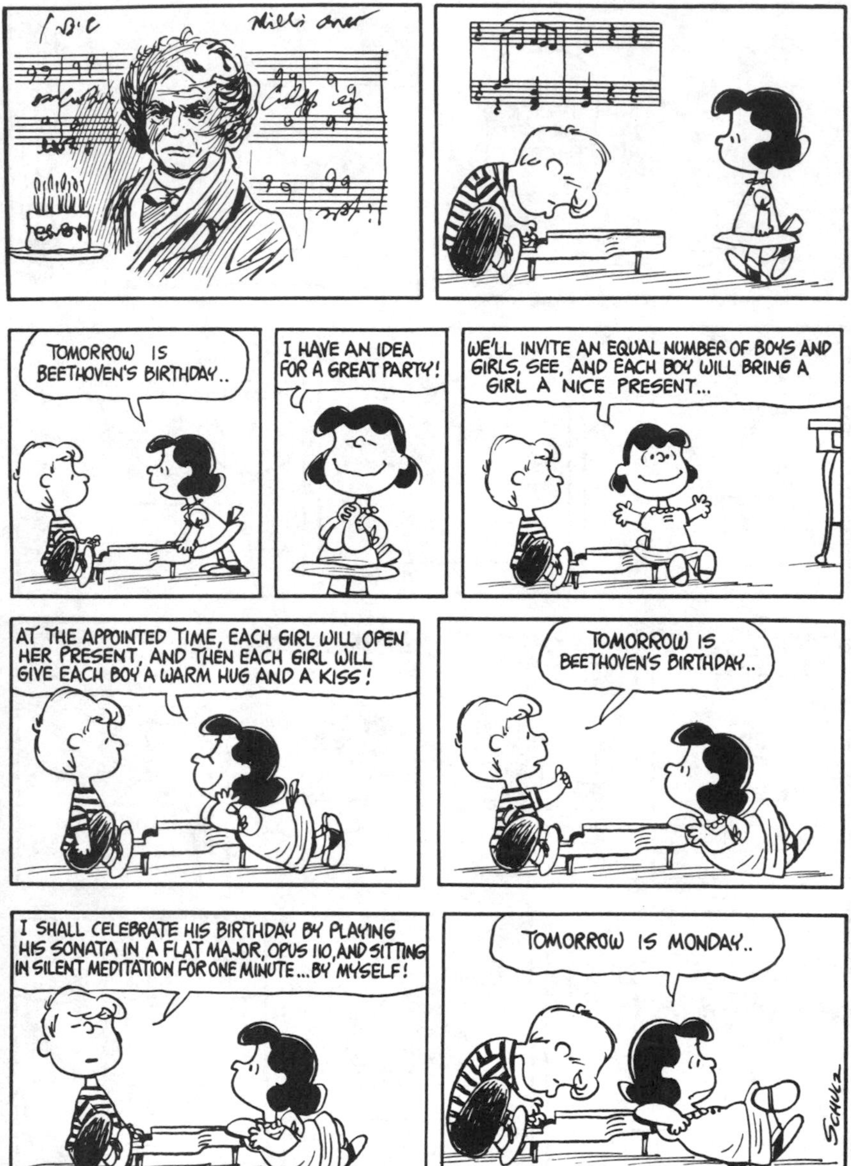
TOMORROW IS BEETHOVEN'S BIRTHDAY..
I HAVE AN IDEA FOR A GREAT PARTY!
WE'LL INVITE AN EQUAL NUMBER OF BOYS AND GIRLS, SEE, AND EACH BOY WILL BRING A GIRL A NICE PRESENT...
AT THE APPOINTED TIME, EACH GIRL WILL OPEN HER PRESENT, AND THEN EACH GIRL WILL GIVE EACH BOY A WARM HUG AND A KISS!
TOMORROW IS BEETHOVEN'S BIRTHDAY..
I SHALL CELEBRATE HIS BIRTHDAY BY PLAYING HIS SONATA IN A FLAT MAJOR, OPUS 110, AND SITTING IN SILENT MEDITATION FOR ONE MINUTE...BY MYSELF!
TOMORROW IS MONDAY..
SCHULZ

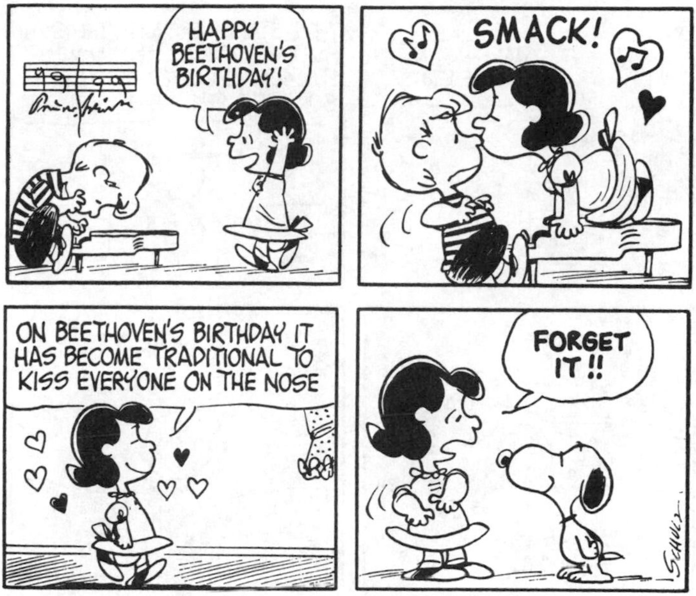
HAPPY BEETHOVEN'S BIRTHDAY!
SMACK!
ON BEETHOVEN'S BIRTHDAY IT HAS BECOME TRADITIONAL TO KISS EVERYONE ON THE NOSE
FORGET IT!!

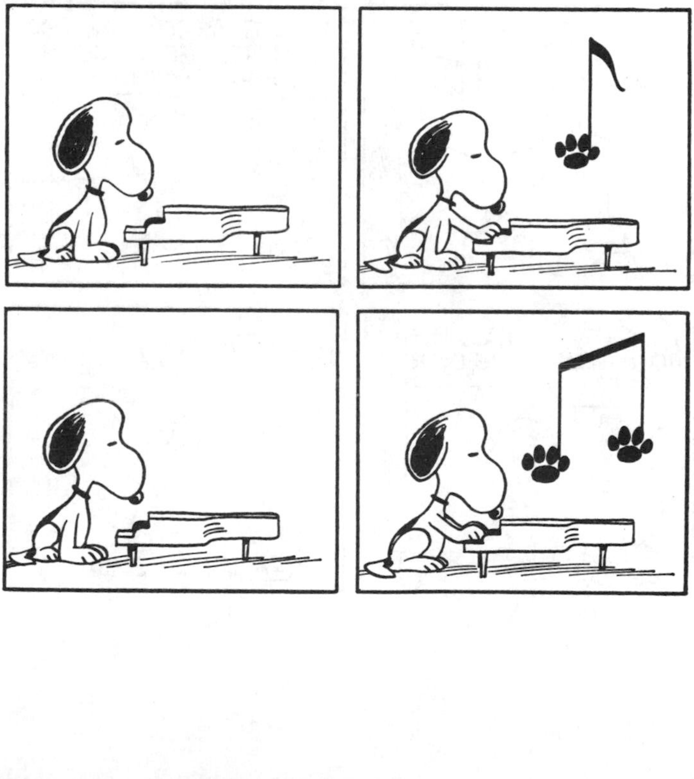

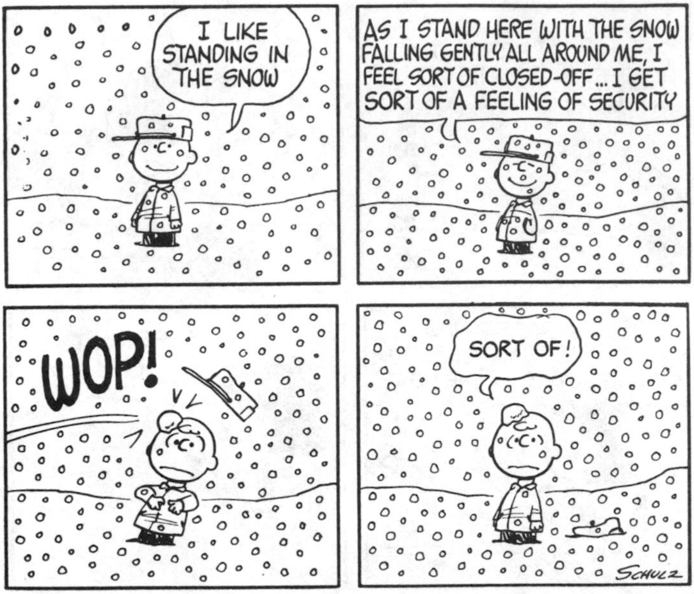
I LIKE STANDING IN THE SNOW
AS I STAND HERE WITH THE SNOW FALLING GENTLY ALL AROUND ME, I FEEL SORT OF CLOSED-OFF... I GET SORT OF A FEELING OF SECURITY
WOP!
SORT OF!
SCHULZ

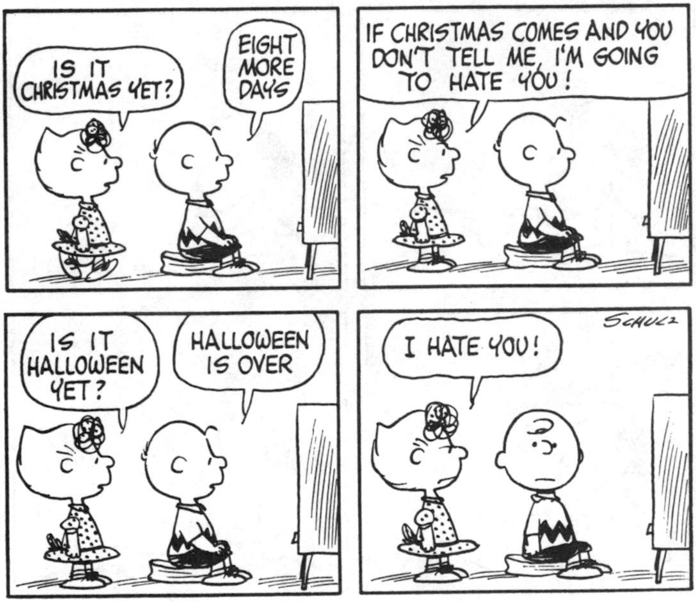
IS IT CHRISTMAS YET?
EIGHT MORE DAYS
IF CHRISTMAS COMES AND YOU DON'T TELL ME, I'M GOING TO HATE YOU!
IS IT HALLOWEEN YET?
HALLOWEEN IS OVER
SCHULZ
I HATE YOU!

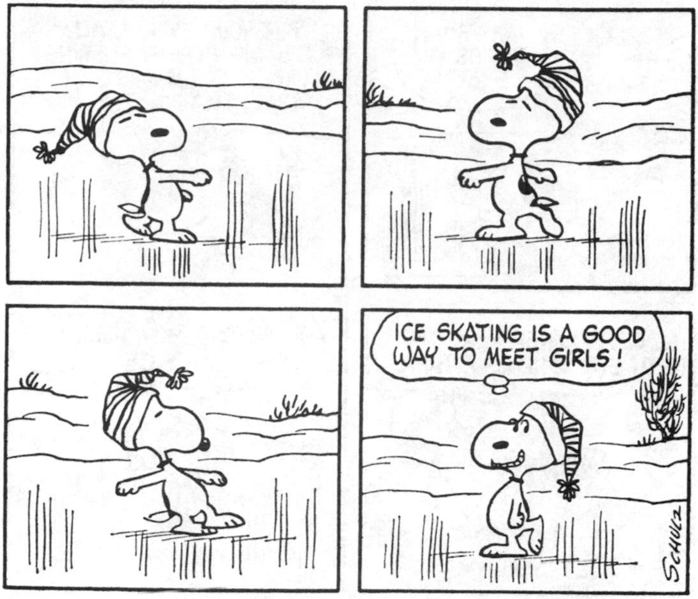
ICE SKATING IS A GOOD WAY TO MEET GIRLS !
SCHULZ

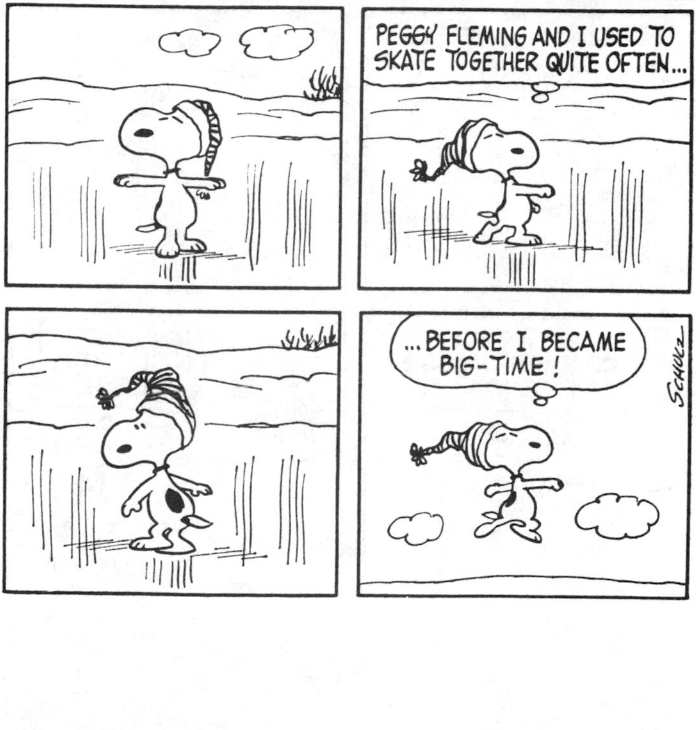
PEGGY FLEMING AND I USED TO SKATE TOGETHER QUITE OFTEN...
...BEFORE I BECAME BIG-TIME !
SCHULZ

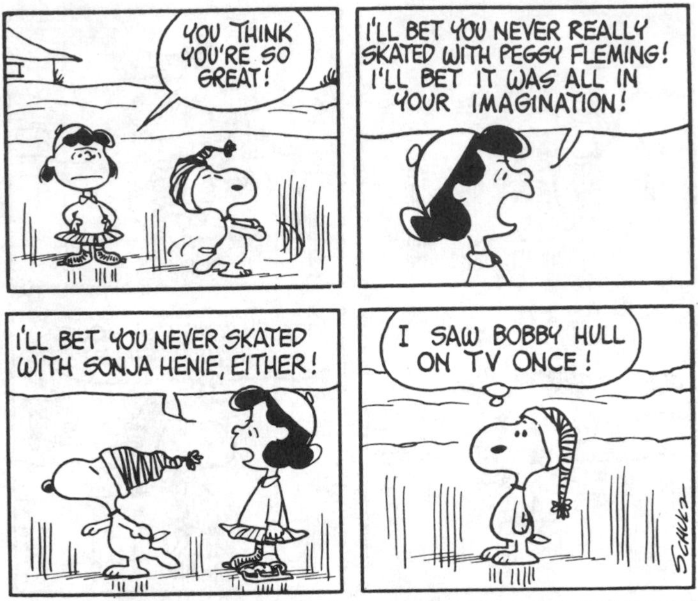

YOU THINK YOU'RE SO GREAT!
I'LL BET YOU NEVER REALLY SKATED WITH PEGGY FLEMING! I'LL BET IT WAS ALL IN YOUR IMAGINATION!
I'LL BET YOU NEVER SKATED WITH SONJA HENIE, EITHER!
I SAW BOBBY HULL ON TV ONCE!
SCHULZ

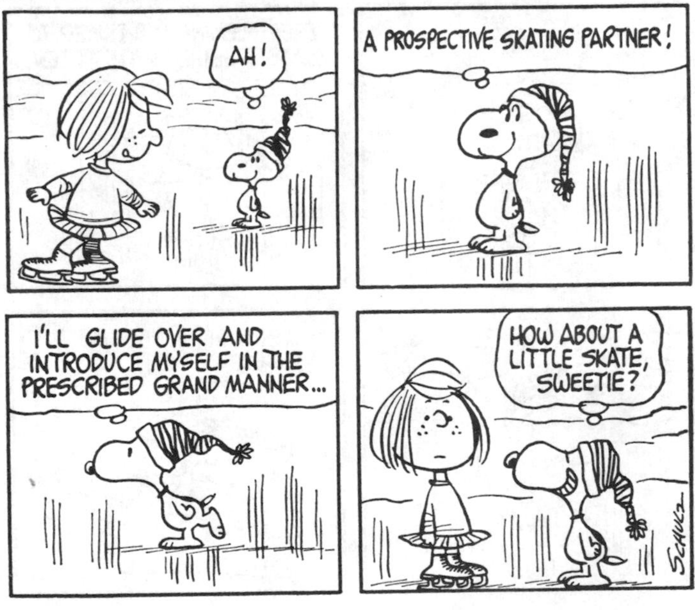

AH!
A PROSPECTIVE SKATING PARTNER!
I'LL GLIDE OVER AND INTRODUCE MYSELF IN THE PRESCRIBED GRAND MANNER...
HOW ABOUT A LITTLE SKATE, SWEETIE?
SCHULZ

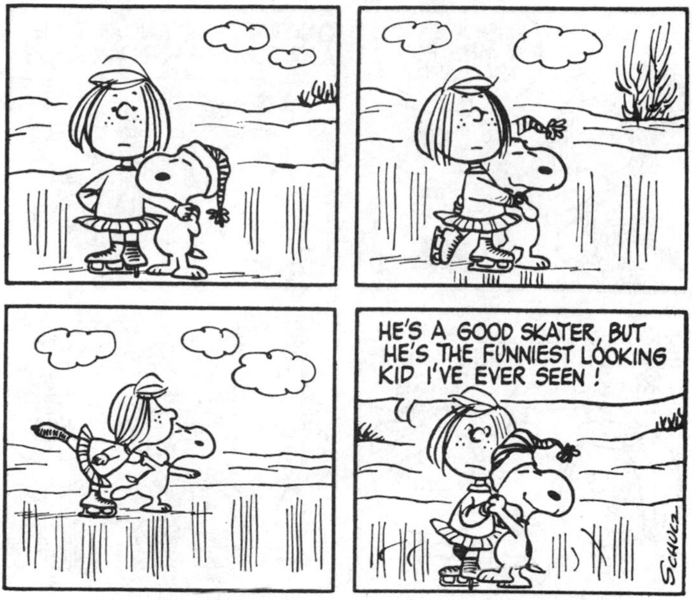
HE'S A GOOD SKATER, BUT HE'S THE FUNNIEST LOOKING KID I'VE EVER SEEN!
SCHULZ

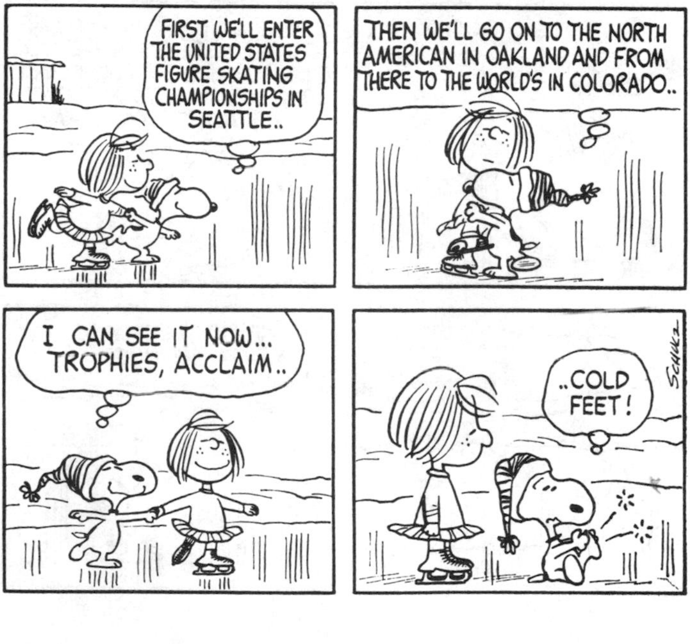
FIRST WE'LL ENTER THE UNITED STATES FIGURE SKATING CHAMPIONSHIPS IN SEATTLE..
THEN WE'LL GO ON TO THE NORTH AMERICAN IN OAKLAND AND FROM THERE TO THE WORLD'S IN COLORADO..
I CAN SEE IT NOW... TROPHIES, ACCLAIM..
..COLD FEET!
SCHULZ

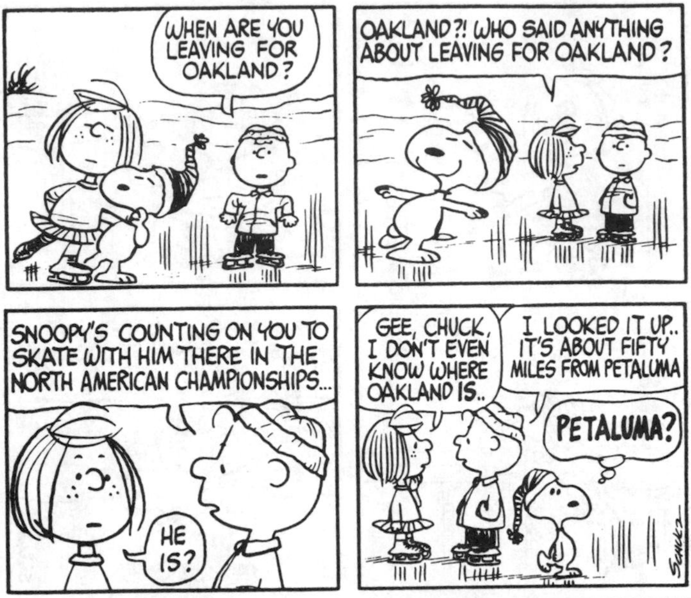
WHEN ARE YOU LEAVING FOR OAKLAND?
OAKLAND?! WHO SAID ANYTHING ABOUT LEAVING FOR OAKLAND?
SNOOPY'S COUNTING ON YOU TO SKATE WITH HIM THERE IN THE NORTH AMERICAN CHAMPIONSHIPS...
HE IS?
GEE, CHUCK, I DON'T EVEN KNOW WHERE OAKLAND IS..
I LOOKED IT UP.. IT'S ABOUT FIFTY MILES FROM PETALUMA
PETALUMA?
SCHULZ

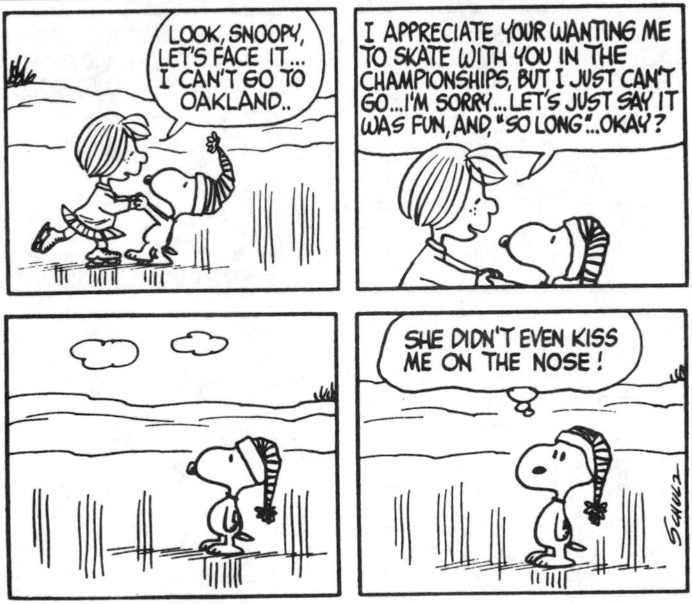
LOOK, SNOOPY, LET'S FACE IT... I CAN'T GO TO OAKLAND..
I APPRECIATE YOUR WANTING ME TO SKATE WITH YOU IN THE CHAMPIONSHIPS, BUT I JUST CAN'T GO...I'M SORRY... LET'S JUST SAY IT WAS FUN, AND "SO LONG"...OKAY?
SHE DIDN'T EVEN KISS ME ON THE NOSE!
SCHULZ

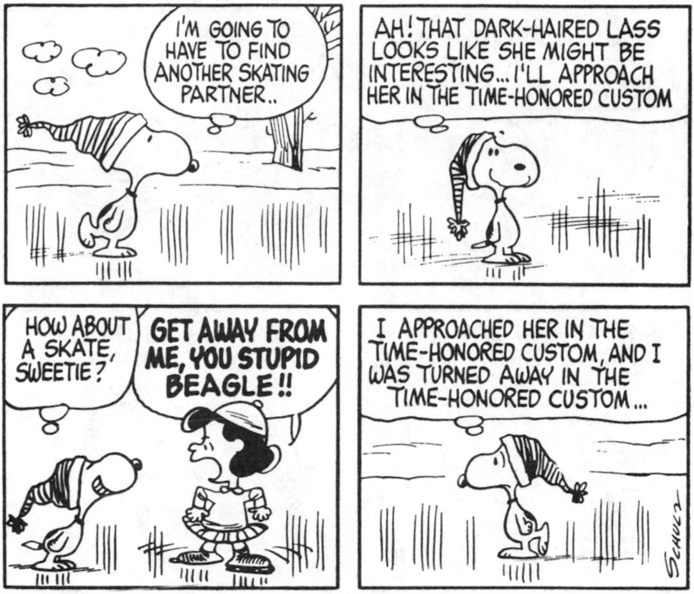
I'M GOING TO HAVE TO FIND ANOTHER SKATING PARTNER..
AH! THAT DARK-HAIRED LASS LOOKS LIKE SHE MIGHT BE INTERESTING... I'LL APPROACH HER IN THE TIME-HONORED CUSTOM
HOW ABOUT A SKATE, SWEETIE?
GET AWAY FROM ME, YOU STUPID BEAGLE!!
I APPROACHED HER IN THE TIME-HONORED CUSTOM, AND I WAS TURNED AWAY IN THE TIME-HONORED CUSTOM...
SCHULZ

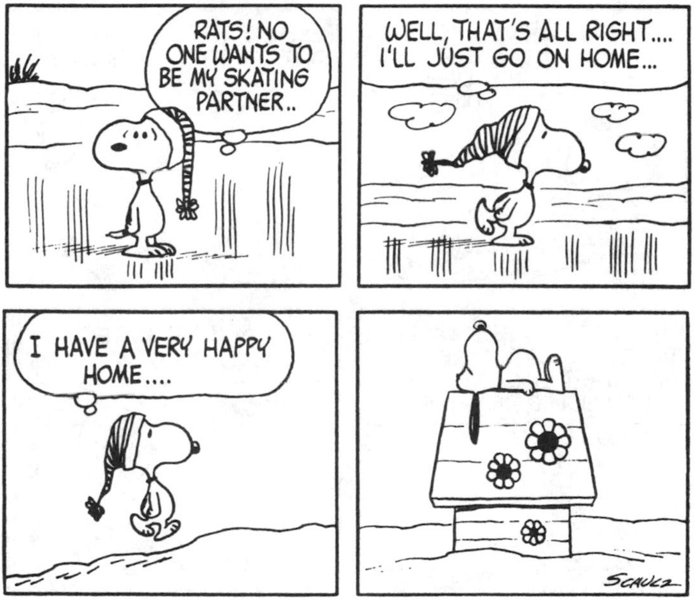
RATS! NO ONE WANTS TO BE MY SKATING PARTNER..
WELL, THAT'S ALL RIGHT.... I'LL JUST GO ON HOME...
I HAVE A VERY HAPPY HOME....
SCHULZ

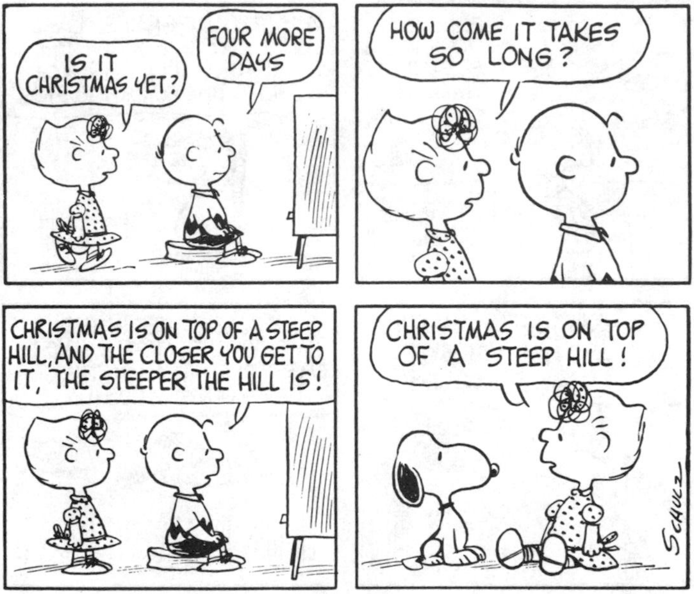
IS IT CHRISTMAS YET?
FOUR MORE DAYS
HOW COME IT TAKES SO LONG?
CHRISTMAS IS ON TOP OF A STEEP HILL, AND THE CLOSER YOU GET TO IT, THE STEEPER THE HILL IS!
CHRISTMAS IS ON TOP OF A STEEP HILL!
SCHULZ

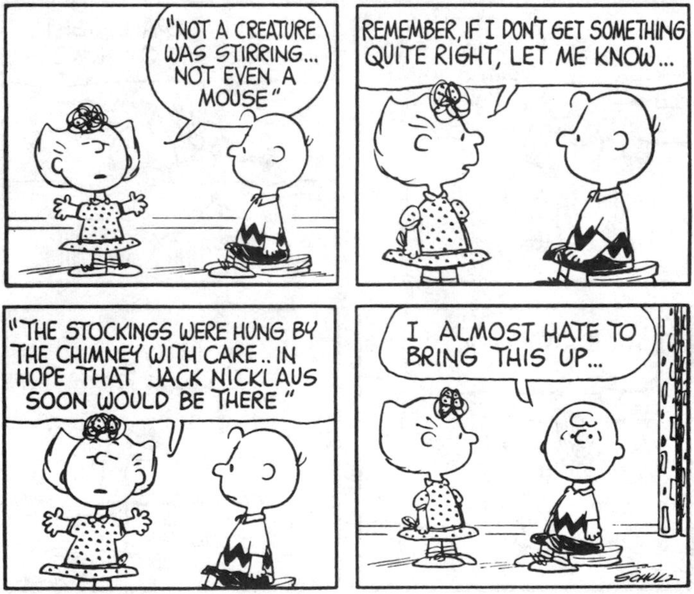
"NOT A CREATURE WAS STIRRING... NOT EVEN A MOUSE"
REMEMBER, IF I DON'T GET SOMETHING QUITE RIGHT, LET ME KNOW...
"THE STOCKINGS WERE HUNG BY THE CHIMNEY WITH CARE.. IN HOPE THAT JACK NICKLAUS SOON WOULD BE THERE"
I ALMOST HATE TO BRING THIS UP...
SCHULZ

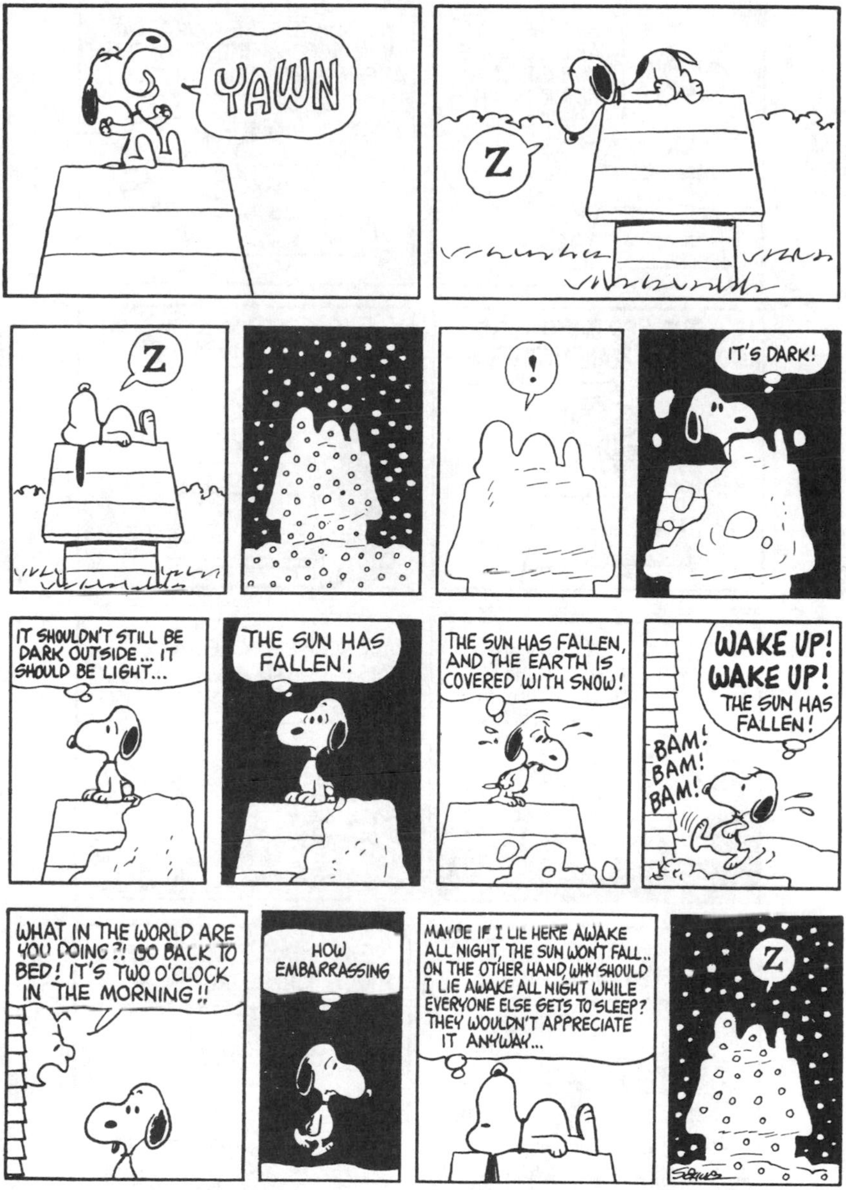
YAWN
Z
Z
!
IT'S DARK!
IT SHOULDN'T STILL BE DARK OUTSIDE... IT SHOULD BE LIGHT...
THE SUN HAS FALLEN!
THE SUN HAS FALLEN, AND THE EARTH IS COVERED WITH SNOW!
WAKE UP! WAKE UP! THE SUN HAS FALLEN!
BAM! BAM! BAM!
WHAT IN THE WORLD ARE YOU DOING?! GO BACK TO BED! IT'S TWO O'CLOCK IN THE MORNING!!
HOW EMBARRASSING
MAYBE IF I LIE HERE AWAKE ALL NIGHT, THE SUN WON'T FALL.. ON THE OTHER HAND, WHY SHOULD I LIE AWAKE ALL NIGHT WHILE EVERYONE ELSE GETS TO SLEEP? THEY WOULDN'T APPRECIATE IT ANYWAY...
Z

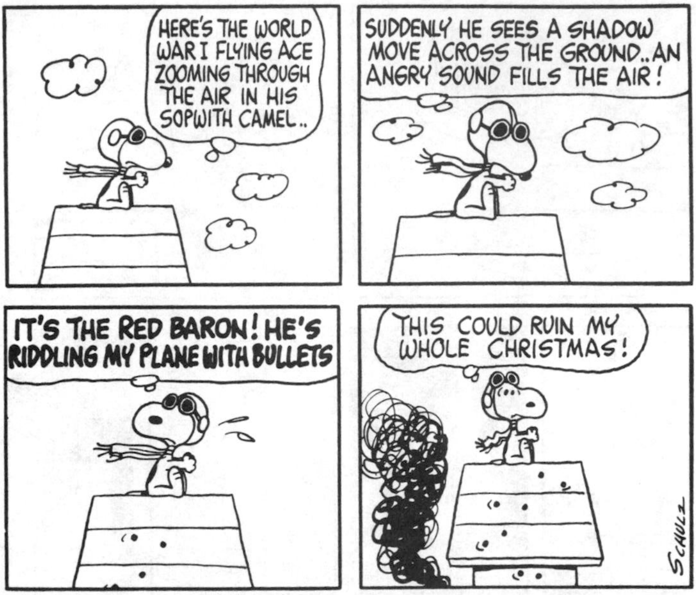
HERE'S THE WORLD WAR I FLYING ACE ZOOMING THROUGH THE AIR IN HIS SOPWITH CAMEL..
SUDDENLY HE SEES A SHADOW MOVE ACROSS THE GROUND..AN ANGRY SOUND FILLS THE AIR!
IT'S THE RED BARON! HE'S RIDDLING MY PLANE WITH BULLETS
THIS COULD RUIN MY WHOLE CHRISTMAS!
SCHULZ

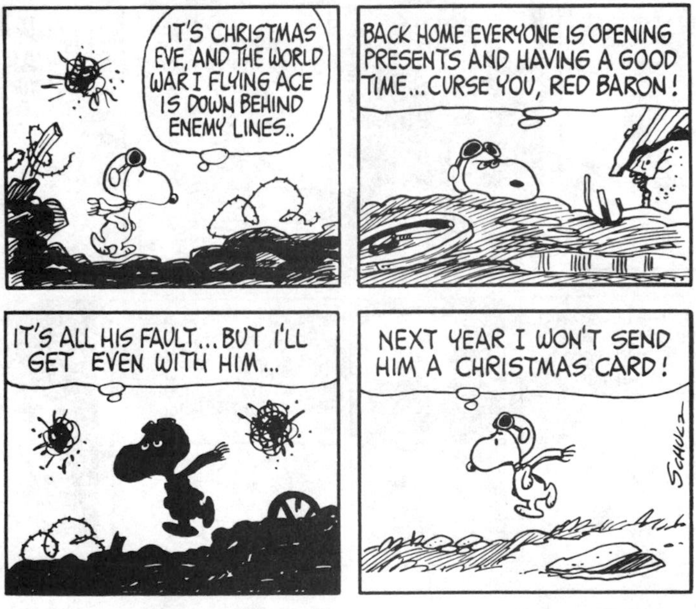
IT'S CHRISTMAS EVE, AND THE WORLD WAR I FLYING ACE IS DOWN BEHIND ENEMY LINES..
BACK HOME EVERYONE IS OPENING PRESENTS AND HAVING A GOOD TIME...CURSE YOU, RED BARON!
IT'S ALL HIS FAULT...BUT I'LL GET EVEN WITH HIM...
NEXT YEAR I WON'T SEND HIM A CHRISTMAS CARD!
SCHULZ

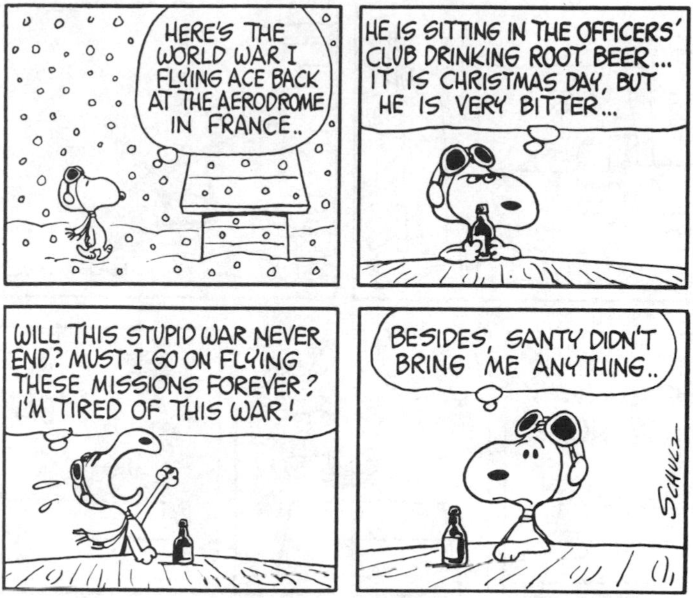
HERE'S THE WORLD WAR I FLYING ACE BACK AT THE AERODROME IN FRANCE..
HE IS SITTING IN THE OFFICERS' CLUB DRINKING ROOT BEER... IT IS CHRISTMAS DAY, BUT HE IS VERY BITTER...
WILL THIS STUPID WAR NEVER END? MUST I GO ON FLYING THESE MISSIONS FOREVER? I'M TIRED OF THIS WAR!
BESIDES, SANTY DIDN'T BRING ME ANYTHING..
SCHULZ

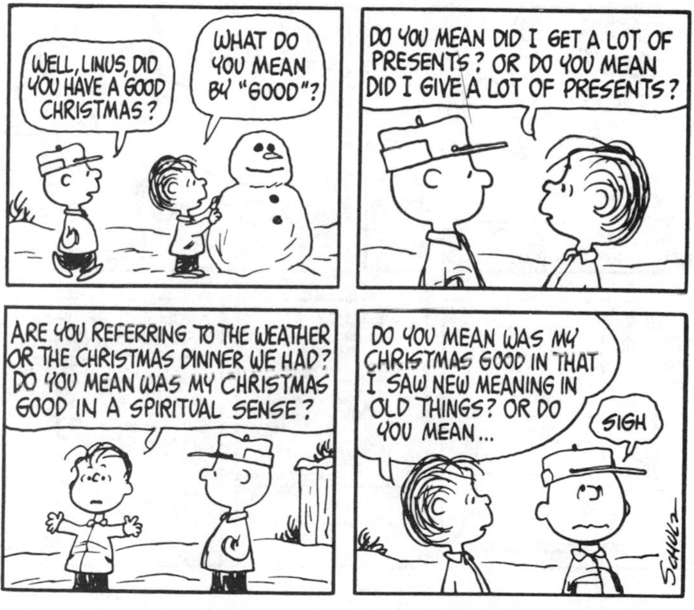
WELL, LINUS, DID YOU HAVE A GOOD CHRISTMAS?
WHAT DO YOU MEAN BY "GOOD"?
DO YOU MEAN DID I GET A LOT OF PRESENTS? OR DO YOU MEAN DID I GIVE A LOT OF PRESENTS?
ARE YOU REFERRING TO THE WEATHER OR THE CHRISTMAS DINNER WE HAD? DO YOU MEAN WAS MY CHRISTMAS GOOD IN A SPIRITUAL SENSE?
DO YOU MEAN WAS MY CHRISTMAS GOOD IN THAT I SAW NEW MEANING IN OLD THINGS? OR DO YOU MEAN...
SIGH
SCHULZ

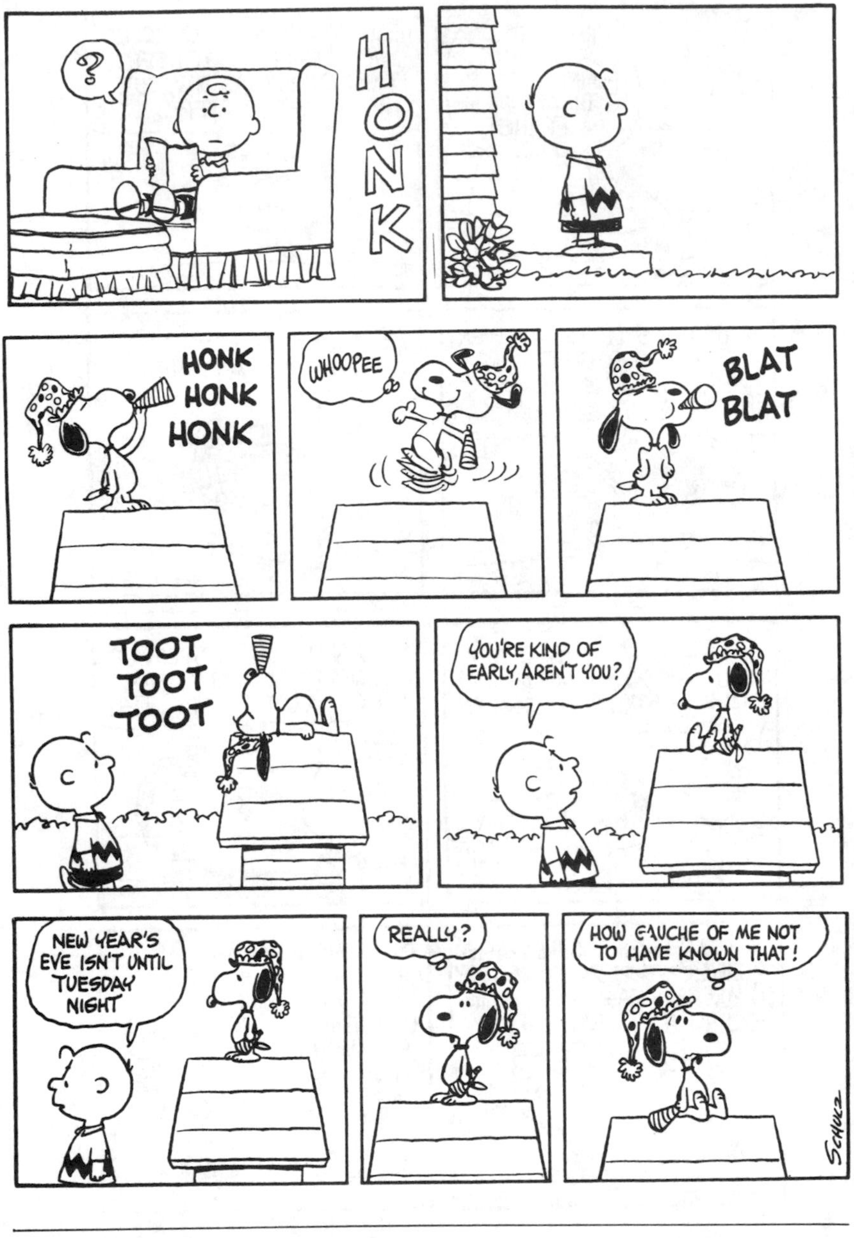
?
HONK
HONK
HONK
HONK
WHOOPEE
BLAT
BLAT
TOOT
TOOT
TOOT
YOU'RE KIND OF EARLY, AREN'T YOU?
NEW YEAR'S EVE ISN'T UNTIL TUESDAY NIGHT
REALLY?
HOW GAUCHE OF ME NOT TO HAVE KNOWN THAT!
SCHULZ

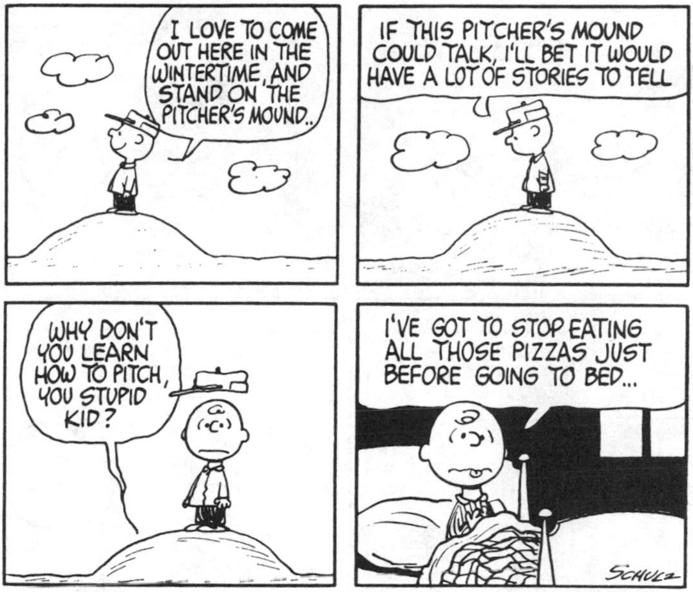
I LOVE TO COME OUT HERE IN THE WINTERTIME, AND STAND ON THE PITCHER'S MOUND..
IF THIS PITCHER'S MOUND COULD TALK, I'LL BET IT WOULD HAVE A LOT OF STORIES TO TELL
WHY DON'T YOU LEARN HOW TO PITCH, YOU STUPID KID?
I'VE GOT TO STOP EATING ALL THOSE PIZZAS JUST BEFORE GOING TO BED...
SCHULZ

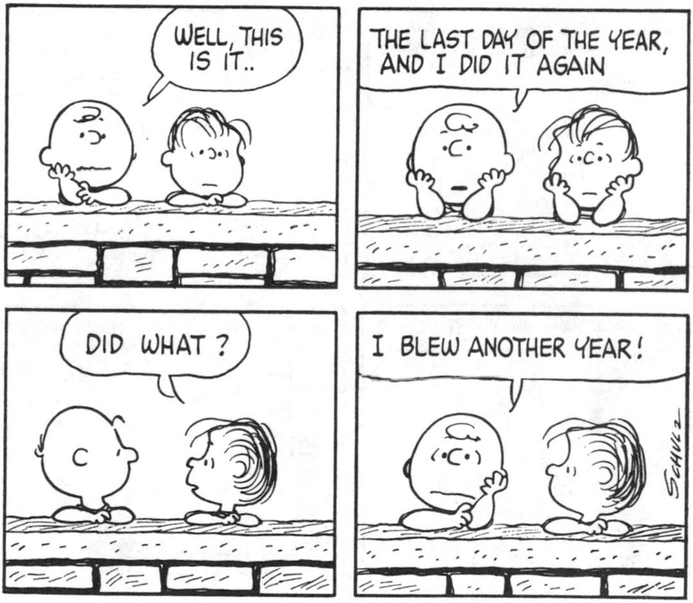
WELL, THIS IS IT..
THE LAST DAY OF THE YEAR, AND I DID IT AGAIN
DID WHAT?
I BLEW ANOTHER YEAR!
SCHULZ

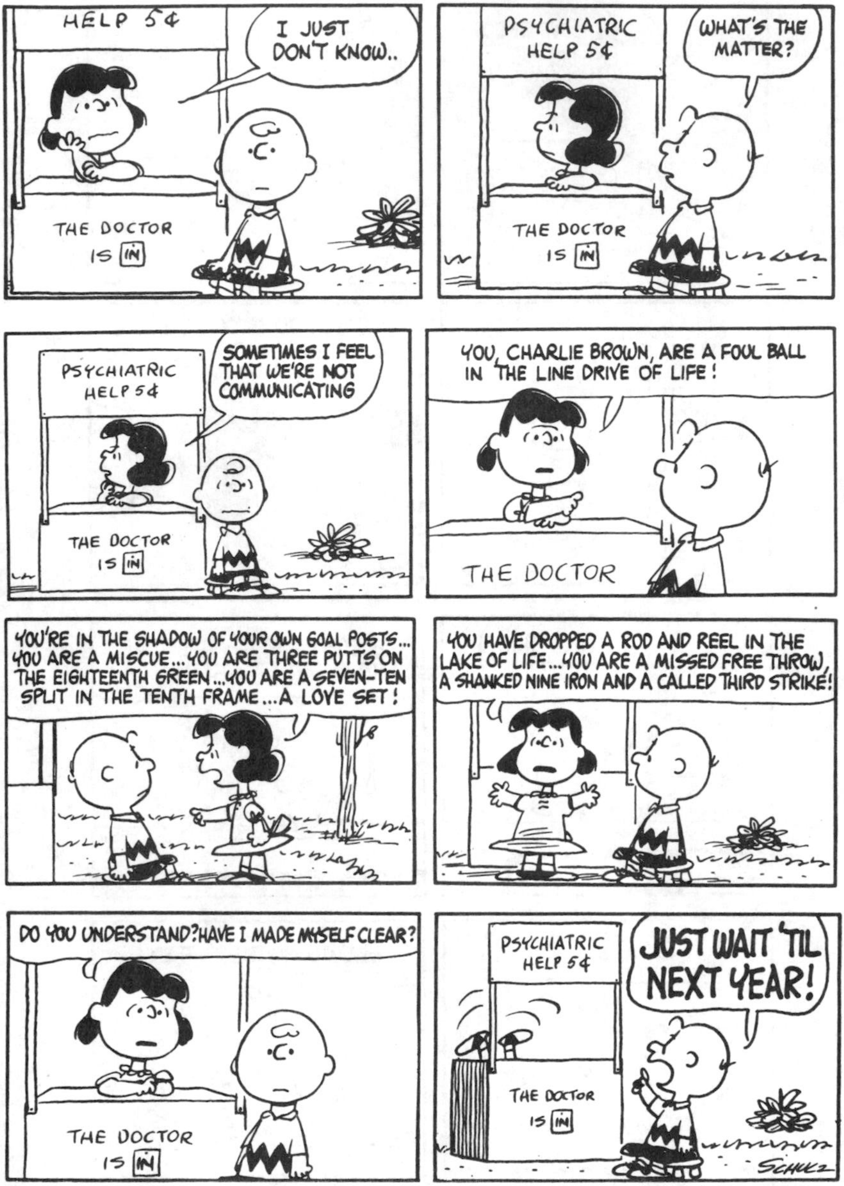
HELP 5¢
I JUST DON'T KNOW..
THE DOCTOR IS IN
PSYCHIATRIC HELP 5¢
WHAT'S THE MATTER?
THE DOCTOR IS IN
PSYCHIATRIC HELP 5¢
SOMETIMES I FEEL THAT WE'RE NOT COMMUNICATING
THE DOCTOR IS IN
YOU, CHARLIE BROWN, ARE A FOUL BALL IN THE LINE DRIVE OF LIFE!
THE DOCTOR
YOU'RE IN THE SHADOW OF YOUR OWN GOAL POSTS... YOU ARE A MISCUE...YOU ARE THREE PUTTS ON THE EIGHTEENTH GREEN...YOU ARE A SEVEN-TEN SPLIT IN THE TENTH FRAME...A LOVE SET!
YOU HAVE DROPPED A ROD AND REEL IN THE LAKE OF LIFE...YOU ARE A MISSED FREE THROW, A SHANKED NINE IRON AND A CALLED THIRD STRIKE!
DO YOU UNDERSTAND? HAVE I MADE MYSELF CLEAR?
THE DOCTOR IS IN
PSYCHIATRIC HELP 5¢
JUST WAIT 'TIL NEXT YEAR!
THE DOCTOR IS IN
SCHULZ